"Lists are kind of my thing."

"Trust me, Taylor, I remember," Alex said. As he took a swig of beer, he noticed the open notebook. He pulled it closer, intrigued by what had to be her precise handwriting.

Requirements

1. Driven

2. Intelligent

3. Successful

4. Considerate

5. Well-respected

6. Conservative

7. Neat

8. Optimistic

9. Polite

10. Health-conscious

Requirements for what?" he asked. "A Bill Gates clone?"

She crossed her arms. "It's a list."

"Yes. We army guys may seem dense, but I figured out all by myself it's a list. What's it for?"

She stared at him, her cheeks pink. The ideal male. Which, it occurs to me, is a fictitious being."

"So, what if you meet someone who gets your heart rate up but he's an up-and-coming artist? Not yet successful?"

"Then I have no interest in going out with him."

He nodded in complete disagreement. "Black and white."

"Precisely."

Dear Reader,

When people ask me what kinds of books I like to read, I usually answer romance and military nonfiction. Sometimes they give me an odd look at the combination, but then I'm used to odd looks.

I especially love reading romances that have a military hero. I finally decided I'd try my hand at writing one, and Alex Worth was born in my imagination. He's a tough, competent, been-through-hell-several-times-over guy whose helicopter was shot down in combat. His best friend was killed in the crash, and Alex is left, seriously injured, to live with the aftermath. Ever conscious of his duty, he feels obligated to watch out for his best friend's younger sister, Taylor McCabe.

Most of the heroines of my books have been self-confident, sometimes mouthy or witty (at least in their minds), socially adept people—the type of woman Alex Worth would normally go for. I thought it would be fun to give him the exact opposite.

Taylor is a super-intelligent, socially challenged computer and math geek who never knows what to say, especially around the sexy, virile helicopter pilot. To add to her unease, she's had a crush on Alex since she was a teenager.

I hope you enjoy reading how the army pilot and the computer geek fall in love, because I had a great time writing their story. Please feel free to write to me at amyknupp@amyknupp.com. Learn more about my books and writing life at www.amyknupp.com.

Thank you for picking up *Because of the List!*

Best wishes,

Amy Knupp

Because of the List
Amy Knupp

Harlequin®

TORONTO NEW YORK LONDON
AMSTERDAM PARIS SYDNEY HAMBURG
STOCKHOLM ATHENS TOKYO MILAN MADRID
PRAGUE WARSAW BUDAPEST AUCKLAND

Recycling programs
for this product may
not exist in your area.

ISBN-13: 978-0-373-78493-6

BECAUSE OF THE LIST

Copyright © 2011 by Amy Knupp

www.Harlequin.com

Printed in U.S.A.

ABOUT THE AUTHOR

Amy Knupp lives in Wisconsin with her two sons, five cats and her very own computer geek, in the form of a husband. She graduated from the University of Kansas with degrees in French and journalism and feels lucky to use very little of either one in her writing career. She's a member of Romance Writers of America, Mad City Romance Writers and Wisconsin Romance Writers. In her spare time, she enjoys reading, college basketball, addictive computer games and coming up with better things to do than clean her house. To learn more about Amy and her stories, visit www.amyknupp.com.

Books by Amy Knupp

HARLEQUIN SUPERROMANCE

1342—UNEXPECTED COMPLICATION
1402—THE BOY NEXT DOOR
1463—DOCTOR IN HER HOUSE
1537—THE SECRET SHE KEPT
1646—PLAYING WITH FIRE*
1652—A LITTLE CONSEQUENCE*
1658—FULLY INVOLVED*
1702—BURNING AMBITION*

*The Texas Firefighters

Other titles by this author available in ebook.

Sincere thanks go out to
Larissa Ione and her husband, Lieutenant Bryan
Estell, for so willingly answering my numerous odd
questions about the military.

Dayna Hughes for helping me with physical therapy
questions and scenarios.

Jim Davies for setting me straight on guns, or
wholeheartedly trying to.

Sharon Muha for embracing my plans to write a
female computer geek. Her enthusiasm pushed me
on days I needed a nudge.

Melanie Scallon and family, for letting me give their
cats cameo roles in my story.

Jeannie Watt, Kay Stockham, Ellen Hartman and
Kim Van Meter, who were involved in the birth of
the book's hero. He may have evolved a bit, but he
still has his roots in rogue-ness.

Victoria Curran for championing the story from
the very first version of the first proposal, and for
making it, and every other book I've had published,
stronger with her mad editing skills.

CHAPTER ONE

As someone who'd recently vowed to find herself a man, Taylor McCabe should've been at least a smidgeon excited to discover a good-looking one on the back deck of her house.

But no. *Excited* wasn't the word she'd use as she drove her car past him and into her garage after a long day at work.

Dread. That was the word. It rose steadily in her gut as she sat summoning the courage to climb out of the front seat and face him.

Two facts held her back: A) She was Taylor McCabe. B) He was Alex Worth—the target of an impossible, embarrassing schoolgirl crush that she'd kept secret all these years.

To avoid the humiliation of being caught hiding, she slipped the straps of her purse and leather laptop satchel over her shoulder and opened the door, muttering a pep talk as she forced herself out of the car.

Eyes glued to the crumbling driveway, she emerged from the safety of the garage and did her best not to focus on the rugged, virile army helicopter pilot who was most likely watching her every step and wondering why she was such a perpetual misfit.

As she neared the deck, she managed to raise her chin and peer at him—or rather, just barely past him—as he slowly stood.

"Look at you," he said with a hint of amusement in the low voice that always surprised her with its smoothness. "Nearly nine o'clock at night and you're just as laced-up and proper as you were when you went to work this morning, I'll bet."

She glanced down at her white blouse with mother-of-pearl buttons, khaki pleated slacks and her latest nod to the shoe monster that raged inside her, dark-brown zebra-print slingbacks with three-and-a-half-inch heels. Acquired at a killer clearance, thank you.

When she looked back up at him, she noticed he, too, was staring at her shoes with…distaste? Confusion?

Her cheeks warmed and no doubt reddened. She nudged her glasses up on her nose and couldn't think of a response to his comment. "When did you get back to town?"

"Yesterday. You missed the party." He frowned as he stared absently into the distance.

Drat. Had she forgotten something? "I'm sorry, Alex. I didn't know—"

"Kidding, Scarlet." The nickname he and her brother had always used for her caused a sharp pain. No one had called her Scarlet since before the accident that had killed Quinn. And though she'd never liked the name, there'd been recent days when she would've given anything to hear her brother say it again. "Just my mom and sister trying to act like I belong here in Madison."

Something in his tone distracted her from the ache in her chest and she finally dared to really look at him. His dark hair hung over his forehead, making him less clean-cut all-American and more overgrown and shaggy, reminiscent of the devil-may-care attitude he'd projected in school—and yet it didn't quite ring true today. The gunmetal-gray cargo pants, black T-shirt and combat boots he wore were the off-duty dress of a soldier, but something was missing from his stance. Confidence, maybe. The spirit he'd always been full of.

A two-inch scar marred the side of his face, not far from his left ear, and though it had obviously been caused by the helicopter crash seven months ago, she wondered precisely what had sliced his skin.

Their eyes met and, though she was embarrassed to be caught examining him so closely, she was taken by his uncustomary weariness, the edginess deep in those steely gray orbs, so unlike the guy who'd been her brother's best friend since junior high.

"Are you back…permanently?" She'd gotten a couple of updates on his condition right after the accident and knew his leg had been seriously injured. But she hadn't heard anything for months. She didn't know his family well enough that she felt comfortable checking in on how he was doing.

"That's what the army docs would have you believe." He shrugged one shoulder. "They'd be happy to turn me into a desk jockey."

"Don't take this wrong, but you don't seem like you'd enjoy a desk job." From what she knew, he lived to fly. Quinn had loved being in the military and, in fact, had convinced Alex to enlist originally, but once Alex had started learning to fly Blackhawks, Quinn had commented repeatedly that Alex had finally figured out where he belonged.

"That'd be an accurate assessment." There was quiet anger underlining his words. "I have every intention of flying again."

Taylor jerked her gaze away. "Why are you here? At my house?"

"Quinn would want me to check on you."

"True." Some girls had to worry about an overprotective father, but ever since she was five and their dad had walked out on the family, her older brother had taken on the job. "He's not here to force the issue, though, and I'm fine. You're off the hook." She smiled, but immediately felt self-conscious.

"You know your deck needs some work?"

He gestured to the opposite side where the railing and bench that ran around the perimeter got the most direct hit from the weather. The bench was rotting in places, she suspected, but she wasn't sure because she tended to ignore the problem.

"Add it to the list," she muttered. "I'm not much of a home-improvement guru." She and Quinn had inherited the house when their mother died eight years ago, and Taylor had always been thankful for it. But with Quinn on active duty, the upkeep had fallen to her—an area she didn't excel in.

Before he could respond, she ducked her head and slipped by him. She jogged up the two wooden steps and unlocked the back door. She turned to thank him for stopping by, knowing they would both be relieved when he left. What she saw, however, struck something inside her. It wasn't that he was following her up, though any other time that would've caused a minipanic attack. It was the wince that twisted his rugged features into a man she didn't recognize. It lasted only an instant. She turned away, somehow knowing he didn't want her or anyone else to see his pain.

"Come in for a drink if you want," she said awkwardly, half hoping he'd refuse.

He grabbed the screen door and held it for her as she removed her key from the lock and pushed the heavy wooden door open.

"Have a seat." Taylor indicated the scarred, round kitchen table that was almost as old as she was as she set her bags, keys and smart phone down on it. "What would you like?"

He, of course, didn't sit. She'd bet he ignored official orders as often as he could get away with it.

"I'll take a beer if you have one."

A beer. Naturally. As if she regularly stocked the stuff. She should probably break down and buy a six-pack just for times like this, but she felt certain she wouldn't choose the right kind anyway. And there was the small matter that she rarely had visitors and even rarer were they males. But if she was going to start dating... She had lots of changes to make. Maybe stocking beer was one of the easier ones.

ALEX WAS OFF HIS GAME in more ways than one.

Not only was he suddenly a man with his career in the shitter and enough self-blame to choke an entire platoon, but it'd been an eternity and a half since he'd been with a woman.

The evidence of this was never so clear as when Taylor bent over to search a lower shelf of the fridge. He caught himself checking out her backside and considering that beneath those no-frills, all-business clothes, she was hiding some intriguing curves.

Taylor McCabe. His best friend's little sister.

Quinn would track him down with an M16 if he knew. If he were alive.

"I do have a couple of Quinn's beers left in here," Taylor said, reaching to the back of the shelf and pulling out two bottles of his dead friend's brand. Just like that, he was thrown painfully back in time. "Will that work? I'm afraid it's all I've got."

"Works fine. Thanks." He took the bottle she held out, twisted off the top and swigged the cold beer past the lump in his throat, doing his damnedest to ignore the label.

Of course, Taylor hadn't bought her own brand. She wasn't a beer woman. She was about the furthest thing from it. Girls with IQs higher than God's didn't kill brain cells with hops and malt on a regular basis. As if to hammer that fact home, she took out a pitcher of sun-brewed tea, probably some mind-boosting formula, and poured herself a glass. Then she dug around in the bottom of the refrigerator again—he made a point of not looking closely at her body this time—and added a wedge of lemon. That was Taylor, wholesome and healthy. He and Quinn had often ribbed her for exactly that, but it didn't seem right now that his buddy was gone.

"Beer isn't the only thing I have of Quinn's," Taylor said hesitantly as she set her glass down. "I've given away his clothes and books, sorted through his sports trophies and personal things, but I'm down to the hard stuff. Guns, fishing gear, exercise equipment. All the testosterone gear. I need to go through it, decide what to sell and how."

"I know a thing or two about 'testosterone gear.' I can help if you need it."

Weekend of suck, anyone? Sitting here in the kitchen where Quinn had grown up, the only place he'd lived besides army bases and camps, was manageable thanks to some hard-core denial. Going through his belongings… There'd be no ignoring reality, ugly and incriminating as it was.

"I suspect you know more than a thing or two. I'd appreciate that. Maybe this weekend?"

"Pretty full schedule of sitting around and feeling useless, actually. But I can try to pencil you in." He attempted something he hadn't done much in the past few months—a smile.

Taylor returned another self-conscious grin, then looked away. She took a package of fig cookies down from the cabinet, opened it and began arranging the squares on a yellow-rimmed plate.

Alex eyed the chair she'd offered him as the ache in his leg again morphed into a stabbing pain. Son of a bitch. The trip from D.C. to Wisconsin was kicking his ass. He didn't want to take any more pills, but the hell if he was going to be the crippled man taking the chair in every room.

"Does it hurt a lot?" Taylor asked, and he jerked his head toward her, silently swearing at himself.

"Does what hurt?" His tone was curt. Unfriendly.

"I don't know. Your leg? Your head? That's twice since you've been here that it's happened."

"What's happened?" So what if he was avoiding her question?

She shook her head and looked down again, in some ways still so much like the unsure teenager he and Quinn had defended more than once against school bullies. And now here *he* was being the asshole.

His constant companion, guilt, was the only reason he took one of her healthy biscuits when she held out the plate to him.

"These aren't that bad," he said as he chewed.

"I could see on your face you were in pain, Alex." Her voice was quiet, but, for once, not unsure.

"It's nothing. Just a flash here and there. Bad

day." The physical stuff was the least of it when you got down to it.

She studied him, as if doubting what he said. He shut out the ache in his leg and forced himself to the table, away from those prying green eyes. As he lowered himself to the ladderback chair, he avoided bending his left knee as much as possible.

"What exactly do the doctors say?" she pressed.

"That I'd be lucky ever to have enough muscle control to fly a helicopter again."

Maybe he snapped the words out at her. Tough. His medical file, three goddamn inches thick though it might be, was his business. Besides, what did it matter what the doctors said, anyway? He hadn't had any intention of accepting their opinions, not three months ago when they'd examined his progress and not today.

"Sorry to pry. I'm not stupid, though. That wasn't *nothing*." Taylor turned her back to him and adjusted the set of three canisters so they were perfectly lined up on the counter.

Oh, yeah, compulsive straightening meant she was pissed. Quinn used to needle her about it whenever she went on an OCD binge. The tendency had amused Alex in the past, but he didn't like being the cause of it.

"The trip wore me out is all."

She didn't respond, didn't turn to face him. Just kept straightening the stuff on the counter.

Alex again made a point of not looking too closely at Quinn's sister. Instead he checked out the kitchen as if he hadn't been here a million times before. Noticed details he hadn't in the past. The place needed some work.

"Why don't you let me do a little repair and up-keep for you. I see some of the trim around the floor is missing. Splintering outward over there." He pointed.

"That's not your responsibility. I'll hire some-one one of these days."

He got up and walked to the spot. Without bend-ing his leg too much, he inspected the damaged trim. "I know how to replace it. Why pay someone when I have loads of spare time?" He straightened and met her gaze.

She shook her head. "I know you're offering because you feel obligated. You're not."

"I'm not obligated, I'm bored, Scarlet. Come on, I'm sure there's other stuff besides the deck and the trim. Right?"

"It's a long list."

"I don't have a job. Only thing I have to do for months is physical therapy a few times a week."

She bit her lip and examined the trim her-self. "I've been thinking about selling the house.

Maybe moving on to something of my very own. The family home has so many ghosts..."

"No-brainer for me to spruce it up, then. You can pay me if it makes you feel better."

Taylor went back to the counter, picked up a cookie and took a bite. She clicked her fingernails on the Formica as she chewed.

"If you'll take payment, the help would be appreciated," she finally said.

"Do you actually have a list of everything that needs to be done?" He headed back to the table and sat, thinking maybe one of the pain pills he'd been avoiding wouldn't be a bad idea tonight. Only tonight.

She shook her head. "But I'll make one. I've been in denial. Ignoring as much as possible. It's such a hassle."

"Not if you know what you're doing."

"Thank you. I know Quinn would appreciate it, too."

She'd hit precisely on the reason he'd volunteered. That and the desperate need to do something, anything useful while he was stuck here in town. He planned to do PT as much as he could but that would only pass a few hours at a time.

So what if his reasons were selfish. It was win-win. "Have the list ready by this weekend. I can come over and figure out supplies and get started next week."

"I'll do that. Lists are kind of my thing." She bowed her head as if embarrassed.

"Trust me, I remember."

Absently, Alex tapped out a rhythm on the table to break the awkward silence that fell over them. As he took a swig of beer, he noticed for the first time the screen on her phone sitting next to him. He pulled it closer, intrigued by what appeared to be a checklist on a virtual yellow legal pad. It was numbered one through ten.

REQUIREMENTS
1. Driven
2. Intelligent
3. Successful
4. Considerate
5. Well-respected
6. Conservative
7. Neat
8. Optimistic
9. Polite
10. Health-conscious

"Requirements for what?" he asked. "Bill Gates clone? You forgot *philanthropic*."

Taylor rushed over to him and tried to grab the

phone away, but he held it on the opposite side, his arm outstretched fully.

"How did you get that?"

"It was just lying here, begging for my attention," he teased. "Relax. I already read it. What is it anyway?"

She crossed her arms and straightened. "It's a list."

"Yes. We army guys may seem dense, but I figured out all by myself it's a list. What's it for?"

She stared at him for a good twenty seconds, her cheeks light pink. "It's a joke. Traits of the ideal male, which, it occurs to me, is a fictitious being."

"Is this for you? Are you *seeing* someone?"

"You don't have to say it like that."

"Like what?"

"Like it would be the most astounding thing if I went on a date." Taylor morphed from shy to quietly outraged.

"I've never known you to go out much."

It was the way she was, the way she'd always been. Quinn had once said her disinterest in dating suited him fine because it gave him fewer asses to kick.

She dropped her arms and walked to the counter and the plate of cookies. Her shoulders slumped. "I'm twenty-six. I live alone. I have no social life and no family. I need to get out of this house more often."

He studied her back, and the fleeting thought about the body she hid snuck its way in again. Her long auburn hair hung past her shoulders in her usual low ponytail and he stopped to think when he'd last seen her with her hair loose. He couldn't recall glimpsing it out of its usual style for years, at least not since she'd been an adult. She wasn't ugly—not at all. She was just…unadorned. More concerned about bits and bytes or whatever the hell a programming wizard dealt with. From what he'd seen, she was obsessed with her work, and as far as he knew, that had always been enough for her. Of course, that was before the accident that had claimed her only family.

"So what are you going to do with a list?" he asked.

"Isn't it obvious? That's what I'm looking for." She waved a hand toward the phone. "I did a lot of thinking about what I want in a companion and that's it."

"It's so…scientific."

"I'm a scientific girl."

"What if you meet someone who…" He glanced at the list. "Gets your heart rate ramped up but he's an up-and-coming artist? Not yet successful?"

"Then I have no interest in going out with him."

He nodded his head in spite of his complete dis-agreement. "Black and white."

"Precisely."

"How are you going to meet all these men? There must be a lot of single guys at—where is it you work until all hours of the night, anyway?"

"Halverson Systems. I'm leading an artificial in-telligence project right now for the…" She paused and pushed her glasses up, more out of nervous-ness than necessity if he had to guess. "You don't want to hear details. No, I won't look for dates at work. I'll start online."

He didn't say a word, though he hated to think what a full-time job it would be to sort through the idiots and creeps.

"What? It's a viable method of finding love."

"Quinn would go into cardiac arrest."

"He's not here, as we already discussed."

That fact threw Alex into one heck of a dilemma. Quinn wasn't here—some could easily point out *because* of Alex—and therefore no one was looking out for Taylor. No one was here to ensure that she wasn't taken advantage of or hurt. He had a younger sister himself. He was plenty well-versed in the art of playing watchdog, but…

Damn.

As Quinn's best friend, he'd just gotten a pro-motion to head ass-kicker.

CHAPTER TWO

ONE PROBLEM WITH staying at the Worth family home, even temporarily, was the lack of peace. Living with two women—especially when those two women were Alex's always-on-the-go mother and his overachieving sister—required a strong constitution.

Alex sat at the kitchen table late Saturday morning finishing the last of the bacon and eggs he'd fried as he tried to make headway on his search for a vehicle. He hadn't owned one for years, hadn't needed to, and didn't care for the idea of purchasing one now. But it was that or be at his sister's mercy.

He'd buy three cars to avoid relying on her whims and insane schedule.

At that moment, Vienna, who was also the baby of the family, stormed into the room, her typical hurricane self, and went straight for the refrigerator. She emerged with a twenty-four-ounce can of Red Bull.

"You're up early," he said dryly, glancing at his

watch. It was nearly eleven. Normally his sister was awake in time to coax the sun to rise.

"Huge marketing strategies project due Monday. I was working on it till six this morning." She opened the can and chugged several gulps. "Caved for a short nap and ended up sleeping through my alarm."

Beyond bedhead, there were no external signs of sleep deprivation. Alex half chuckled. "Sure you need caffeine, Vee?"

"I need an IV of it. Doubt I'll be sleeping for the rest of the weekend."

"You'll do fine," he told her, meaning it.

Alex had long ago figured that, at five feet tall when she stretched, his sister had to bluster around as she did to make people notice her. And notice her they did. Though she was half-pint in size and wore her dark-brown hair short and pixie-style, she had enough drive for all three Worth siblings—and you could tell that just by looking at her. Of course, Alex was the only one of them who had ever been short on drive.

That was pre-army. Things had changed since he'd last lived here. *He'd* changed. It had never been so evident to him as when he hung out in the small hub of the family home with the country-French decor. His long frame dwarfed the round-backed wooden chair he now sat in, making it creak whenever he moved.

Vienna set her drink on the counter and opened the pantry next to the refrigerator. Without hesitation—he wasn't sure she ever hesitated about anything—she pulled a family-size box of chocolate-and-marshmallow cereal down from the shelf. Instead of bothering with a bowl, she cupped her hand, poured in a pile of sugar-coated crap and shoved it into her mouth. One would think having a dental hygienist in the family would dictate a less sugary grocery list, but their mom had always joked that people like her children kept her employed.

"Get a bowl, Vienna." Cheryl Worth marched in and beelined for the fridge next.

"No time, Mom." Vienna refilled her hand and poured more cereal down her throat. "What are your hours today?"

"Noon to nine. I'm going to the post office and the bank on the way."

Their mother had worked weekends at a department store in addition to her Monday-through-Friday dental gig for as long as Alex could remember. Though there'd been a time after their dad had taken off when it had probably been necessary, she maintained that she did it now because she wouldn't know what to do without it. Wouldn't know what to do without the employee discount was more like it.

Cheryl laid an assortment of veggies out on the counter and sliced a fat carrot into a plastic container. The women continued to discuss sales, shoes, schedules and God knew what else as Alex pushed his now-empty plate aside and drew the next freebie newspaper closer. They'd both disappear soon from the sound of it.

The side door to the garage slammed shut as someone else entered the house. Alex couldn't see the hallway from where he sat.

"What happened to *you?*" Vienna asked whoever had just come inside.

"Bite me." Marshall, the oldest Worth sibling, sauntered into the room, making it seem crowded.

Alex gaped at his disheveled brother. "Your shower broken? Somebody die?"

"Good to see you, too, soldier."

The moniker never failed to grate on Alex's nerves. "That's officer to you, big guy." Who could blame him for replying with the nickname he'd come up with years ago as a subtle reminder he had about three inches and twenty pounds of muscle on his brother? "You look like hell."

Marshall grunted in response and took his turn at the fridge.

"Help yourself," Alex said dryly, feeling territorial over the groceries he'd picked up this morning in a bout of sympathy for their mom. She was only used to having one Vienna to feed and, though she meant well, her foraging attempt for Alex's return hadn't been sufficient.

"Welcome home," Marshall said as he closed the fridge door, a shiny, dark red apple in his hand. Without rinsing it off, he sank his teeth noisily into it and leaned against the counter, chewing. His eyes were hollow, perpetual-stress style. His hair, normally short and neat, could use a trim by Marshall's pretty-boy standards. His pale blue, button-down shirt, his version of casual, looked as if he'd slept in it and hung untucked over his dark blue jeans.

"Apparently I've missed a lot," Alex said.

"Going to war will do that." Marshall took the chair next to Alex, falling wearily into it.

"Among other things." Alex registered the ache in his left leg that was always there, so constant he almost managed to forget it at moments like this when it wasn't flaring up.

"I'm going back in," Vienna said after returning the cereal box to the pantry. "If I don't resurface by tomorrow night, send in nourishment." She sped down the hallway and up the stairs to the big bedroom above the garage that she'd taken over when the rest of them had left the nest.

"I'll be glad when she finishes her MBA," Cheryl said, shooting a concerned glance over her shoulder at her only daughter. "I don't know how she exists on so little sleep."

"Like mother, like daughter," Alex said.

Their mom returned the vegetable bags to the refrigerator and covered her lunch container with a plastic lid, then stuffed it and a can of pop into her pink, insulated lunch bag. She flitted around the house, collecting everything she'd need for an eight-hour shift. "There are chicken patties in the freezer. Buns in the bread bin," she coached from the hall as if they were teenagers staying without parents for the first time. "Maybe you boys can catch up today."

"Later, Mom."

Alex and Marshall weren't best buddies but Alex could handle his brother most days. Marshall was calmer, quieter than the women.

"Forgot how much noise the two of them can make," Alex said, standing slowly, taking time to stretch his leg now that his mom wasn't around to witness it. He went to the counter and prepped the coffeemaker. "Want some coffee?"

Marshall ran his hand over his face and nodded. "Extra-strength."

Alex eyed his brother as he scooped grounds from the large can. Something was definitely up.

Either Marshall had uncharacteristically tied one on last night or something was eating away at him. Alex wasn't one to pry, though.

"What's with all the bird-cage liners?" Marshall indicated the stack of fliers and newspapers.

"I need some wheels."

"You sticking around, then?"

Alex started the pot brewing and turned, leaned against the counter. "Are you kidding? What would I do here?"

"What choice do you have? Thought the alternative was paper-pushing stateside."

"Would be if I accepted the army doc's opinion."

Marshall studied him, head tilted slightly. Old habits died hard and Alex became antsy under the scrutiny. Amazing how nine-plus years in the service, building an admirable career prior to the crash, could go out the window when you were stared down by your older brother.

"So what's the plan? Some kind of surgery you haven't had? Wonder drugs?" Marshall didn't sound judgmental, to Alex's surprise.

"No big miracle. Just hard work with the PT. It's been three months since the army evaluated my leg and I've been working out the whole time."

"How long do you think it's going to take to get back up to speed?" Marshall actually seemed interested and fully alert for the first time since he'd stumbled in.

"Couple of months if I'm lucky. It so happens one of the best therapists in the country is a woman in Chicago."

"You plan to call her?"

"I plan to meet her next week," Alex said, taking a pair of mugs from the ancient mug tree. "Which is why I need wheels."

"If you don't find anything, I'll take you."

Alex poured coffee and raised his brows at his brother as he set the mugs on the table. Marshall wasn't known for going out of his way for Alex. Chicago was two hours each way on a good day.

"No need to take time off work," Alex said. "I'll find a car." He crossed the room again to grab the sugar bowl. He couldn't stand unsweetened coffee. Back at the table, he spooned in two heaping piles of the white stuff and started to stir.

"I had to shut down Worth Publishing."

Alex froze. "What did you say?" His brain wasn't processing right.

"Add it to the long, sad list of belly-up businesses."

Alex turned to scrutinize his brother's face but it only took half a second to ascertain that he was dead serious.

Worth Publishing was Marshall's life. He didn't

have a wife because he was married to his job, cliché or not. From the time he was nine years old, he'd inundated the family with "magazines" he'd created himself, or so the story went. He'd planned on a journalism degree from ninth grade on and followed his plan to start up his own publication. A year and a half after he graduated from college, the first volume of *Lake Life,* a full-blown hoity-toity bimonthly magazine focused on Wisconsin living, was released. The last Alex knew, the company had something like nine or ten full-time employees and had moved to publishing every month.

"What the living hell?"

Marshall pushed his chair back as he stood abruptly, and it slammed into the wall beneath the windowsill. He took off down the hall and out the door to the garage. Alex swore out loud, hesitated, then followed him. He found him on the driveway, shooting hoops with an old basketball that had lost its bumpy texture.

Alex rebounded his brother's shot and took one of his own. They continued without speaking for several minutes, politely taking turns. That gradually led to a one-on-one battle, during which Alex schooled Marshall.

"I'm out of practice and out of shape," Marshall said as they huffed for breath.

"I have a bum leg, man. I'd beat you blindfolded." Alex wiped sweat from his forehead with the bottom of his T-shirt and steeled himself against the pain in his leg. "So what are you going to do?"

"Do? About my career?" Marshall dribbled the ball hard, punishing it. "Hell if I know. I hear fast food is a lucrative field."

"You have money to get by?"

Marshall's jaw tightened. "I haven't taken a paycheck for four months."

Alex swore again and Marshall said, "Amen, brother."

"Does Mom know any of this?"

Marshall shook his head as he blew out a tense breath. "Haven't figured out how to tell her. I'm thinking 'I need to move back home' might be a starting point."

"She'll be so happy to have both of her sons back she won't know what to do," Alex said sarcastically. Their mom loved them plenty, he fully acknowledged, but who wanted a couple of grown, jobless sons bunking and tripling the grocery bill?

"Never thought I'd be in this position. No idea where I'm going, what I'm doing. No direction."

"I've lived like that half my life," Alex replied. "Guess it doesn't matter whether you know what you want all along or if you figure it out when you're nineteen years old. Losing it is a big pile of crap."

Either hell was freezing over or, for the first time in his twenty-nine years, Alex and his older brother had something in common.

"Truer words were never spoken." Marshall drilled the ball into the ground again, forcing it to bounce off the pavement so hard it went as high as the top of the two-story house. "I believe I've figured out the one thing I'll do first." He checked his overpriced designer watch. "Close enough to noon. Think I'll have myself a beer."

"Never thought I'd say this to you, big guy, but that's a damn good idea. I believe I'll join you."

CHAPTER THREE

NOT. GOING. TO CRY. TODAY.

Taylor kneeled on the bathroom floor next to the tub. She stretched her fingers, taking a break from scrubbing the shower grout with an old toothbrush. Scrubbing it to within an inch of its bloody life, as Quinn had always said.

No tears, no tears, no tears.

She'd repeated the words like a mantra. All day long. Maybe if she said them enough, she'd believe them and get through the afternoon without having a complete system failure in front of Alex.

Why in creation had she agreed to have him help her sort through Quinn's remaining belongings? The rest of it—the clothes, high-school trophies, yearbooks—that'd been a traumatic task. In truth, she probably could've figured it out herself if she'd tried, but she hadn't felt up to tackling it. Really, the task could wait another year... or twelve.

She knew why she'd jumped at Alex's offer, though. She was a coward. Terrified of facing the basement alone, because if she did, her control could slip, and she'd already cried her eyes out for a week straight when she'd sorted through his bedroom. The loneliness, the emptiness of Quinn's downstairs workout room, where he also kept his gun collection, might just kill her. She might never stop crying. Having someone with her was a safety net.

Having that someone be Alex Worth was the dumbest plan she'd formulated yet.

Taylor checked her watch through tear-blurred eyes, cursing the painful ball in the back of her throat. Fifteen minutes till he'd said he would arrive. Maybe if she bawled her eyes out now, she'd get it out of her system. Yeah, and then she could greet him looking like she'd been staring at a computer monitor for a week straight.

Biting her lower lip and shaking her head resolutely, she attacked the grout again. It was difficult to tell where she'd stopped cleaning because, truth be told, it didn't need to be done. There was no marked difference between before and after. That's what a death in the family could do to a cleanaholic. A couple of months ago, she'd considered replacing the old tub and all the tile around it—original to the fifty-five-year-old house, she was certain—with one of those one-piece, tile-free models. But then what would she do for therapy?

If she was really going to sell the house, though, she'd have to look into the possibility.

A knock on the back door startled her. She dropped the toothbrush in the tub and jumped up. Checked her watch again. Drat. He was early. Normally that was a trait she appreciated, but today she needed every second she could get to force the lump out of her throat. Steel herself. Start believing that mantra of hers.

The knock came again as she hurried through the living room into the kitchen.

Lord help her. *Not going to cry today.*

She gave the corners of her eyes one final swipe with her index fingers and hoarded oxygen. Opened the door. And for the thousandth time was jolted by the mere sight of Alex Worth. Those broad shoulders, the narrow hips. The stubble on his chin that partially camouflaged his scar and somehow made him even more attractive. The sharp gray eyes that could've been dreamy on another, softer face. On his they were arresting. To her, disconcerting.

His virility seemed to suck out her IQ like a straw in the last drops of chocolate shake.

"H-hi. You're early."

"You're flustered and you smell faintly like bleach."

Heat flooded her cheeks. "Sorry. I was cleaning…"

"No need to apologize, Scarlet. I didn't intend to be early. Wasn't sure how long it'd take me to walk."

"You walked from your mom's house? Isn't that a couple of miles?"

"Three and a half last time I checked."

"With your leg? If you needed a ride—"

"I needed a walk. May I come in?"

She jumped back so he could enter, the blush not receding at all. Alex brushed by and she made the mistake of breathing in just so, catching his masculine, woodsy scent.

"Would you like a drink? Some cookies?" Taylor opened the cabinet and searched for anything she could feed him. "I…didn't get more beer yet but I have tea."

Alex chuckled behind her—she wasn't sure why—and said, "No. No tea. Thanks."

"Water? Cookies?" So what if she was trying to put off walking down into Quinn's "man room"?

"I'm good. Do you have the home-improvement list done?"

Grateful for the stall, she took the list from the side of the refrigerator where she'd hung it with a magnet and handed it to him. "That's the exhaustive version. I don't expect you to do all of that," she said, regretting writing every last task down.

He perused it, flipped it over to the back. "Looks like you're losing your touch."

Alarmed, she moved closer and read over his shoulder, or rather, next to his shoulder, trying to figure out her error.

"I expected you to have each one weighted for priority," he said, shoving the list into his back pocket.

"Oh. I did consider that, but I'd rather you just do the things that you want to take on. I didn't know if your leg would hold you back…"

"My leg isn't going to hold me back." His words came out harshly, as if driven by anger or frustration. Or both.

At that moment, Taylor believed he would fly a helicopter again. Soon. This Alex was decidedly different from the apathetic high-school kid she remembered.

"Let's get started," he said.

Taylor sucked in a fortifying breath. "Okay. Yes, let's get started."

ALEX FOLLOWED TAYLOR down into the basement. As he took the last step with his good leg, he was blindsided by the dank, dim familiarity. The wood-paneled family room seemed to vibrate with Quinn's presence.

They'd spent hours down here, in high school and after. Summers, weekends. There were times when Alex had practically lived down here himself. They'd played video games, Ping-Pong, worked out, watched TV…when they weren't fishing or playing sports, chances were good you'd find them in this cave.

Alex swallowed hard and faked a smile when Taylor glanced back at him, apparently noticing he was slow getting down the stairs. This time the pain wasn't so much in his leg. His head throbbed and threatened to explode.

"Does it hurt?" she asked, frowning.

Like he'd been flattened by a goddamn tank. "I'm fine." He was tired of being asked how he was, if his leg hurt, if he was okay.

Taylor paused at the door to the other finished room, straightened her shoulders and then forged inside.

At the doorway, Alex steeled himself against the feeling that Quinn should be sitting there on the bench waiting for him to spot while he lifted. He shut out the pang of sharp grief as he scanned the room he knew so well. Nothing had been moved an inch. The workout equipment, covered now with a thick blanket of dust, still loomed in the center of the polished concrete floor. He tried not to notice the weight level still sitting at three hundred pounds. Refused to think about the time Quinn had finally hit that goal.

The gun cabinet was in the far corner. The large heavy-duty container where Quinn stored his fishing gear whenever he wasn't in town stood near the door to the furnace room. The stereo on the folding table, considered gargantuan by today's standards, dated back to tenth grade when Quinn had saved his allowance to buy it. Alex knew without looking that the banged-up cardboard box next to it held the CDs that hadn't made the cut when Quinn had gone into basic training years ago, pre-MP3 era.

Shit, this blew.

Or it would if he hadn't had months of practice shutting it all down.

"The guns," Taylor said, her voice hoarse with sadness. "Let's do those first."

She took a key chain out of the pocket of her baggy hoodie sweatshirt and attempted to unlock the cabinet. The third key worked. Once she opened it, she stood back and gestured toward it.

"Go ahead," Alex said.

"No, thanks. I don't like guns."

"He always made sure they were unloaded, you know."

Taylor shrugged. "You're the expert. That's why you're here, right?"

Something like that. Alex opened the door she'd unlocked and pulled on Quinn's gloves to keep oil from his hands off the guns. He took out the Winchester rifle first. He wasn't the gun fan Quinn had been, but he could appreciate the collection just the same.

"Whatever you want is yours," Taylor said. She slid her back down the wall to sit on the floor a few feet away, where she could see but wasn't close enough to handle the guns.

"Don't you want to keep any of them?"

"I've never liked having them in the house. If you don't take them, I'll just sell them. Post them online or something."

"No."

"No?"

"Absolutely not. You can't put a gun up for grabs on the internet. You could get all kinds of crazies showing up at your door." He cringed to think what a cluster that would be. Thank God she'd brought the suggestion up so he could prevent it.

"Oh." He could see her imagining the possibilities as she frowned. "I hadn't thought about that. So what do I do?"

"If you really want to get rid of them, I'll take care of it for you. I know some guys who might be interested in a couple of them. The rest I can take to gun dealers, see who will give us the best price."

Alex continued to unload the cabinet, inspecting each one. He leaned the rifles carefully against the wall and set the smaller guns on the folding table by the stereo. For now, he treated the process like business. He wasn't an expert and hadn't purchased a gun himself for a couple of years, but he silently estimated what she could get for each one. Not that she needed the money with her all-powerful computer-wizard job.

"What about this one?" he asked, pulling out Quinn's AR-15. "It was his favorite. The one he bought himself for Christmas three or four years ago. Remember that?"

Taylor glanced at the gun he held and nodded. "I remember. You should definitely take that one."

Alex looked it over, admiring the bluing of the metal. "I don't know."

It didn't seem right taking any of them. They were Quinn's, dammit. He'd spent years acquiring these, starting when they were still in school, with Marshall's help when they were too young to make the purchase.

And Quinn was no longer here to clean them, use them—hell, even decide to sell them.

"If you don't take it, some stranger will end up with it," Taylor said.

He nodded slowly, thinking how that would've made her brother crazy. "I might. Let me know before you do anything else with it." He went to hand the AR-15 to her to set on the table.

Taylor stared up at him but didn't take the gun.

"What's wrong?" He stepped closer to her. "You won't touch it? Really?"

"Guns scare me," she said quietly, and his surprise disappeared, the old protectiveness replacing it even though she was completely safe and there was nothing here, right now, that could harm her.

"Think of it as just a bunch of metal. No ammo. It's safe."

She eyed the weapon as if it was a cobra dancing out of a basket. "No, thanks."

"If you want to get rid of them, a coat of oil might be advisable. Which presents a challenge if you don't want to touch them."

She stared up at him hesitantly. "I was hoping maybe you could help me?"

"You were hoping, huh?"

This was one of those times she looked so young, like an unsure little girl who could easily get hurt. It was difficult for him to say no to that version of Taylor.

She sat forward, and before he realized what she

was doing, she touched the side of the gun he held with one finger then quickly retracted her arm.

"There." She looked smug.

Alex almost grinned. "Really?"

"I touched it. Now will you help me oil them? Please? Or do you require further bribery?"

"What did you have in mind?"

"I'd offer to do your math homework but..."

He couldn't help cracking a grin at that. Even though she was three years younger than him and Quinn, there'd been plenty of times when they had convinced her to do exactly that—and she always had been more than capable. Of course she was the whiz kid who'd graduated early from high school and already had college credits under her belt when she did.

"Home-cooked meals hold a lot of leverage," he said, reacting to the rumble in his stomach.

She stared at him for a moment, maybe to gauge whether he was serious.

"I'll help you with the guns—no cooking required," he relented. He'd convince Vienna to take him for carry-out when he got home.

Her shoulders seemed to relax and he wondered why she was always—still—so tentative around him. They'd known each other for years. This house had been like a second home to him.

"Nothing to worry about, Scarlet. I'll handle it.

Okay if I keep them down here until I find homes for them?"

"Of course. Thank you. I'm making a list of them for you." She held up her phone to show him she'd typed the heading Gun Inventory.

"List time, is it?"

She frowned and he resolved to try to stop teasing her so much.

"Tell me what each one is," she said, "and I'll email you the information."

Even if Alex hadn't known much about guns, he could've given her a detailed summary of every one Quinn owned. He'd gone with him to purchase most of them and had listened to Quinn debate with himself every time he'd gotten the urge to add to his collection. He rattled off the info now, slowly, as Taylor entered it into her phone.

"What's next?" he asked when they were finally through the list of rifles and handguns.

Taylor blew out a long breath that made the loose wisps of hair around her face fly upward. "Take your pick. Exercise equipment or fishing." She stood slowly, wearily, and typed something else into her phone.

Alex might be blocking out the significance of their task but he could tell it was taking a toll on Taylor. "Want to take a break?"

Her eyes fluttered shut and she leaned her head

back against the dark wood paneling. Her long lashes beneath her glasses caught his eye and he took a step toward her without thinking, instinctively wanting to reassure her. Of course there was no reassuring. Quinn was gone and there was no way to make that easier to swallow.

She opened her eyes and met his gaze, determination suddenly emanating from her, taking him by surprise. Moments like this served to remind him she was a fully competent adult, not just Quinn's kid sister.

"I'd like to get through all the man stuff while you're here, if you have enough time."

"Let's get it done, then."

The workout equipment was quick, since most of it would be sold as a set. They wiped it down and made sure everything worked. Quinn suggested a price and she made a note to put an ad online. Then they moved on to Quinn's fishing gear. Rods and reels, tackle and the rest of it— even more than the guns, this was who Quinn was. His preferred brand of rods, stored vertically in one section of the cabinet. Neon orange and yellow bobbers that Quinn had sworn were luckier than other colors. An entire tackle box full of nothing but line, organized neatly, secured with wires. If you compared his gear to Alex's, it was immediately evident they were opposites, at least in this, and you'd wonder how the heck they could be friends.

Alex laughed quietly. "My tackle box always made him cringe."

"He mentioned that. A couple of times."

"Couple of hundred, more likely. He wasn't overly neat in any other area of his life but his fishing gear made me think he hired you to organize it."

Her glance skimmed the floor shyly. "Somehow I think that might be an insult."

He shook his head absently, fortifying himself again against the grief. Over the next forty-five minutes, as they sat on the cool, hard floor and sorted through more fishing gear than the entire army could make use of, he kept an eye on Taylor for signs she was losing it. A woman in tears could level him as a hand grenade couldn't. If she was going to break down, he wanted as much heads-up as he could get.

Taylor had kept it together so far, though. She'd been fighting tears the entire afternoon. Fighting them hard and doing an impressive job of it, in his estimation.

She continued to make the sorting as business-like as she could. Efficient. Organized. Lists on her phone. And then he opened the hinged lid of the last plastic box.

Alex didn't immediately notice her reaction. Then a knot formed in his chest as realization dawned.

"This is the box he always took with him when he fished."

It wasn't as neat as the others, but everything in it reflected the last jaunt Quinn had taken—a river trip, Alex guessed from the gear.

Taylor's thin, pale arm came into his view as she reached across him and grabbed something. She held it in front of her carefully to avoid getting sliced by one of the multiple hooks on the neon pink lure. He looked at her face in time to see a tear escape and trail down her lightly freckled cheek.

Damn, but he needed to get out of here.

Instead, he touched her forearm briefly, helplessly.

"I gave him this when I was seven," she said in a choked voice after quickly drying her face with the back of her hand. "I don't think he ever once used it—for all I know it's only good for catching salmon in the Bering Sea."

"It was his good-luck charm," Alex told her. "He took it with him wherever he went. Lakes here locally, rivers, a trip up north. He always triple-checked to make sure that lure was in the box."

"You can have everything else. This is all I want."

He made the mistake of looking her in the eye. The depth of the sadness there did it. Did him in.

He'd been over and over the crash that had killed Quinn. Could remember every second of it, recall his every decision as the helicopter had come under attack and he'd attempted to bring the disabled Blackhawk down safely. He'd thought through it ad nauseum during the never-ending weeks he'd spent in the hospital and then rehab. He'd thought about Quinn every day since he'd been back in the States. Tortured himself with questions and doubts. But despite all of that, the repercussions had never been so painfully clear to him as they were at this moment, when he looked into Taylor's haunted, desolate eyes.

He was ultimately responsible for the pain that was tearing this woman apart.

CHAPTER FOUR

ALEX WENT FROM one silent emotional woman to one frantic hysterical one when he answered his cell phone on the walk home.

"Yo," he said, forcing a lightness he didn't feel, knowing by the number on the screen it was either his mom or his sister.

"Alex, where are you?" Vienna spoke even faster than usual.

"On my way home. What's wrong?"

"You're not at Taylor's still? My computer, it's freaking out. Dead. I don't know. I can't fix it and my project is due in less than two days. I'm going to die if I can't get it to work—"

"Vee, stop. Breathe."

"I can't breathe, Alex! Do you know how long I've been working on this thing? On my MBA? It all rides on this project! If I can't turn it in on time, it's F city for me."

"Don't you think your professor would understand?"

She laughed but there was only crazed desperation in the sound. "Not a freaking chance. This guy's motto is 'No excuses.' I think he's a direct descendant of Hitler. He's been rubbing his hands together all term, just waiting for us to fail."

"What do you want me to do?" Alex asked, knowing there was no talking his sister down when she was so worked up.

"Fix it!"

"You want me to fix a computer."

"It's…electronic. You can fix anything, Alex."

He knew his way around helicopters, a few military planes, and he might be able to fake it on a car as long as it was an older American model. "I can barely turn a computer on, Vienna."

"But Taylor can, right? You said she's got a high-power computer job. Can we call her?"

"I don't think computer repair is her strong point…"

"Can you ask? If she spends eight hours a day with these stupid things, maybe she knows more than you and me combined?"

More like eighteen hours a day, he thought.

"Aren't there companies who will come to your house for problems like this? Mobile geeks or something?"

"It's Saturday night." Her voice was starting to sound genuinely panicked. "Please, can you at least ask Taylor? Where are you? I'll come pick you up and we can take my laptop over."

Call him a selfish bastard but the prospect of not having to walk another three miles on a leg that was now throbbing after bending, stretching and squatting all afternoon had definite appeal. And maybe Taylor could help.

"I'll call her and ask," he said. "Wait to hear back from me."

"Thank you thank you thank you." She disconnected before he could tell her not to get her hopes up.

TAYLOR GAZED AT HER reflection as she combed through her wet hair. Her skin was pink from the scalding shower she'd taken in an attempt to wash off all the basement dust as well as the soul-deep sorrow that'd been dogging her all afternoon.

Although she dreaded the long empty evening that stretched before her, she was relieved Alex was gone. His presence put her on guard as nothing else could. She couldn't explain it, really, but she felt as if he constantly scrutinized her every clumsy move. Logically, she guessed most of it was in her head, but that didn't matter. He made her feel edgy and inadequate just by being in the same room.

Still, she couldn't have gotten through today's task without his assistance. At least not so quickly. It would've taken her weeks to research everything, look up models and brands and retail prices to try to figure out what prices to ask. Plus the bit about being naive enough to consider selling the guns online. Honestly, without him, either the guns would sit in the basement for eternity or she'd end up dead from a crazed killer.

The pile of dusty clothes on the bathroom floor began buzzing and she realized she'd forgotten to remove her phone from the pocket of her sweatshirt. Lorien, her blue point Siamese, had sneaked in and curled up on the heap. Taylor tossed the comb on the bathroom counter, tugged her sweatshirt out from under the cat and dug in the pouch for the vibrating cell.

"Hello?" She didn't recognize the number.

"Hi, Scarlet, it's Alex. Is this a bad time?"

"Um, no?" Was there a good time? She felt shaky just hearing his voice.

"Sorry to bother you. My sister's having a crisis and I promised her I'd call." She listened as he explained about Vienna's grad-school project and her potentially dead computer, and the shakiness gradually went away. She could deal with computers so much better than testosterone-laden, stormy-eyed helicopter pilots.

"I can see if I can figure it out. My diagnostic skills are mediocre."

"Apparently she doesn't have many options at

this point. I'll call her. I imagine she'll be there as soon as she can drive over if that's okay."

"It's fine." Pathetic as it was, the thought of company—less intimidating female company—brightened her outlook for the evening, even if it meant fighting with a machine. "Anytime."

"Thanks, Scarlet."

Taylor frowned at herself in the mirror as she set the phone on the counter. She was forever Scarlet, Quinn's redheaded little sister who needed to be looked after. She wondered if Alex would ever see her as more than that. As a capable woman who could write some pretty world-rocking computer code. Not likely, since she seemed stuck on stuttering and blushing whenever he was around.

She threw on a pair of black leggings and an oversize T-shirt she sometimes slept in, thinking only of being comfortable as she tried to solve Vienna's computer problem. She'd seen Alex's little sister from time to time over the years when their families ran into each other. Though Taylor wasn't well-acquainted with her, she knew one thing for certain—Vienna was a lot less nerve-racking than Alex. Easy to talk to, relatively speaking. She'd come to Quinn's funeral, along with their mother. Alex had been stuck on the East Coast at the time, unable to walk and in pretty bad shape. Vienna's warm embrace at the visitation had seemed genuine in a long line of uncomfortable hugs of obligation.

Taylor had just finished blow-drying her hair when the doorbell rang. Elanor, Lorien's seal point sister, beat a hasty path to Taylor's room, no doubt to hide under the bed. "Coward cat," Taylor called out, shaking her head. Lorien peered up at her with disinterest as she left the room.

Taylor opened the door and greeted Vienna. Again, something about the girl's manner was open, friendly, and any nervousness Taylor had harbored lessened.

Vienna was dressed in denim shorts, a plain white tank top and glittery purple flip-flops that Taylor coveted on sight. A faint darkness below Vienna's eyes was the only hint that she wasn't on top of the world. What Taylor wouldn't give to look half as put-together with so little effort.

"Taylor." Vienna pulled her into a friendly one-armed hug, holding her laptop to her chest with the other. "You're an absolute doll for agreeing to look at this thing. If my life didn't depend on it, I would've winged it into the street by now."

"It's no problem, really. I just hope I can find the issue. I love your shoes, by the way."

"Brand-new," Vienna said enthusiastically. "Sales at Laurel's are the best."

"My favorite store." Taylor smiled, her two favorite subjects—computers and shoes—relaxing her to a degree.

The ancient, rusted-around-the-edges car backing out of her driveway caught her eye.

"I sent Alex to pick up pizzas for all of us. You haven't eaten, have you?"

"No," Taylor said, suddenly self-conscious at how sloppy she looked in her almost-pajamas. Changing now would make it seem like Alex's opinion mattered, and really, it didn't.

"Is pizza okay? It's the least I could do."

"Pizza sounds delicious but you really didn't have to."

"Ha! You don't realize how much my ass is in a sling until I can get this thing working." Vienna energetically entered the house as Taylor watched Alex speed off down the street.

"Let's see what we can figure out." She closed the front door, took the laptop from Vienna and headed to the kitchen. The sooner she got started, the sooner she could finish and the less time Alex would be stuck hanging out with her.

Twenty minutes later, the front door opened and Taylor tensed automatically—which was stupid. Why should she worry what he thought of her?

Back to the task at hand, she told herself. She was making progress on Vienna's problem, bit by bit. Losing herself in the challenge again wasn't hard. She belatedly looked up when Alex entered the kitchen and noticed he was limping subtly. His back was to her as he set two large pizza boxes, two smaller ones and a paper sack on the counter. He opened the sack and took out a six-pack of beer, a different brand from Quinn's. He turned around and did a double take when he glanced in Taylor's direction.

She self-consciously ran her hand over her loose hair, adjusted her glasses and tucked her baggy shirt more tightly underneath her rear. "I'd just gotten out of the shower when you called," she explained, realizing as she spoke the words how inane they sounded.

"Don't know when I've seen you with your hair down," Alex said.

Taylor studied the screen, unsure what to make of his comment. His tone sounded about a half step from teasing.

"It looks good down," Vienna said. "Gorgeous copper color. I'm jealous."

Taylor felt heat climbing up her neck at the compliment. "Your hair always looks good. It must be easy to take care of."

Vienna ran a nonchalant hand over her short locks. "It works. I don't have the time or patience for anything else."

"Hate to interrupt the hair fest," Alex said, "but I'm eating. Anyone want a beer?"

"No, thank you." Taylor returned her attention to the stubborn hunk of plastic in front of her.

"What's your rush, brother mine?" Vienna stood and walked over to the counter. She helped herself to a beer and a slice. "Got a hot date tonight?"

Alex scoffed. "Hell no." He put the rest of the six-pack in the refrigerator then took out a breadstick and shoved half of it in his mouth at once. "Taylor's the one who might have a hot date."

She pretended she didn't hear him and typed in a command.

"Are you going out tonight?" Vienna asked, not-so-subtle excitement underlining the question. She sat back down at the table, pulling one foot up on the chair and hugging her knee.

"No." Lorien rubbed up against Taylor's leg as if offering moral support.

Alex's sister continued to stare at her expectantly and Taylor feigned deep absorption in the computer screen.

"Are you dating someone? What's he talking about?"

Taylor bit the inside of her lower lip hard. Closed her eyes briefly and considered how to make this less embarrassing. "I'm ready to meet someone. The right someone. I haven't dated much and I just decided it's past time to go for it." Her voice got stronger as she spoke. She dared to meet Vienna's gaze and braced herself, just in case Vienna was as amused as her brother by the prospect of Taylor finding a man.

"That's awesome, Taylor." Vienna's cerulean eyes shone with encouragement. "Some guy out there will be lucky to find you."

Taylor couldn't help herself. She shot a vindicated glance at Alex, who leaned against the counter stuffing pizza in his mouth. She could swear he momentarily froze when he spotted the cat at her feet.

"So you don't have someone already picked out?" Vienna asked.

"Actually, maybe. I signed up with one of those online dating sites. One of my coworkers met his wife online." She was talking too fast but couldn't help it. "I've kind of met a guy on this site."

Alex gave a disapproving grunt, still staring at Lorien uncertainly.

"Excellent." Vienna leaned forward and practically rubbed her hands together. "So you're going to meet him in person?"

"He asked me to go out this Tuesday." Her cheeks warmed and she cursed the blushing gene.

"You can't go out with some guy off the internet," Alex said. Lorien padded toward him and rubbed against his legs. He stepped to the side. The cat followed.

"Why not?" Taylor had started a process on the laptop that would take a few minutes, so she went to the counter, picked up a paper plate from the pizza place and grabbed a slice of the veggie-heavy pie from the bottom box.

"How do you think serial killers meet their victims?"

"Nice," Vienna scolded him. "Shut up, killjoy. Don't listen to him, Taylor."

"Lorien, leave Alex alone. He's afraid of you," Taylor scolded her cat.

"Am not."

Taylor tried not to laugh. "You've been staring at her. Cats always go to someone who stares at them."

"I don't like cats."

"Don't listen to him," Taylor said to the feline, mimicking Vienna's words to her.

"Come here, kitty," Vienna said, holding her hand down. Lorien, being an attention hog, strutted over to Vienna and allowed her to pet her. "Back to the internet guy. Have you seen his picture?"

"Does he look like a serial killer?" Alex actually sounded worried as opposed to just giving her a hard time. He glanced at the cat, caught himself and looked away.

"He isn't wielding a knife in his photo." Taylor grabbed a plastic fork and cut herself a bite of pizza.

She had many concerns about meeting this guy—any guy—in person, but being offed wasn't at the top of her list. Not even in the top ten. She was too fixated on what she would say, what she would wear, what she'd do if he turned out to be a jerk...what she'd do if he turned out *not* to be a jerk.

"I'm sure she's being cautious," Vienna told her brother.

"Where are you planning to meet this guy?"

"It's nothing formal. Just happy hour at Ian's." She cut another bite, leaning over the counter to pop it in her mouth.

"See?" Vienna told him. "Taylor's smart. Big, busy public place, daylight hours."

Taylor was torn between feeling annoyed that Alex was trying to fill the conspicuously vacant big-brother role and being a teeny bit touched that he cared enough to not want her massacred by some psychopath. That was twice in one day, come to think of it. First the potential gun nuts and now the serial-killer date. She finished chewing and straightened. "I'm a big girl, really."

Alex stood up straight as well and peered down at her, towering over her and emphasizing their eight- or nine-inch height difference. "No. You're not."

"Bully." Taylor took her plate and returned to the table to check on the computer's progress. Setting her plate to the side, she typed rapidly, her suspicions about the problem beginning to be confirmed. "It looks like your hard drive is dying."

"That doesn't sound pretty," Vienna said, frowning and taking a swig from her bottle. "What does that mean exactly? Can it be fixed?"

Taylor typed some more, checking one last possibility. It confirmed her diagnosis. "It means you'll need to replace the computer."

"Tonight? Is it completely dead?"

"I've got it working for now. You need to save everything on an external drive just in case, but you should be able to finish your project. I wouldn't rely on it for more than a few days."

Vienna leaned her head back and groaned. "Nooo. This," she told Alex, standing and taking her plate to the trash under the sink, "is why I'm so frantic to secure a job for the fall. I'm sick of being a broke grad student. Tired of asking mom for another lump of cash."

"I can loan you the money for a new computer,"

Alex said, adding his plate to the trash after devouring at least half of the food he'd brought.

"Ha, you think I want to be in debt to *you?*"

"I won't charge you too much interest."

"Good, because I won't pay you any." Vienna crossed her arms over her chest, her shoulders sagging.

The two of them reminded Taylor of how she and Quinn used to get along. They gave each other a hard time, but when you got down to it, they were there for each other. Family. A sharp pang of longing struck her, took her breath for a long second.

"I have several old laptops that still work," Taylor said, pushing the overwhelming wave of emotion aside as best she could. "You're welcome to borrow one for as long as you need it."

"Taylor, you've done too much already."

"They're sitting in the closet in my office wasting away. Nothing's wrong with them, just that newer models come out and, well…never mind about that. I've been meaning to do something with the better ones but haven't gotten around to it. Please. Take one off my hands."

"When you put it that way…." Vienna said. "If you're really sure, I'll take you up on the offer."

"I'll dig out one of the newer ones this week and

get it cleaned off for you. Just let me know when you can pick it up."

"Let me get this straight," Alex said, looking slightly incredulous. "You have a computer *collection?* Enough to 'dig' through?"

"Yes. I guess I do, though it's more of an occupational hazard than an intentional collection."

"How many computers do you have?"

Taylor thought about the closet in her home office. It was her one lapse in neatness. A militant clutter remover in every other way, she had a difficult time parting with old laptops. It was odd, she realized, but she couldn't seem to help herself. "More than a handful," she admitted.

"Ten?"

She smiled sheepishly and shook her head.

"More?"

It was closer to fifteen but he didn't need to know that. She shrugged noncommittally.

"Alex is allergic to computers," Vienna explained.

"Damn straight," he said proudly. "Fishing gear and guns are my speed."

"Ah, that's why we love you so much. Every family needs a Neanderthal fish-catching bear-killer." Vienna patted him affectionately on his very tight abdomen—not that Taylor had noticed.

No, she hadn't noticed at all when he'd raised

his arms to lift something in the basement earlier and his shirt had ridden up. Not more than a dozen times, anyway.

Alex grabbed his sister and pulled her to his side, rubbing the top of her head roughly. There was no mistaking the bond between them.

The emptiness in Taylor swelled and she looked away so they wouldn't notice the wetness in her eyes.

She missed her brother. Though he'd spent the past ten years in the military, this had still been the place he landed when he had time off. Taylor had treasured the few days here and there when he came home.

She longed to have someone around now, someone to keep her company, tease her. Yearned to have someone else breathing in the house besides furry critters who lacked conversation skills. She was aching for someone who could love her.

As soon as Alex and Vienna left, she'd go online and tell Dan yes to Tuesday night. Having company here this evening was a rarity. She wasn't sure how many more nights she could face in this silent, somber house.

CHAPTER FIVE

DAN DRUMMOND WAS decidedly not what Taylor was looking for.

If she had to listen to one more word about video games, guilds or levels, she was going to... well, she didn't know what she'd do. She hadn't gotten that far in her pre-blind date freaking-out session because she'd been too caught up in important matters, like whether or not to put on lip gloss and which potential conversation topics she'd use in case of awkward silences.

An hour and fifteen minutes into the date and there'd been plenty of awkward. Not enough silence.

Dan was not her dream companion. And she hated to be prematurely judgmental but he was crawling closer to nightmare status.

She closed her eyes, savoring the break in his incessant chatter. He'd gone to the bar to get himself another "fully leaded" soda. As he'd explained, he had plans to play the online game that apparently ruled his existence later tonight and needed to be able to stay awake till all hours. If she wasn't so relieved that he didn't intend to take up too much of *her* evening, she'd be annoyed by his double planning.

Maybe it was just nervousness on his part, Taylor thought as she picked up the last piece of fried mozzarella from the combination appetizer platter they'd shared. Maybe she just wasn't trying hard enough to ask him questions that didn't involve his beloved game. She was, after all, rusty on dating. Had never been good at small talk, either.

The sight of him heading through the happy-hour crowd back toward their table had her stifling a groan of dread. Surely this couldn't last much longer. She could get through a few more minutes, be pleasant. Act interested. Well, not *interested* interested, just…polite.

"So…" She searched her mind for one of those topics on the list, something they hadn't covered in the first five minutes—the slot of time before he'd delved into his disturbing video-game obsession. "How long have you lived in Madison?"

He sat on the raised stool and set down his third non-alcoholic drink as well as a basket of cheese fries. "Couldn't resist a little more food," he explained.

Before he could answer her question, he took his phone out of his pocket.

"Excuse me just a second. A text from one of my guild guys."

For the love of all things holy...

Taylor glanced around, desperately wishing for a graceful way out. Come to think of it, graceful wasn't that important at this point. She just needed to cut her losses and escape.

She didn't know what she was looking for, but she did know precisely what she wasn't looking for. Or who, more specifically. Her pulse picked up when she recognized none other than Alex Worth sitting at the bar. He stared directly at her and she wanted to throw her head back in frustration. Even better, to duck.

Was it coincidence that he was here? No. He'd pried out of her when and where her date was. *Pried* wasn't the right word—she'd offered up the information like a naive little lamb. Was he spying on her? Really, what did he think she was going to do? She prayed desperately that he was too far away to ascertain how horribly her rendezvous was going.

She pretended she hadn't recognized Alex and returned her attention to her oh-so-engaging date.

"Oh, no." Dan's fingers moved over the letters on his phone in a frenzy. He frowned, his entire face falling.

"Is everything okay?" She leaned forward and nearly reached out but caught herself.

He didn't answer right away, just kept punching the mini keyboard. Then he seemed to realize she'd spoken and he looked at her. "I'm sorry, Taylor. I'm not usually this rude. Got a bit of a situation here...."

His phone vibrated again and he read the new message. "Well, crap." He tapped in another response. "Yeah. Taylor, I'm really sorry but I'm going to have to cut this short."

"What's wrong, Dan?" She was starting to wonder if someone had died or had some horrible catastrophe.

"Oh." He surprised her with a grin and waved his hand. "Just a guild emergency. But we've got to take care of it right away or one of our main guys is threatening to leave the group."

Her jaw must have dropped to the floor. "A... guild...emergency," she repeated slowly.

"These guys aren't a patient lot. This one is key to our success and he knows it."

"Oh, well, then he holds all the cards." Sarcasm wasn't normally something she used aloud, but it had been building in her for the past hour. She couldn't care less what Dan the Guild Man thought of her.

"Exactly." He picked up the glass of cola and

swigged a third of it down. "Thanks for being so understanding. I'll be in touch."

Not if she could help it.

Before she could wish him insincere luck with his crisis, he was gone.

Fantastic.

She could feel the people at the surrounding tables glancing in her direction, as if they knew her date had walked out on her. Her face heated as she picked up her purse, ready to make a quick getaway, but then the still-hot basket of fries caught her eye.

Oh, lord. Had he paid for *any* of this?

Humiliation balled in her throat. She lowered her chin to her chest, squeezed her eyes shut tightly and willed hot tears away. When she'd composed herself, she raised her head to track down the waitress who'd originally served them.

Just in time to watch Alex step up next to the stool Super Dan had occupied.

Someone really needed to invent a way to disappear.

"Is this seat taken?" Alex said with a sympathetic half grin, and she could tell he'd seen what had happened.

This was where she should have a cute, sassy line to throw back at him, to show him it didn't matter that she'd been walked out on. Unfortunately, in typical Taylor style, she had no catchy lines and it did apparently matter. She simply shook her head in response.

He sat on the stool and indicated the fries. "Can I steal one?"

"Steal the whole basket. My treat." She tried to smile nonchalantly but just wasn't feeling it.

"Did that bastard really leave you here?" All hint of amusement was gone and the anger in his tone surprised Taylor.

"It appears so." Taylor took a sip of her soda more for something to do than because of thirst. "What are you doing here?"

"It's happy hour. Great drink specials."

"Right. Ian's doesn't seem like your kind of place."

He stuck another cheese-drenched fry in his mouth. When he'd finished chewing, he said, "What *is* my kind of place?"

Something with a less-sedate clientele, she thought. A room full of beautiful women dressed to kill. Even at happy hour, Ian's catered to the business crowd. Guys in Dockers and women with non-trendy hairstyles.

"Why don't we just get this over with," she said.

"Get what over with?"

"The whole I-told-you-so lecture. 'Can't date a guy you met online.' Et cetera."

He started to speak but then stopped himself. "I was worried about you getting hurt physically. It didn't occur to me the asshole would go AWOL on you."

"I hadn't anticipated that, either." She swished her straw around in her nearly empty drink. "It wasn't a bad thing, frankly."

"He wasn't worth your time, Scarlet." He continued to devour the fries.

"If you only knew…"

The waitress stopped by their table then and asked if she could bring anything else. She did a double take, as if noticing Alex wasn't the same guy as before. Then Taylor watched her whole manner change from business to flirty.

"Just the check, please," Taylor said, unwilling to witness Alex landing a date without even trying.

The man at the next table gestured to the waitress. "You got it," she said to Taylor and hurried off.

"Seriously?" Alex said, staring at her in disbelief. "He left you with the tab?"

"He was charming."

"I've got to ask…what made him retreat?"

"Guess I'm just a scary date." The truth seemed worse than taking the blame herself.

"Sure you are. Terrifying. I don't buy that for a second."

The waitress reappeared, moving in closer than necessary to Alex and putting her hand on his shoulder as she set the black vinyl sleeve in front of him. Really? It took a lot of nerve to be so forward when he was with another woman. Of course, that woman was Taylor, and obviously a man like Alex wouldn't be on a date with her.

Too bad for the waitress that Taylor was the one leaving the tip.

Alex smiled blandly at his new friend and she told him to have a great evening before walking away.

He took out his wallet and was sliding his credit card into the plastic pocket before Taylor realized it. She reached out and grabbed it away from him, handing his card back.

"No way are you paying a dime," she said.

"You don't deserve to be left with it." He held out his hand.

"I'm humiliated enough," she said in a low voice as she counted out enough cash to cover the total plus a measly tip. "I just want to leave."

He backed down, as if he understood.

"Thank you." She wasn't sure why she said it, but then she'd never been accused of being smooth.

"I'd offer to give you a ride home but I don't have a car yet."

"Tell me you didn't walk here."

"I didn't walk here."

She didn't entirely believe him. "*I'll* give *you* a ride home unless you plan to stay. I need to get out of here. Immediately."

"I'm not staying. Not my kind of place, you know." He smirked when she met his gaze.

No one should have eyes that alluring, she decided. In this light, they looked more blue than gray. There was no question many women had gotten lost in those depths.

Taylor wasn't going to be one of them. She slipped off the stool and headed through the throngs toward the door, not allowing herself to check whether Alex followed.

He fell in beside her once they hit the parking lot. They walked in uncomfortable silence as Taylor flipped through her list of conversation starters for Dan the Dork. None of them were adequate. She couldn't imagine Alex wanting to discuss the *New York Times* article about Cloud computing or the latest electronic tablet releases. And she already knew about his family and his background.

The click of her open-toed hot-pink heels on the pavement seemed magnified by their lack of conversation. She compulsively counted the last steps to reach the driver's-side door. Punching the remote to open the locks, she climbed in and started the engine. Alex squeezed into the passenger seat and slid it all the way back, drawing her attention to his long, cargos-clad legs. His muscular thighs stretched the material tight and she momentarily imagined those legs without the pants. She suspected they would match the tautness of his picture-perfect abs—or at least they would have at one time. She was curious about how his injury had affected his leg.

"What's wrong?" he asked, and she whipped her head away and put the car in Reverse.

What *was* wrong with her? She tried to rationalize with herself, get herself to believe she had merely wondered about scarring or other evidence of the trauma he'd been through. She wasn't a lusty person and didn't tend toward fantasies inspired by six-pack abs or sculpted pecs. Now that she thought about it, though, she'd bet a large sum that his chest was photo-worthy, as well.

"You going to tell me why the wonder ass walked out tonight?" Alex asked as she turned out of the parking lot onto the street.

"No. Are you going to tell me how you got to Ian's?"

"Vienna dropped me off on the way to some talk for one of her classes."

"Nice of her. She got her project in on time, I assume?"

"Of course. Nothing will stand in that girl's way when it comes to school or getting a job. She's obsessed."

"There are worse things to obsess about."

"*Determined* is a better word," he said, lowering his window to let the early-summer air in.

"What kind of a job is she interested in?"

"Her concentration is in marketing. I don't know exactly what she's looking for, but she claims she wants more than a run-of-the-mill entry-level assistant-peon position."

"Does she have a lot of connections around town?" Taylor asked. She turned the air conditioner off.

"Beats me. I try to stay out of her way."

"I could introduce her to some of the marketing people at my company. I don't know if they have any positions open but it couldn't hurt."

"She'd eat it up. Don't go to too much trouble, though."

"No trouble." An idea popped into Taylor's head that would serve both her and Vienna well. "I'll talk to her about it when she comes by to get the loaner laptop."

They fell into another silence as she stopped at a red light. She stared straight ahead at the bread truck in front of them, hyperaware that Alex was looking right at her. Heart pounding, she fidgeted with the sideview-mirror controls, minutely adjusting hers. She lowered her window halfway and tapped the steering wheel, willing the traffic signal to turn green.

"Are you going to try the online deal again?" Alex asked out of nowhere.

"I might."

She wouldn't. Because he was right. Dan had been able to hide his weirdness from her in spite of several long emails. Who was to say another man's hidden interest wasn't collecting corpses? After tonight's epic failure, she wasn't willing to take another chance on going out with someone she hadn't previously met in person. It might work for millions, but not for her.

But Alex didn't need to know that.

She couldn't bring herself to admit it out loud. To own up to her poor judgment.

"What's it going to take to convince you?" Alex asked. "What if I introduce you to some men. Guys I know."

"First problem, who could you possibly know that would be willing to go out with someone like me?" She could just imagine what his friends would say if he brought her name up.

"What's that supposed to mean?" he asked.

"Never mind."

"Scarlet, I'm trying to help you. I don't agree with the way you're going about the manhunt thing so I offered to introduce you to people you can trust. That's all."

She felt him staring at her again and tried to ignore the need to squirm.

"I don't get you," Alex said.

"You don't want to get me."

She pulled into the Worth driveway.

"You remembered where I live. Impressive."

"I have an above-average brain," she muttered, only half paying attention to the pointless conversation.

"Some guy will fall in love with that. Just not someone you'll find on the computer."

"Alex," she said, keeping her gaze fixed straight ahead. "Could you…go now? Please." He continued to study her then shrugged.

"See you Saturday."

Saturday. To start the work on the house, she reminded herself.

She should cancel that whole arrangement, or at least Alex's part in it. But not right now because she had about twenty seconds before she broke down and cried her eyes out, and frankly she was maxed out on humiliation for the evening.

CHAPTER SIX

IN SPITE OF EVERY MUSCLE in his body screaming at him after forty grueling minutes of physical-therapy hell, the need to hit something rumbled through Alex like a volcano getting ready to erupt.

The news from Helen Vossmeyer, the highly respected physical therapist, wasn't roses and unicorns. She hadn't sat across from him, after poring over his medical files and putting him through a workout, and smiled hopefully. None of them ever did, and he understood that they couldn't guarantee anything. Didn't want to get someone's hopes up to have them crushed yet again. He wasn't an idiot. But was an optimist too much to ask for?

Because, dammit, he was grasping on to hope the way an orphan clung to a ratty old teddy bear.

He entered the parking garage, walked up to the passenger side of Marshall's eggshell Acura and opened the door before noticing his brother sat there.

"What the hell? Move over," Alex said.

"You can drive home."

Alex swore at him. "You said you'd give me a ride. That suggests that you drive the car."

He shifted his weight off his bad leg and leaned heavily against the back door, waiting for Marshall to get out of his way. Instead of climbing out, his brother lifted his right hand, which held a bottle of Jack Daniels. A third of the amber liquid was gone.

"You bought whiskey?" Alex didn't know whether to be impressed with his foresight or disgusted with the implications.

"Liquor store down the block and across the street. I'd offer you some but you're driving."

This was not the perpetually motivated brother he knew. Nothing like him. Marshall wasn't a complete abstainer, but his version of tying one on was having a second glass of wine at a business dinner. Alex had never seen him hit the hard stuff. Maybe that was why he pushed off the car and headed around to the driver's side without another word.

He got in, found the keys hanging from the ignition and started the engine.

"You better be able to hold your liquor. I don't want to have to pull over if you get sick."

"I don't want to mess up my car even more than you don't want to stop."

They were silent until Alex had merged with the

relatively-light-for-Chicago midafternoon traffic on I-90.

"So how'd it go?" Marshall asked after taking another swig.

Alex was just about picking up a buzz from the smell alone. "It went." With one hand steering, he tapped the bottom of the wheel agitatedly, trying to release some of his pent-up energy.

"What'd she say? Was she encouraging?"

"Somewhat. More so than the army doc three months ago."

"She thinks you can recover fully?"

"Said it's possible. I've made a lot of progress since March."

Marshall nodded and took another drink.

"Keep that out of sight, would you?" Alex snapped. "I'm not looking to be pulled over today, either."

Marshall lowered the bottle below window level. "So?"

"So what?"

"What do you think? You going to give it a chance?"

"I think to hell with 'possible.' I'll get it all back. I have to."

Silence filled the car for several minutes.

"I'm the one with everything at stake," Alex said, maybe more to himself than to his brother.

"That's what they don't take into consideration when they give you their official opinion. Willpower. Determination. I've *got* to get back."

"Why are you so bent on returning to that hellhole?"

"Just…need to." His hand started tapping on the steering wheel again, without his conscious thought.

"Army's not exactly running a four-star hotel over there. You've got a compelling, understandable reason to walk away. What gives?"

"It's just…what I do. What I know."

Marshall stared at him again. Alex forced his hand to still on the wheel. He hit the CD player's power button and was pleasantly surprised when the cacophony of Rob Zombie blared through the expensive speaker system at a brain-busting volume. Suited his state of mind perfectly.

After tipping the bottle up again, Marshall reached over and killed the music. "You can do something else."

"Like what?"

"Whatever you want to. You're the only one who bought your act of drifting around uselessly before you joined."

"Flying's in my blood."

"Don't have to be military to fly."

It was all so damn easy, wasn't it? "I know that!"

Alex exploded. If he couldn't punch something, yelling would have to do.

His brother didn't take the bait, didn't give him the fight he was itching for. Marshall just sat there, infuriatingly calm, sipping his Jack like a baby with a bottle of milk. Irritation built, welled up from deep in Alex's gut. He could feel his blood pressure ticking upward. He let out a stream of crude obscenities and again Marshall didn't even flinch.

"I have to go back," Alex finally said. "For Quinn." Speaking his dead friend's name had a sobering effect. Tightness gripped his chest as oxygen seemed to leak out of the car.

They crossed the Wisconsin border without a word, the silence tense, expectant.

"I don't understand that," Marshall said just when Alex thought he was going to get away with the admission. "What's going back to hell got to do with Quinn?"

"Quitting now..." Alex took his time to form an answer, maybe because he was figuring it out as he went along "...is the easy way out. I just get a guy killed and then go get a job at Radio Shack and live easy?" A foul taste filled his mouth. "I don't think so."

"So it's like penance?"

"Hell if I know." He wasn't in the mood to be

psychoanalyzed by his cerebral brother. "No. It's not like penance. It's going back and doing what I do because that's what Quinn would've done. If he could've. He was over there for a reason, more of a reason than me. I just wanted to fly. He believed in the cause to his core. I owe it to him to keep doing it because he can't."

Marshall chewed on that for a good five minutes before speaking again. "You don't have anything to make up to him, you know. The enemy shot you down. You did the best you could to land safely."

"Easy to say," Alex snapped. "Hard to prove. I don't expect you to understand."

"I goddamn understand more than you know." The rage in Marshall's voice took Alex by surprise, but before he could question him, his brother pounded on the CD player and Rob Zombie serenaded them with his angry growling once again.

Suited him just fine.

It wasn't until they hit the outskirts of Madison that Marshall reached over and swatted the music off as violently as he'd turned it on.

"I screwed the hell up," Marshall said quietly, but with so much conviction it dripped from the words.

Alex knew his brother wasn't talking about today, but he didn't ask any questions. More than half the bottle of whiskey was gone. Maybe this was Marshall working through some hard-core crap.

"Nine people are out of work because of my mistakes," Marshall continued, self-loathing evident in his tone.

"Businesses go under. I'm sure you tried to prevent it."

Marshall scoffed. "Two years ago I had a company trying to get me to take the magazine electronic. 'Where the future is,' they said. Did I listen to them?"

"I'll guess no."

"Hell, no. I was one of those fools who swore print would never go away. Couldn't imagine newspapers going under. And high-end glossy full-color magazines people could hold in their hands…they'd never choose a computer monitor over that." He laughed bitterly. "I know a thing or two about self-blame."

"That sucks," Alex said sympathetically.

"Screwing the hell up sucks."

"Agree completely."

"It's humiliating." Marshall's voice had lost all its bluster and he was barely audible over the sound of the road.

Alex nodded once, understanding all too well what Marshall was talking about.

Wasn't it funny how things changed, he mused. After a lifetime of being the family member who never really belonged, Alex now had more in common with his brother than he could ever want. He wasn't going to acknowledge that out loud, though. What was the point?

Instead, he was going to funnel all the self-blame, all the anger and the doubt into PT. He couldn't change what had happened or take anything back, but he was going to somehow move past it all by honoring his dead friend. The best way to do that was to get back to the Middle East and continue the work Quinn had believed so fervently in.

CHAPTER SEVEN

TAYLOR BREATHED EASIER the farther she and Vienna got from the crowd near the lakeshore park on Friday evening.

Another work function survived—the annual picnic and concert. They'd endured the dinner part and had escaped as the local band was setting up. Taylor had done her duty, made her appearance, and now she was done in more ways than one. Ready to wilt into a puddle and decompress for the next hour or two.

Ready but not able to quite yet.

Though Vienna was friendly, Taylor still felt a bit ill-at-ease with her, especially now that it was just the two of them. It wasn't Vienna—that's just how Taylor was. Once a social failure, always a social failure.

They opened her car, climbed in and sat with the doors ajar for a few seconds to let the remaining late-afternoon heat escape. Taylor was just starting to become antsy, thinking she needed to say something, when Vienna broke the silence.

"That was excellent. Thank you so much for introducing me to practically everyone in the marketing department, Tay. Awesome connections."

"It was no problem. I hope it goes somewhere. Did they say whether they expect to be hiring in the fall?"

"It sounds promising, actually. They're working on creating a new position that would be a perfect fit for me. Hugh Samuels said he'd contact me when it's concrete."

"That's encouraging. He seemed interested in you."

The shake of Vienna's head was so subtle Taylor would've missed it had she not been looking directly at the woman.

"Not the kind of interest I'm looking for, you know?"

No, Taylor didn't know. The marketing vice president had been overtly friendly to Vienna. Had maybe held her grip a touch longer than necessary when they'd shaken hands, but you couldn't prove it by Taylor whether he'd crossed a line. She'd never had anyone be anything but professional with her, so she wouldn't know.

They both pulled their doors closed and Taylor considered turning on the radio to avoid the need to talk. Would that be rude?

She decided against music and settled for the air

conditioner on High. She backed out of the parking space and headed toward their side of town.

"What's wrong, Taylor? You're practically white-knuckled. Something bad happen back there that I missed?"

Taylor forced her fingers into a stretch on the wheel, unaware until Vienna had spoken that she'd been grasping it so hard. "Work things like that aren't my favorite."

"You were great when you did all the introductions."

"The business part I can handle…" She nervously pushed the strands of hair that had come out of her ponytail behind her ear. "You're good at the social thing," she said simply.

Vienna laughed. "If only you knew. I was so nervous I talked five hundred miles an hour. About nothing! I'm not usually such a mess but I felt like a college student among grown-ups."

The admission relaxed Taylor a bit. "I never would have guessed. You seemed at ease. Enviably so."

"I hesitated to shake anyone's hand because mine was so sweaty."

"I'd say you made a good impression."

"Thanks. You know, we need to recover. That was trying."

"Recover," Taylor repeated dumbly.

"Absolutely. Let's go have a drink. It's Friday night, we've been through trauma."

"Wh-where?"

"Nothing fancy. The opposite, in fact. There's a bar two blocks from my house, Saint Patty's. Do you know it?"

"I'm afraid not."

"Most people don't, which is the beauty of it. It's smack in the middle of a bunch of houses. No idea how it got zoning approval. It's about as big as the backseat of your car. Low-key. We'll probably be the only two there."

Taylor had never gone out to bars with girlfriends. She didn't have girlfriends, never had. Kind of a fact of life when you were two years younger than your classmates and, well, a geek.

She apparently hesitated too long.

"Patty's a family friend. She makes a wicked white chocolate martini."

"I'm embarrassed to admit I've never had a martini."

"Do you drink?" Vienna asked in a rush.

"Some. Usually wine. Mostly because I don't care for beer and I don't know what else to drink."

"You have to try Patty's martini. She doesn't advertise it, only makes it for someone who knows to ask. It's not really a martini kind of place."

Taylor didn't exactly know what a martini kind

of place was, but as they walked toward the front of Saint Patty's five minutes later, she could see clearly that this was not the classiest watering hole in town. Likely not in the top five hundred.

"Told you it's a dive," Vienna said, holding the rickety screen door open for her. "Don't worry, it's safe."

The exterior was white and in desperate need of a coat of paint. Centered on either side of the entrance was a small window with an empty, weathered flower box hanging haphazardly beneath it. The one to the left was more vertical than horizontal. The concrete walk was crumbled in places, and Taylor was thankful she'd worn two-inch floral wedges to the picnic. She wasn't sure she could navigate it in heels.

This wasn't a place where heels were commonplace, she surmised as they went inside. Motorcycle boots, work boots, maybe.

A shabby bar with three sixties-era light fixtures stretched along the near wall, perpendicular to the front door. Small tables were scattered throughout the room—six of them, Taylor counted. Nothing matched, not even four chairs at a single table and Taylor itched to rearrange them to achieve at least some degree of symmetry.

"Table or bar?" Vienna asked.

"You choose." Taylor felt the two men at the

far table watching them and longed for her own kitchen and a fresh-tossed green salad.

Vienna took one of the stools with a back midway down the bar. Taylor uneasily sat to her right on a simple round stool with no back.

"It's the baby Worth," a woman's voice called out. There was a service window in the wall behind the bar, and though no one was visible, that's where the sound came from.

"Hey, Patty," Vienna hollered.

The woman appeared in the doorway at the far end of the bar, wiping her hands on a powder-blue towel. She was in her late fifties, Taylor guessed, with short, russet hair, round cheeks and a genuine smile. Wide-shouldered and ample-chested, she carried extra pounds around her middle. Her pink T-shirt declared, *I'm not good at empathy, will you settle for sarcasm?*

"How you doing, honey?" She came around on their side of the bar and hugged Vienna.

"Fantastic." Vienna swiveled to include Taylor. "This is my friend Taylor McCabe. Taylor, Patty Wyman."

Taylor's stool didn't twist so she rotated partway around, extending her hand politely and saying hello. Patty threw her off by ignoring the hand and pulling her into a quick hug. "Welcome, Taylor. Have you girls eaten yet?"

Vienna nodded. "We're here for dessert, if you know what I mean."

A conspiratorial smile spread across Patty's face. "White chocolate for each of you?"

"You in?" Vienna asked Taylor.

"I have my car—"

"We'll make sure you get home safely, sweetie," Patty said, somehow brash and warm at the same time. "I don't let anyone drive outta here who can't."

Taylor liked this woman. She was welcoming and motherly and yet Taylor suspected she could and would knock skulls together when necessary. "Saint Patty's white chocolate martini sounds like something I have to try at least once."

Patty slapped the counter lightly. "On their way. You girls sit tight."

"How you doing, Vee?" one of the guys at the table called casually.

Vienna smiled and waved at him.

"How often do you come here?" Taylor asked, surprised Alex's sister knew the man, who wore some kind of uniform.

"I worked here last summer. Had to quit when school got too intense. I miss the tips."

"You'll get a job easily," Taylor said, "with much nicer paychecks."

"Hope you're right."

Patty came out carrying three full martini glasses and set them on the counter in front of them. "I only allow myself one of these babies a day." She winked at Taylor. "Keeps the doctor away."

Vienna held her glass up to Taylor. "To surviving corporate picnics."

"I'll drink to that."

"You didn't tell me that," Patty said. "Sounds like I should've made these doubles." She held her glass up as well and all three clinked.

Taylor took a tentative sip and raised her brows in surprise. "That tastes amazing. Like white chocolate chips. Are you sure there's alcohol in there?"

Patty chuckled and nodded. "And a two-drink limit on those for newbies."

"They kind of sneak up on you," Vienna confirmed.

Half a drink later, Taylor felt warm and more relaxed than she'd been in a long time.

And then it all blew to pieces as the door opened and Vienna looked past her.

"Dearest Alexander," she said, and Taylor stiffened.

Sure enough, Alex took the stool on Taylor's right.

"How's our favorite high-flyer today?" Patty asked.

"Not flying too high. Physical therapy's kicking my ass."

Taylor angled toward him in greeting. "Alexander, huh?" It didn't fit him.

"Only in Vee's mind. She knows it annoys me."

"Which is a hobby of mine," Vienna said.

Patty took Alex's order for fried cheese curds, a burger and a beer. She drew the beer from the tap and slid it three feet down the counter to him, then disappeared again.

"What are you two doing together?" Alex asked, not bothering to hide his bafflement.

That was all it took for Taylor's insecurity to rage once again. She, too, wondered at Vienna's motives for hanging out with her. "I think your sister's trying to thank me for subjecting her to my company picnic to meet marketing types."

"Nah, we just both needed girl time."

"So you met marketing types? Did you meet any 'list' types?" He leaned his elbows on the bar and stared pointedly at Taylor.

She studied the counter in front of her, thankful the lighting in here was too poor for anyone to tell whether she blushed. She prayed Vienna had missed what he'd said or would ignore it.

"What's a list type?" Vienna asked after sipping her drink.

Alex's gaze rested on Taylor—the top of her head, to be precise, because she couldn't bring herself to look at him. Couldn't think of what to say.

"You didn't tell her?" he asked gently. "I figured that was fodder for girl talk."

"You have to tell me now," Vienna said. "What's a list type?"

Before Alex could twist it around or say something else that embarrassed her, Taylor jumped into the explanation. "I made a list of the traits I want in any man I go out with."

Vienna nodded slowly. "I can get behind that. Kind of the ideal-man thing."

"Exactly. If a guy doesn't meet one of my requirements, why should I go out with him?"

"Amen, sister. So what's on the list? What are we looking for?"

Taylor pulled her phone out of her purse and opened the list. She could probably recite it from memory but not with Alex sitting so close and judging her.

Patty came out and set a plastic basket of steaming bar food in front of Alex.

"Thanks, Patty," he said. He picked it and his beer up and stood, hovering behind Taylor and his sister. "You girls make it sound like you're looking for a stud at an auction or the perfect job applicant."

"Taylor definitely needs a stud," Vienna said with a wicked laugh.

Taylor smiled, Vienna's enthusiasm bolstering her confidence. "And it *is* a job position when you get right down to it."

He shook his head gravely. "Enjoy your girl time. If the beer goggles make an appearance, refer to the almighty list."

CHAPTER EIGHT

"I COULD'VE GOTTEN HOME by myself," Taylor insisted as she climbed out the passenger side of her own car. Her boldness, the very fact she'd found the courage to argue with him, proved to Alex he'd been right to insist on driving her.

"Ever been drunk before?" he asked as they emerged from her garage.

"Not really. I'm not drunk now."

"Have you seen the public service announcements that explain your blood alcohol level can be above the legal limit even when you don't feel loopy?"

She went up the two steps to the deck and opened her screen door.

"You had how many martinis?" he continued, holding the screen while she dug in her purse for her keys.

"Two."

"And you weigh about eighty-seven pounds."

Taylor laughed freely, no hesitation or inhibition. Alex wasn't sure he'd heard that from her before.

"The more you argue with me, the more you prove I'm right, Scarlet," he said when she was about to speak.

Still grinning, she shook her head, then finally located her keys. Several seconds passed and they stood there, Alex behind her, holding the door.

"You pass out already?" He looked over her shoulder and watched her repeated attempts to get the key in the hole.

"It's dark," she said, determined. Stubborn. "Didn't plan on going out so I didn't turn on my light."

"So I see." He gently took the keys from her and unlocked the door.

"Hey!" Taylor burst into the kitchen ahead of him. "I'm not drunk. Tipsy, maybe, but I could do constant coefficient linear differential equations right now if I wanted."

"You could do differential equations in your sleep."

She stared up at him and opened her mouth as if she was about to argue. Then she laughed. "You got me there. Now if I can just find a guy who isn't scared by that. *That* is my ideal date."

"Better add that to your list."

That damnable list.

She actually swatted him on the arm. Alex

caught her hand briefly before easing a step back. He liked this relaxed side of her.

"Why are you here?" she asked, tilting her head slightly as she peered at him.

"Originally it was to be a gentleman, but now that I'm here, I'm going to measure for the kitchen trim. We're still on for the hardware store tomorrow morning, right?"

"Bright and early, like you said."

"If you're up for it."

"The secret," she said as she took a glass down from the cabinet, "is hydrating to get the poison out before you go to bed." She filled the glass with water and gulped it down.

"Excellent advice from an obvious authority on the subject."

"It's science." She filled the glass again. "I can do science." Once more, she chugged all the water. "The other thing is to stand under a stream of hot water to rinse it all off."

"Just wash off your drunk, huh?" He could no longer hide a grin.

"Not drunk. Going to take my shower and go to bed. Just lock the door when you leave. Good night."

Either she was more intoxicated than she seemed—she didn't slur her words or have trouble walking—or she trusted him. Whether she should or not.

Alex opened the one drawer in the McCabe kitchen that had always been less than militarily neat, the one that held an assortment of random, non-kitchen items, like a tape measure. He searched for a piece of paper so he could write the measurements down. Typically, Taylor hadn't left much lying around. He'd grown used to Spartan surroundings overseas, but there was a difference between a neatness inspired by lack of belongings and space and that dictated by a compulsion to keep all things in their places. That was Taylor, he thought, chuckling to himself.

There was nothing to write on in the kitchen, which surprised him until he remembered she pecked everything into that phone of hers. Surely in her office... He walked into the living room and spotted, in the dim wash of light from the kitchen, a notebook on one of the end tables. He grabbed it and returned to the kitchen.

As the shower turned on, Alex fought to block out the sound. He didn't want to consider what she was doing on the other side of the wall. Stripping her conservative clothes off and...

Longing for his ear buds, he whistled, loudly and tunelessly, as he measured the first stretch of wall that required new trim.

The shower stopped, snapping his attention back to the task at hand. He turned to the first blank page and jotted down the measurement. The kitchen was small and it didn't take him long to finish. He added all the numbers to get an idea of how much trim they'd need to buy in the morning.

He took the project list Taylor had written for him out of his wallet and skimmed it to make sure there wasn't any other information he needed to collect. Replace kitchen light fixtures, repair deck, replace trim in kitchen, new shower and countertop in bathroom, closet doors, basement ceiling, paint interior...

Alex was in the living room jotting down estimates of how much paint they needed when Taylor emerged from the steamy bathroom wearing light green pajamas. A camisole and shorts. He swallowed hard and raised his eyes to her face. Eventually.

She startled when she saw him and crossed her arms over her chest. "I thought you were leaving."

Her uneasiness was back but he barely noticed. He noticed all the wrong stuff instead—wet strands of her auburn hair curling around her face, nearly perfect circles of pink on her cheeks from the hot water, the moist shine of her lips...

"I am. As soon as I figure out how much paint we need. Every room, correct?"

She nodded. "I hadn't thought about colors yet...."

"If you're still thinking about selling, you need to keep it neutral."

"You're right." She studied the walls thoughtfully. "Do you know a lot about selling a house?"

"My mom's addicted to the home channel. I got sucked in the other night."

"A neutral cream color would look nice, don't you think?" She stood next to him now, surveying the room, squinting slightly as she imagined something other than the light green currently on the walls.

"Cream, white, whatever."

As he breathed, he caught her scent. Apples and sugar. Sweet, pure. More alluring than he would have guessed. He watched her, intrigued. She was so consumed by her plans for the walls that he could just about see the gears in her head turning. He'd always admired her intelligence. Never been intimidated by it, even when she'd passed him and Quinn in math and been doing science projects that were over his head.

Not scared off by her brain.

Go figure. That was the single qualification on

her list that Alex met, and she hadn't even bothered to write it down.

Her eyes shot to his as if he'd said the words out loud, and their gazes held. Gold flecks sparkled in the emerald as seconds ticked by with neither of them moving.

Alex closed the space between them with a single step, paying no heed to the voice in the far corner of his mind that was screaming to slam on the brakes.

Faint freckles dusted skin so creamy he longed to run his fingers over it. Her lips were partway open, and the subtle sexiness of that contradicted the simple purity that was Taylor. He followed the curve of her mouth with his eyes, entranced by the dip at the top, the natural coral-pink tint, the hint of moisture....

He leaned down and brushed his lips to hers, unable to resist the urge to touch them, to sample the soft warmth. A jolt went through him, jumpstarted his pulse at the whisper of contact. He pulled back just enough to gauge the look in her eyes, expecting to see confusion or blame but finding...hunger. Need tangled with a hint of vulnerability. The combination did him in.

He cupped the back of her neck and pressed their lips together, breathing her in. He trailed his hands down her sides, tantalized by the curves he'd previously only guessed were hiding beneath her modest clothes. He rested his hands at her tiny waist and caressed her ribs with his thumbs.

Her hand was suddenly on his chest, gripping his shirt, drawing him nearer. She wound both hands around his neck, into his hair.

Urgency pounded through him to taste her, know her. He parted her lips with his tongue and Taylor was there with him, responding, her tongue tangling with his, twisting him into a blindsiding lust.

He never would have suspected Taylor had this kind of response in her. Shy, unassuming Taylor. His best friend's little sister.

Alex abruptly broke their contact and moved back a step, reeling. He closed his eyes as regret flooded him. He was damn lucky Quinn wasn't around.

What the living hell had he done? He'd made protecting Taylor from the bad guys his job, in a sense…and he was the one who'd moved in on her.

That didn't fly with him. At all.

She stared at him hard, searching for an explanation.

"That…" He was straddling a thin line here and struggled for the right words.

"What?" Heat still emanated from her eyes.

"That…compatibility." He refused to use the

word *chemistry*. That took things down a road he wasn't able to travel. He paced away from her. "I meet very few, if any, of the criteria on your list."

She frowned, lost in thought. "You're intelligent…"

"Not in a Taylor McCabe way."

"You seem to be driven to get back to the army."

"Scarlet. You're missing the point."

He saw the exact moment he hurt her—her eyes fluttered shut for a fraction of a second and her shoulders dropped almost imperceptibly. That wasn't his intent, dammit.

"Why don't you enlighten me?" Her voice was soft but tightly controlled.

"All I'm trying to say is that your list is not the answer to finding what you're looking for. You're trying to make it black and white but relationships are…gray. There's a lot of factors besides traits on a checklist. We both know there can't be anything between you and me but…" How much more could he fumble over this? "My point is that you might be attracted to someone who doesn't meet your qualifications, and that's okay."

She nodded once. Dismissed what he said. Didn't even consider it.

Hell. He'd screwed up twenty times over tonight. Instinct had him wanting to touch her, to make her understand, but he'd already done too much touching. "I'm sorry, Taylor. I'll let you get some sleep."

Her eyes had done a one-eighty from heat to hurt, and that told him more than anything why he wasn't the right man for her.

"That's…for the best." She walked to the door and opened it, no hesitation whatsoever.

That was Taylor…always the smartest girl in the room.

HOT TEARS BURNED TAYLOR'S eyes as soon as she closed the door behind Alex.

Wasn't she just the dumbest girl alive? Maybe *pathetic* was a more appropriate word, but nuances of vocabulary failed her right now.

She sagged against the door, eyes closed, then slid down it until she landed hard on the wood floor.

Why would a man like Alex Worth, with all his muscles and bravery and, *lord,* those eyes, ever kiss her? More important, why would she ever fall for it and let herself be kissed by him?

And then to get into it like she had? The first instant of contact had sparked through her, turned her into a quivery mass of neediness. Instead of acting shocked and backing away as she should have, she'd let herself lean into him. Kiss him back. Be affected by his touch like…

She hit the door with the back of her head, forcibly and intentionally. Three minutes of Alex's lips and hands on her had affected her the way no other man ever had.

She'd been with men before—okay, one man, really, but she'd been kissed by several—and she'd never gone from zero to all over them in three-point-five seconds.

And with a man who just wanted to prove a point to naive "Scarlet," to save his army buddy's little sister from her inexperienced, misled self.

She couldn't even blame it on alcohol. The slight tipsiness that had necessitated the ride home had been washed away completely by the time she'd emerged from the shower. She'd been tired but clearheaded as they'd discussed paint colors.

Now it was obvious that teaching her a lesson about the foolishness of her checklist had been his reason for sticking around and taking measurements. She should've guessed something was up when he didn't immediately leave after getting her and her car safely home.

Lorien and Elanor strutted into the living room.

"Beasts, I suppose you think you need food even though I'm dying a slow death of humiliation, huh?" The seal point sat, pear-shaped, in the doorway to the kitchen while Lorien climbed up on Taylor's lap, full of self-entitlement. She scratched behind the cat's ears and stood, picking her up and carrying her to the kitchen. "Everyone should be so pampered." Both felines wove around her legs as she opened a can of smelly seafood delight and divided it between two bowls.

As she absently set the bowls down, she could see Alex in her mind, the way he'd been looking at her just before he kissed her. She'd thought she'd discerned something in his eyes, some kind of emotion. Hunger. Obviously she'd thought wrong.

The whole debacle proved two things. One, she had an overactive imagination. Two, she was way out of her element with someone like Alex Worth. He'd been set on proving her list was "wrong," but he'd done the opposite. She was convinced now more than ever that she'd be more comfortable and have a more successful relationship with a man who met each of her carefully thought-out qualifications.

CHAPTER NINE

ALEX HATED HIMSELF more than usual when he woke up the next morning.

The first thing he discerned, before he even cracked his eyes open, was the pain in his lower body from yesterday's PT session. Which veered his thoughts directly to Quinn, who was never far from his consciousness anyway. And that... He bit out a crude curse.

Taylor.

He rolled onto his stomach and pounded the pillow. His head throbbed and all the shit that'd gone down last night filtered through his brain as if he'd been drunk and only half-conscious. Talk about irony. Only thing he'd drunk was the one beer with his dinner. He'd made a point of staying sober, maybe as an attempt to counteract all the liquor Marshall was sucking down lately. Seemed like one of the Worth siblings ought to be able to walk a straight line. As soon as he'd finished his burger at Patty's, he'd gone home. Wasted several hours in front of the idiot box until Vienna had called and asked him to drive Taylor to her house.

He should never have walked through her front door last night.

Alex dragged his wrist near his face to check his watch. Nice. Who'd be surprised that he'd overslept and was two hours late for the hardware-store date with Taylor? He groaned. *Date* was entirely the wrong word.

He kicked the sheet off as he turned over the other way, digging deep, trying to find a reason to get his ass out of the sack. For Taylor? Yeah, that was a plan. Because he'd done so much *for Taylor* already.

He'd kissed her when he had no right even to think about kissing her. Worse, he'd liked it.

He couldn't have her thinking there was anything between them, or even the potential for anything, because there wasn't. She wasn't the kind of girl who played around. Alex wasn't the guy for her, could never live up to what she deserved. A well-educated, suit-wearing computer geek or finance geek or whatever, that was the type Taylor needed, even if the guy only met half the traits on her list. A quarter. To hell with the list—it was irrelevant. Taylor deserved the very best, and Alex was a jackass on a good day.

Embracing that undeniable truth, he turned over and went back to sleep.

IF TAYLOR EVER NEEDED a new career, carpentry offered some surprisingly attractive possibilities, even if she didn't particularly have a gift for it.

Thanks to the do-it-yourself book the man at the hardware store had recommended, she was getting the hang of beating the life out of the nails as she drove them through the kitchen trim. And if she happened to picture Alex's head as she pounded, who could blame her?

As the hammer connected with her thumb, she yelled and growled her frustration loudly. Darn that man for getting in her thoughts and making her lose her concentration.

Someone knocked at the front door. She tossed the stupid hammer down and got up, sucking on her thumb as if that would take away the pain.

She checked out the peep hole before opening and growled again, more quietly this time.

Why did her heart speed up at the sight of Alex standing on her front porch? Was it rage-induced? Lingering embarrassment? The usual nerves he brought out?

Yeah, sure. Lying to herself was fine as long as, in the back of her mind, she knew she was lying. Right?

He knocked again, harder, and she jumped. Lord, why now, when he'd blown her off all day? She looked tired, dirty and generally awful. At nine o'clock this morning when he was supposed to pick her up, she'd at least smelled clean. She'd even considered putting on some lip gloss and mascara but that idea had fizzled when she discovered her rarely used mascara was dried and crusty.

"I know you're in there, Taylor. I heard you yelling your head off."

She opened the door. "I did not yell my head off."

"Heard you clear out here."

"You're eleven hours and seventeen minutes late."

He shoved his hand in the pocket of his cargos and glanced toward the driveway at nothing. Dusk was falling, spilling streaks of pink and lavender across the sky. "May I come in?"

She pressed her lips together, moistening them. When his gaze lowered to them, she took a quick step back and let him inside. They stood in the entry, two feet and a heavy silence between them.

One would think she'd made peace with awkward moments after twenty-six years, but no. She pushed loose strands of her hair behind her ear and fumbled for what to say. "You don't need to help me with the house," was what finally came out.

"I think I have someone to buy Quinn's Winchester."

"Okay." That was the last topic she'd expected. "You know where it is."

"That's not why I'm here."

"Oh. Then why?" She was curt with him and it felt good, but not as good as the hammer action.

He craned his neck to see into the kitchen. She'd pushed the table to the middle of the room to access the walls. "What are you doing in there?" He stalked past her with purpose, as if he needed to save the day.

"I'm getting my house ready to put on the market."

"You're doing the trim? By yourself?"

"*Myself* was the only one around when the work needed to be done," she said pointedly.

The only sign he even remembered he was supposed to have helped her this morning was the flicker of his lids downward. Or maybe he was just blinking.

"What do you know about replacing trim?"

"Before today, hardly anything." She took the hardcover book from the table and waved it in the air. "But, amazingly, when there's something a girl needs to learn, there's always a book out there that will teach her."

"How are you cutting the pieces?"

She wasn't yet. She'd put that part off for as long as possible while she removed the old trim, then started with a long piece that didn't need to be cut. "With a saw."

"What kind of saw?"

"The right kind. I rented one."

He looked around for it, but it was out in the garage.

"It wouldn't be very bright to bring it in here, would it?" she said smugly. "It's big, messy. I don't want sawdust in my orange juice."

"Garage?"

She nodded and he headed out the back door before she could say anything. Baffled, she followed him.

The light in the garage was on, the door closed. Alex opened the small side door and went in. She'd left her car in the driveway and placed the saw, the trim and everything else she'd bought this morning where her car was usually parked.

"You left the garage unlocked with all this stuff in here? What is it worth, a couple of grand?"

"In case you hadn't noticed, I was still working. I'll lock up when I'm done for the night."

"I'll do the cutting."

She was dying to have someone, anyone but her, work the saw. That sharp blade terrified her. But her stubborn streak was even stronger than her fear. "I've got it covered."

He turned and stared at her, disbelieving at

first. Then his shoulders dropped a notch. "You're really pissed."

"No." Okay, maybe.

"You have every right."

"You think?" Apparently she was loosening up with him enough to say exactly what popped into her head. That was progress, in a twisted way.

"Scarlet…" He turned away, rubbed his palms together.

She leaned against the wood stud of the unfinished wall, studying him. Something was up. He was…nervous? Around her? Maybe just contrite. As he should be.

Alex turned around, looking at the cracked concrete floor. "I'm sorry."

"This was never a good idea. You're trying to recover, get your leg healed. I meant it when I said I could do this—"

"That's not what I'm talking about." He walked over and stood in front of her. Crossed his arms over his chest. Made eye contact, and she felt the impact of that gaze down to her toes. "I'm sorry I kissed you."

He might as well have punched her in the gut. She took in a shaky breath. "That's not exactly what a girl wants to hear…"

"That's not what I mean. Don't twist it around."

"'Sorry I kissed you' is pretty straightforward."

He reached out, squeezed her shoulder. Let his hand linger on her upper arm for a second before dropping it. "It can't happen again. I'm...look, I know Quinn's not here. God, do I know that. Every second of every day, I have to live with that..."

He broke off and his throat moved as he swallowed.

"It's a guy thing," he continued. "Because of me he's not around to do what big brothers do. Carry the heavy stuff, work the saw, scare off assholes who could hurt you. Last thing I want to do is *be* the asshole."

"What do you mean, Alex..." she barely heard the last part of what he said "...it's *because* of you?"

He shook his head and looked away. "Not going there." Before she could argue, he stormed out the side door.

He was blaming himself for Quinn's death?

She stood a moment, stunned, trying to wrap her brain around that, then rushed out after him. He sat on the deck steps, in the same spot she'd found him when he'd first come back to town. This time, instead of looking smug, he seemed defeated, his shoulders sagging with the weight of so much sadness.

His wide soldier body took up most of the steps.

"Move over," she said, forgetting the insecurity that normally plagued her around him.

Equally shocking was that he did what she said and made room for her. Taylor sat next to him, their thighs touching.

"Quinn died in combat, Alex." She spoke quietly, as if saying it too loudly would make it more painful. Instead of focusing on her own heartbreak, she needed to get this point across to Alex, who'd gone completely silent. "The other side tried to blow up your helicopter. You can't really think it was somehow your fault."

"You don't know the first thing about it."

She gritted her teeth and used her short thumbnail to scrape away dirt that had caked around the base of the railing support. She didn't remember ever feeling the urge to punch a man, didn't really know how to throw a punch when you got down to it, but she clenched her left fist against the temptation now. With her right, she continued to assault the dried dirt on the step. "Why don't you tell me about it, then?" she said tightly. "I'd like to understand."

The last streaks of light had disappeared, the silhouette of the leaves against the sky barely visible. Cicadas filled the dusk with soothing music that contrasted with the storm of emotion contained in their little corner of the universe. A cricket hid somewhere nearby and piped out a solo.

Alex supported his elbows on his knees and had his hands steepled in front of his face.

"You can be the strong, silent, manly man another time," Taylor said, abandoning her dirt-removal project and searching for a way to make this stubborn man talk. "He was my brother. If it's really your fault, I have a right to know."

She didn't believe he was to blame for a second, but how else could she get through to him?

He stretched his left leg out and massaged his thigh, seemingly without noticing he was doing it. "My brain knows I'm not to blame," he finally said. "I've been over the accident a thousand times. The army's been over it. If I'd done something undeniably 'wrong,' you better believe they'd make me aware of that."

"And you didn't. You managed to bring the helicopter down safely enough to save everyone else on board from what I heard."

"You can't make this black and white, Taylor."

"Actually, I can."

"The end result is that I wasn't able to bring it down safely enough to save every man." His left leg bounced at hummingbird speed. "And your brother isn't here because of that."

A lump swelled in her throat, for Quinn, for

Alex…for her own grief. "He died doing what he loved, Alex. For something he believed passionately in dying for." These were words she'd clung to in the weeks after her brother's death. Words she knew with all her heart were true.

He stood abruptly and went inside the house, leaving Taylor there with her jaw hanging open. Again. For being such a tough guy, he sure did run away a lot from what she had to say.

When she got into the kitchen, Alex was bending over the one piece of trim she'd almost completed before he'd interrupted.

"We need to angle this end off," he said. "Makes it harder to see the seams."

"Stand up and finish our conversation," she said.

He hesitated then eased himself up. Turned to face her. "What happened to shy Scarlet?"

"She got mad and had to leave. You're stuck with ticked-off Taylor."

One side of his mouth curved up and he shook his head. "She scares me."

"She should."

"I'm going to help you with the house, like we agreed. Sorry I flaked this morning."

She stared him down, debating with herself. She'd welcome the help from someone but…

"I don't want to be an obligation to you," she said quietly.

"You're not an obligation. You're my best friend's little sister. I want to do it."

"What if Quinn was still alive? Would you still insist?"

"I can't say what I'd do or where I'd be if Quinn was alive. I'd give anything to find out."

His voice was so thick with sadness that tears filled Taylor's eyes. Without thought, she stepped forward and wound her arms around him, aching for him. For both of them. For several seconds, Alex stood stiffly, motionless. Eons later, she felt his hands on her torso, hesitantly at first, and then he pulled her close and burrowed his chin into her hair.

She'd initiated the hug to comfort him, but... lord, she must have needed it just as much. More. She closed her eyes and pressed into his solid chest, letting the tears that spilled over be soaked up by his shirt. They stood like that, unmoving, not saying anything for some time. Seconds? Minutes? She should feel awkward. Self-conscious. But she'd been craving this, the comfort of another person, without even realizing it. Not specifically Alex, she told herself. But being in his arms...

Stop thinking so much and just take the comfort while it's there.

Alex loosened his hold on her and ran a hand over her messy hair. "The whole thing is screwing with my head." She felt his breath at her temple. "I'm trying like crazy not to dwell on it. Trying to move forward but not sure how. All I can figure out is that I need to get back to what I do, what Quinn did. What he believed in so strongly."

Reluctantly, she pulled back enough to look him in the eye. "As long as you're doing it as a positive thing. Not trying to punish yourself or something."

"I don't have any damn idea what I'm doing most days. Fixing up your house gives me something to think about."

He seemed lost. Vulnerable and unsure of himself for the first time since she'd met him. He was no longer the godlike beautiful man who could do no wrong, who made her feel inadequate. All those years since Quinn had first brought Alex to their house, she'd never been able to see past the veneer to the man beneath. Now she did.

As his eyes met hers, she wasn't sure if that was a good thing or not. Was she better off getting to know Alex or keeping him in the untouchable category? Because the more she knew, the more she cared.

And it didn't seem wise to care too much about someone who'd never think of her as more than his duty, as a debt to a man who was no longer alive.

CHAPTER TEN

ALEX KNEW FOR A FACT Taylor was still alive. She left little signs around her house: the dishwasher running when he let himself in to work on his non-therapy days, a partially eaten fresh apple coffee cake—locally made and organic of course—on the counter with a note for him to help himself.

He also knew she'd been avoiding him ever since the night a week and a half ago when she'd insisted they talk about Quinn.

At first he'd been relieved by her disappearing act. That scene in her kitchen had left him exposed. Instead of fixing the trim then and there, he'd gotten a spare key from her and promised to get started Tuesday while she was at work. The plan was to let himself in to work two or three days a week until the project list was finished.

Yeah, so he'd played the avoidance game, too, but it was for her own good. Now he was done with it, though, or at least wanted a break from it so he could see how she was doing. That was all he wanted, he told himself. To make sure she was okay. That she hadn't reverted to being upset that he'd kissed her, stood her up, been a general all-around prick.

When the heck was that woman going to call it quits at the day job and come home? It was almost nine-thirty at night. Had she gone on another date with some jackwad?

He climbed down from the stepladder where he'd been replacing damaged ceiling tiles in the basement. His leg nearly gave out on him when he put his weight on it and he bit out a curse.

One of Taylor's cats seemed to think the fact that he was on the ground signified a willingness to pet it, so it walked over and rubbed against his legs.

"You're getting my pants all furry, cat."

The feline stopped and looked up at him. It got up on its back feet and pawed his thigh expectantly. Alex stared it down, then gave in and petted its head for a few seconds. When he moved toward his toolbox, the cat trotted along with him.

"That's all you get, cat. Don't be so greedy."

Alex had pushed hard today. The decision to hang around until Taylor got home had been a subconscious one until the past hour or so. Now he checked his watch every five minutes, wondering where she was. Who she was with.

He put away his tools and supplies for the night and made his way slowly up the stairs, concern and jealousy battling in his gut. He needed to can the jealousy once and for all and just focus on the concern.

The upstairs was dark—the sun had set since he'd been downstairs—so he flipped on the dim light above the kitchen sink. The apple coffee cake sitting there reminded him he'd worked through dinner. He sat at the table with his new friend, the cat, and the remaining three-quarters of the cake. He dug into it with a fork.

The cake was nearly gone when the back door opened and Taylor walked in. Not yet spotting him, she greeted the second cat, who'd walked over to meet her. When she turned around, a scream slipped out and she put her hand to her chest.

"What are you still doing here?"

He held up the last bite of coffee cake on his fork. "Dinner. I owe you one."

She checked her watch. "It's nine-thirty."

"Did you have a date?"

For an instant, she looked confused, then covered with a frown. "What if I did?"

"The guy better have treated you right this time." Alex got up, threw away the empty foil container and put his dirty fork in the dishwasher.

Taylor stood eighteen inches away, watching him in silence, her gentle green eyes hiding behind the specs. Her hair was pulled back at her nape as usual, not a single strand out of place. Her clothing was vintage buttoned-up Taylor—plain black pants and a short-sleeved peach sweater that revealed very little of her milky skin. Once again, she'd put all her style focus on her feet with impossibly high snakeskin-patterned black heels that came to a wicked point in the front. They looked about as comfortable as brand-new combat boots a size too small.

"Well?" He suddenly cared too much about her response.

"I didn't go on a date," she admitted. "I worked late. You know me, Miss Social Life."

A knock at the back door startled both of them. The door opened and Vienna called out.

"Hellooo? Tay, it's me." She stuck her head inside and grinned when she saw them. "Hey, guys. Saw you turn down the street and thought I'd stop by," she said to Taylor.

"Hi." Taylor smiled but seemed uneasy.

"What are you still doing here, Alex? Earning some overtime?" His sister wagged her brows suggestively. Thankfully Taylor missed it.

"Got on a roll today. Did you worry about me?"

"Always," she said sarcastically. "I've been pining away, waiting for you to come home." She walked all the way into the kitchen. "I've been camped out at the library trying to finish some reading. Mom was doing a *Wheel of Fortune* marathon with the week's recorded episodes when she got home from work. I had to bail. And I've got something for you, Taylor." She held out a Laurel's Shoes bag.

"What...?" Taylor hesitantly took the bag and opened it. "Oh, my lord!"

Alex watched, curious as hell. She pulled out a pair of green glittery flip-flops that looked just like his sister's purple ones.

"Are these..." Taylor examined them from every angle.

"For you. Serious clearance, but my way of saying thanks for everything you've done. The laptop, the introductions at your company..."

"This is weird," Alex muttered.

"Not weird." Taylor set the shoes on the floor, slipped a shoe off and tried on a sandal.

"Seven and a half?" Vienna asked.

"You're good. Thank you. I love them." She scuttled over to a drawer and took out scissors. Bending over, she cut the plastic ring holding the shoes together, then slid her other foot into the second one. "I'd offer you some coffee cake but your brother took care of it already."

"I can't stay anyway—still have a bunch of reading for tomorrow. You want a ride, army guy?"

"Affirmative, marketing girl. Give me five to finish cleaning up."

As he walked through the main floor of the house in search of any tools he might have left, he could hear the two talking casually in the kitchen. He couldn't help noticing that Taylor seemed shy, uneasy with Vienna. He'd thought they'd been getting along fine when they were at Saint Patty's.

He glanced in Taylor's bedroom even though he hadn't worked in there today. Or ever. Her closet doors had to be replaced and the walls, like every other room in the house, needed to be painted, but for some reason he'd avoided going in her room. Her bed was neat enough to pass military inspection—except for silky-looking pajamas folded up on her pillow. The sight started his blood pumping faster and made him recall, in detail, the skimpy ones she'd worn after her shower.... This was why he hadn't worked on her closet yet. He needed to get his libido under control.

A quick check through the other two bedrooms assured him he hadn't left anything behind. He headed back to the kitchen and found Taylor alone, fixing herself iced tea.

"Did she leave me hanging?" Alex asked.

Taylor shook her head just as Vee laid on the horn outside.

"Does she feel sorry for me or something?"

Taylor asked, stopping him short on his way to the door.

"Feel sorry for you?" He turned toward her and searched her face. "Why would you think that?"

"She bought me shoes and asked me to Sunday dinner."

Alex processed that idea, imagining Taylor at his family's table. Growing up, Quinn had frequented their one sit-down meal each week and had fit in like another Worth. His mom would love having a guest. Now that Marshall had officially moved back home, it'd almost be like old times.

Taylor nervously tapped the counter with the fingernails of her left hand while squeezing lemon juice into her glass with her right hand.

"My sister likes you. She appreciates the help you've given her, but mostly she's just trying to be your friend. Go with it."

He stood next to her at the counter, watching her from the side. Taylor didn't look at him, just wrinkled her forehead.

"What's wrong?" he asked.

She glanced sideways but not directly at him, shaking her head. "Just me being me. I like your sister." She stirred her tea absently. "I'm not very good at friends."

The horn honked again but Alex ignored it. Thought back to when they'd been kids. Teens.

He didn't remember her ever having a friend over to the house or getting phone calls. At school she'd been a loner. He'd figured it was the two-year gap between her and her classmates. Taylor was different, without a doubt, but it hadn't occurred to him that she'd never made a close friend or two, especially in college.

"Vienna's easy. Just be yourself."

She tried to smile but it was more of a grimace. "Thanks. I wouldn't exactly say I was myself drinking two martinis." She shook her head dismissively. "You better go before she deserts you."

What was it about this woman that evoked some kind of protective response in him? He stared at her a moment longer, wanting to reassure her but settling for squeezing her shoulder lightly on his way past.

She really didn't have a concept of what an amazing, likable person she was. Too bad he wasn't in a position to make her believe it.

CHAPTER ELEVEN

IT WAS DUMB FOR TAYLOR'S insides to be tied in knots before dinner at the Worths' house. She knew them well enough, or at least fifty percent of them.

She pulled her hybrid up to the curb and turned the engine off. Sat there trying to calm herself. Replayed Alex's words about Vienna genuinely liking her.

Logically, Taylor understood her fears were unfounded. Vienna was a sincere, warm person who had done nothing but be friendly. It was that unsure teenage girl inside of Taylor, the one who used to throw up every morning in the school bathroom because she dreaded what the day, what the mean kids would have planned for her.

Vienna was cute, put-together, instantly likable. The embodiment of a "popular" girl. But they were grown up now and Taylor needed to reprogram herself to accept that cliques were a thing of the painful past. Vienna had seen something she liked in Taylor—the grown-up, competent, computer-programmer version—and recognized the things they had in common instead of the ways they were different.

Still…trust didn't come easily for Taylor. Trust in others or in herself.

As she walked up the drive toward the front door, she prayed to God she didn't make a fool of herself tonight, didn't say the wrong thing, spill something, generally make herself look like the social dork she was.

Before she could turn up the walkway, Vienna poked her head around the corner of the house from the backyard.

"Hey, Tay. Come on back here."

Taylor smiled and relaxed slightly. "Hello," she said as she stepped onto the expansive tiled patio. An outdoor fireplace dominated one corner, surrounded by wrought-iron benches. Another corner overflowed with barrels and pots of flowering plants. Vienna sat at a round glass-topped table in the center of the space, a newspaper opened in front of her. "I never knew you had such a pretty space back here."

Vienna shrugged. "It's only a couple of years old. I designed it and finally convinced my mom to foot the bill to have the work done. It's my summer hideout." She gestured at the chair next to hers. "Make yourself comfortable."

The table was shaded by a towering elm tree.

"This is beautiful," Taylor said. "I'm not sure you'd ever get me inside if I had something like this."

"If you ever want one yourself, I'd be happy to plan it out for you. I'm not a pro but I can save you some bucks on outrageous design fees."

"If I wasn't planning to sell the house, I'd have you start today."

"Your new place, then, wherever that ends up being."

"Deal. Reading anything interesting?" Taylor recognized the local weekly business publication. She picked it up when she could and always meant to subscribe. Though she was content at her job, she liked to keep up on what was happening with other companies.

"As a matter of fact..." Vienna flipped back a few pages, her eyes coming alive. "Check this out." She tapped the paper emphatically with each word and set the article in front of Taylor.

"'Madison's Brainiest Bachelors,'" Taylor read aloud. She glanced over the double-page spread, scanned the photos for anyone she knew. "O-kay. What am I looking at?"

"These," Vienna said excitedly, "are your list guys! They're perfect. Exactly what you're looking for."

Taylor frowned and started reading. The feature was the first in a weekly series that highlighted local eligible bachelors who were successful in their fields. And allegedly brilliant. It promised that females would be highlighted the following month.

The five men weren't GQ. They were well-groomed and confident, though. Some were better-looking than others. Most wore suits. Each one radiated success in his own way.

Taylor skimmed the text that told each man's position, his interests, age, professional affiliations and business philosophy. She sat up straighter.

"You're right. These are *exactly* the kinds of men I'd like to meet. I just wish I knew how. I bet they don't leave their offices very often."

"Sure they do." Vienna pulled the paper back toward her. "And this tells us exactly where they go. Bill here is vice president of the local chapter of Entrepreneurs and Inventors. Gregg founded Madison Mathematicians. And look at Joel. He's ideal for you. Not only is he the best-looking but he belongs to Information Technology Professionals."

"I'm pretty certain they don't hang out at bars and it doesn't list the grocery stores they frequent." Taylor laughed. "They probably have a delivery service anyway. I don't know how to find guys like these."

Vienna, whose legs had been propped on the

chair opposite her, dropped her feet to the ground. "We track them down in their natural habitat. Stalk them at their extracurricular meetings."

"We don't belong to any of those organizations."

"But we could join. I'm betting most of them allow anyone to become a member, except maybe the Midwest Manufacturers Guild."

The thought of dropping into professional meetings to meet eligible men tied Taylor's stomach in knots.

"What do you think?" Vienna asked.

"Terrifying." Taylor shook her head.

The back door to the house opened and Cheryl Worth appeared. "Dinner's almost ready. I could use your help, Vienna. Taylor..." Warmth filled her voice. "It's so good to see you, honey. How are you?"

Taylor forced a smile, still rattled by Vienna's idea. "I'm doing well, thanks." She and Vienna stood and headed toward the door. "Dinner smells fantastic."

"It's an old family recipe for bacon mac and cheese. Haven't made it for ages. I just hope it comes out okay." She closed the door to keep the cooled air inside. "I suddenly find myself with a full nest again...and an excuse to cook a real dinner."

"Thanks for including me," Taylor said. If she

was disappointed that the kitchen was empty, she didn't acknowledge it to herself. One part of her wanted to see Alex, but the other, the socially clueless part, didn't. Butterflies fluttered in her gut. Even though she'd made progress and in general felt less inept around him, he still set her balance on edge in a different way. A way she didn't care to examine at all.

"What can I do?" Taylor asked.

"You girls can set the table and get drinks."

Vienna took five dinner plates down and handed them to Taylor. "Silverware's in here. I'll take drink duty."

Taylor was relieved to have a means to occupy herself, even if it was a mindless task. She could hear someone upstairs walking around, and she wondered if it was Alex. Someone thundered up the basement stairs, as well.

"Jeez, Marsh. Remember the shower?" Vienna said as her unkempt brother trundled in silently. "Would it kill you to not smell for dinner?"

"I smell fine, princess." He opened the cabinet and took down a cocktail glass.

"Got you water already," Vienna said.

"Not looking for water."

Taylor watched the interaction between the two as she finished setting the table. She could feel the tension between them and wondered how uncomfortable sitting down together would be.

Her pulse picked up as footsteps descended the stairs toward the kitchen. She placed the last knife just as Alex entered the room. She took in his appearance in mere seconds—faded blue jeans instead of his usual cargos, a plain, dark green T-shirt stretching across his chest, black tennis shoes. His gray eyes zeroed in on hers for an instant. She looked away but not without recording the image in her mind to appreciate later.

"Hey," he said to the room in general. "I smell food."

"Don't you think you could wait till after dinner to start your daily drink fest?" Vienna asked Marshall, standing next to him at the counter.

"Too late," he said.

Marshall turned toward the table and made his way across the room with a glass full of golden-brown liquid. Vienna shook her head and rolled her eyes when Alex looked at her.

"He's okay," Alex said. "Let him be."

Vienna gave him a look that seemed to ask when he and their older brother had gotten so buddy-buddy but she said nothing. Alex had mentioned his brother had lost his company recently, and it appeared he wasn't handling it very well. Or maybe he was just having a bad day.

"You remember Taylor McCabe," Mrs. Worth said to Marshall as she put a steaming hot casserole dish in the middle of the table. "Quinn's sister."

Recognition flashed in Marshall's eyes, quickly followed by sympathy.

Taylor was mostly fine until someone felt sorry for her.

"Nice to see you," she said, hoping he wouldn't break into the typical spiel about tragedy, being sorry, etc. She wanted to believe she wasn't here completely out of sympathy, but doubt nagged at her.

"Sorry I didn't shower. Didn't know we'd have a pretty guest."

Mrs. Worth set a bowl of green beans on the table as Vienna put a glass of water at everyone's place, plonking Marshall's down harder than necessary. Alex wandered over and sat next to his brother. He nodded to Taylor to sit on his other side.

"As far as you're concerned, Taylor's off the market," Alex said, and she braced herself for her old companion, embarrassment. "She's doing the online dating thing. Right?"

That's what she got for purposely not telling Alex she'd dropped the idea and closed her account. "Not exactly."

Marshall smiled at her.

"I mean, the online part. Not anymore." She was sure Marshall was a nice man, but cleanliness was such a given with her, she hadn't even bothered to put it on her list. Maybe this wasn't his typical state but she felt no attraction to him.

"Not having any luck?" Alex asked. Obviously he was still trying to keep tabs on her dating life out of a misplaced responsibility, not because he had any interest in her as a woman. Fortunately for him, keeping track of her dates was an easy job. They were nonexistent at the moment.

"I decided one nightmare was enough," she said, avoiding everyone's prying gazes.

"Some of my girlfriends swear by the online dating scene," Mrs. Worth said. When all three of her children's heads spun her way, she widened her eyes unapologetically. "What? Fifty-somethings need love, too."

"I don't want to hear about that," Alex said, helping himself to some fruit salad.

"I second that." Vienna picked up the serving spoon and heaped some mac and cheese on her plate.

"I didn't say I was doing it," her mother said. "Yet. What kind of bad experience did you have, Taylor?"

The very thought of Dan Drummond killed Taylor's appetite. "Just your average miserable date," she said, not about to go into the details. "It probably wasn't because of the online aspect specifically, but I feel better meeting a man in person before subjecting myself to several hours with him."

"Smart," Mrs. Worth said.

"We have new plans for Taylor anyway," Vienna announced.

"Maybe." It was obvious this family shared a lot at the dinner table but that didn't mean Taylor was comfortable with it.

"What kind of plans?" Of course Alex couldn't have let the comment slide by.

"Well," Vienna said, finishing a mouthful of food. "The biggest challenge is meeting the kind of men Taylor's looking for. You don't find a lot of intelligent, successful guys hanging out in bars. So we're thinking about invading their territory, so to speak."

"Only thinking about it," Taylor insisted.

Vienna explained the idea of joining professional organizations. Taylor wanted to hug her for not going into the brainiest bachelor article. Somehow just the title of the feature made it an embarrassing endeavor.

"Let me get this straight. You join all these business groups and go to their functions to troll for geeks?"

"Not geeks, army guy. Intelligent, professional men. Single ones."

"If they're so in demand, why are they single?" he asked.

"Why are you single?" Vienna shot back.

Alex ignored her and Taylor felt him staring at her. "And you're cool with this?"

She took her time chewing the food in her mouth. Took a drink to wash it down…and stall. When she couldn't avoid him any longer, she met his gaze.

His eyes burned into hers, and for an instant, she saw the same heat in them as when he'd kissed her. The feel of his mouth on hers, his arms holding her close, all of it came back to her now in sensual detail.

She wanted that again. Craved it the way a chocoholic yearned for a Snickers. She'd done her best to block out memories of that evening and normally managed to only let them sneak in late at night when she was at her weakest. Loneliest.

Now was not the time for them to slip past her defenses.

"Well? Are you?" he repeated.

Taylor had to think hard to recall the question. "I'm considering it."

"It's not a bad idea," his mother said. "If you went with her, Vienna, you could make some valuable contacts."

"That's true." Vienna's enthusiasm grew, if that was possible.

Mrs. Worth's point was a valid one, but still, Taylor wasn't about to agree to the plan without weighing all the variables.

"Can't believe you're really considering that," Alex mumbled.

"You didn't like the internet dating idea, either," Taylor reminded him. "So tell me what you would suggest as a way of meeting eligible men who don't spend every night drinking more ounces of beer than they have IQ points."

"Don't ask him," Vienna said. "He's barely left the house in the month since he's been home other than to go to PT or your place to work."

"You must be confusing me with him," Alex said, nodding toward Marshall.

"Go to hell," was Marshall's first contribution to the discussion.

It was obvious Marshall wasn't in the mood for this conversation, and the last thing Taylor wanted to do was annoy him more. She did her best to draw the attention back to Alex. "Something tells me you've never had trouble getting a date, any-

way." Case in point, the waitress's instant interest at Ian's.

"Does that make me a bad person?" Alex asked.

"Your ego makes you a bad person." Vienna
helped herself to a second serving of mac and
cheese.

"I could introduce you to a few 'bad people.'"

"Why don't you take it a step further and go out
and meet someone yourself," his sister suggested.
"You're so opinionated about Taylor's love life, but
really, you can't talk."

"Maybe I could tag along to Geeks Anonymous
with you two."

"We wouldn't be caught dead with you." Vienna
grinned smugly at her brother.

"So what do you think I should do, Miss Marketing?"

"Go to a bar. Meet a girl. In fact, take him with
you." She nodded at Marshall. "Meet two girls.
The house has shrunk since you both moved
back."

"What do you say, Marshall? You don't have to
work tomorrow. Up for a night out?"

Marshall looked more lively and interested than
he'd been since coming upstairs. "I'm game for a
woman hunt."

Their mother shook her head. "I might have to
disown you children."

"I didn't mean you should go track down a one-night stand," Vienna said. "Nasty boys."

"Not dinner conversation material," Mrs. Worth said, putting her hand up.

Taylor became overly interested in the rest of her macaroni and cheese as the Worths reminisced about controversial dinner discussions from the past. She tried to pay attention, but she couldn't help turning a single thought over in her mind… Was Alex planning to pick up a woman tonight?

Undoubtedly he had before. He was a male. In the military. She didn't remember him having any long-term relationships. But then she probably wouldn't have known anyway unless Quinn had said something.

The thought of him going home with someone he barely knew *tonight*… She squeezed her eyes shut.

"Are you okay, Taylor?" Mrs. Worth asked.

Taylor's eyes popped open and she flashed an overzealous smile. "I'm fine."

She wasn't fine. She was jealous of a potential, trashy, one-night stand that Alex *might* decide to hook up with tonight. That was bad news on so many levels that she, the math whiz, couldn't count them all.

Jealousy where Alex was concerned was not a viable option. Caring about him as more than just a friend wasn't, either. He failed to meet more than one of the qualifications on her list. And there was the small matter that the only reason he spent time with her or did things for her was because he was beating himself up over Quinn's death.

As soon as she and Vienna were alone, they had some research to do. Specifically, she needed to choose which brainiest bachelor hangout she was going to target first.

CHAPTER TWELVE

ALEX HAD EVERY INTENTION of meeting a woman tonight.

He was sick and damn tired of worrying about Taylor. Her online dates, her newest scheme to meet men. He could handle keeping tabs on her in a protective, look-out-for-creeps way, the kind of "worrying" he'd set out to do originally, but the thoughts he'd had at dinner were *not* brotherly nor were they welcome.

The fact was a man couldn't go months on end without sex. Not without it messing, hard-core, with his mind and every other aspect of his life. It was that simple. It was time, past time, for Alex to end his dry spell.

Marshall set a beer and a cocktail on the high, stool-less table where Alex stood, then caught hold of the edge to steady himself.

"Place is finally filling up," Marshall said, managing not to slur his words. "Lot of chicks here for a Sunday night."

"Mostly college girls. You could be their father."

"Better yet. Pretty young things."

"You think you better slow down a little?" Alex asked. It was early. At this rate, his brother would be facedown on the table before the end of the Brewers game that played on the large-screen TVs around the room.

"Did you bring Mom with us?"

"Maybe I should have."

"That'd seriously cramp my style."

"Last I knew, sloppy drunk wasn't your style, dude."

"Things change."

A chorus of cheers rang through the bar and Alex checked the closest big screen. Out of the corner of his eye, he saw Marshall pick up his cocktail—likely straight whiskey—and turn to look at the score. The amber liquid sloshed out of his glass and ended up on the shoulder of the woman standing closest to their table. Marshall didn't even notice.

Alex met the woman's eyes as she turned toward them, her annoyance clear. He reached across the table and swatted Marshall's upper arm—the one not holding his drink—to get his attention. His brother's reaction time was delayed but when Marshall finally acknowledged him, Alex nodded toward the woman.

"Major party foul, Marshall."

It took several seconds for Marshall to focus

his eyes on the woman and understand what had happened.

"Ooh, sorry, honey." He took the cocktail napkin that'd been under his drink and went for the spot on her T-shirt. That wasn't going to do a quarter of the job.

Alex searched the surrounding tables for real napkins. He spotted a stack on a nearby ledge and grabbed a handful. He held them out to the woman, but his moron brother took them first and clumsily attempted to dry her shirt as he again rambled out some lame apology.

The woman was obviously not in the mood for a drunk ass to fondle her under any pretense. She snatched the napkins from Marshall and scowled at him. Marshall, ever the idiot, straightened and stuck his hands in the air, surrender-style.

"Sorry. Sorry. No harm intended. Didn't mean to tick off a pretty girl."

Once the woman turned and stepped away, Marshall took another swig of liquor.

"That was ugly, man. You need to slow down."

"You just need to pick up the pace," Marshall said. "Never thought I'd see the day when my little brother couldn't hang with me."

They'd never hung out together in the past. Marshall had never been the bar type.

"Come on, it's brother time. We're both going

through rotten times, might as well have some fun."

Apparently there was a part of Alex, buried deep, that wanted to connect with his older brother, and that part surfaced now. The idea of the two of them flipping the bird to their crappy circumstances and tipping one back together... This wouldn't have happened five years ago. Misery did love company.

Alex reminded himself his brother needed to cut loose. Hell, *he* needed it, too. He relaxed and tapped the neck of his beer bottle to Marshall's nearly empty glass. "Cheers, bro."

Marshall finished his drink and looked toward the bar.

"Give me a minute to catch up," Alex said. Shared misery or not, his brother needed to slow the hell down. Telling him that directly wasn't going to do any good tonight, though. "I'll get the next round if you wait."

He managed to drag out his beer for eight minutes before Marshall got antsy.

"You need a nipple for that thing?" Marshall asked. "I'll get this round. You can get the next." He stalked toward the counter before Alex could stop him.

Alex became engrossed in the ball game and was just starting to realize Marshall had been gone too long when he slid another bottle of beer across the small table and set his half-full whiskey glass down hard.

"Long line?"

"Nah. Was talking to a woman at the bar."

Just then a large hand slammed down on their table, sloshing whiskey over the side of the glass and making Alex's beer bottle skitter an inch to the side.

"That you talking to my girlfriend over there?" A large man with a sleeve of tattoos on each arm and a death glint in his eyes glared at Marshall.

Shit, what had Marshall done now?

"If I did, it was an accident."

Marshall didn't seem as concerned as the situation warranted. Alex could hold his own in a fight, but this guy…he looked like the type that didn't play fair. The kind that carried a switchblade and wouldn't hesitate to use it.

Alex watched the rest of the exchange warily, ready to jump into the fray for his brother if necessary.

Tattoo Man threatened some more, and Marshall pleaded drunken innocence. The guy stared him down. Marshall was too far gone to recognize the danger in his eyes.

"He's leaving soon," Alex said to the big guy, who then turned toward him and scowled as he sized him up. Alex straightened and crossed his arms.

The thug sauntered off and Alex considered beating his brother himself. "Bad judgment, man."

"Said it was an accident. Godzilla was nowhere near when I talked to her." He shrugged as though everyone was being unreasonable. "You owe me a drink."

Alex stared at him, disbelieving. "Forget it, man. You're on your own."

"Works for me," Marshall said as Alex stalked off with his full beer.

He could understand the need to blow off some steam with a few drinks, but he didn't have to stand around and watch his brother make an ass of himself.

With no particular destination in mind, Alex scanned the room. His gaze froze on long copper hair that hung down the back of a woman sitting at the bar. His fool heart raced without his permission. Walking closer, he could easily tell it wasn't Taylor. Besides, she wouldn't be caught in public with her sexy hair down like that. Sadly.

He took the only available seat at the bar, several spots down from her, and kept an eye on the woman. He didn't plan to make the same mistake his dumbass brother had by moving in on someone with a boyfriend.

When she swiveled in her chair, he finally got a glimpse of her face. Pretty. Thirtysomething. And nothing like Taylor.

All good.

He made eye contact. Smiled. She smiled back and his confidence surged. He might be a little rusty but connecting with a good-looking woman was like riding a bike.

He bided his time until he saw Marshall's thug walk out with a short blonde, then made his way toward his redhead.

ALEX WAS MESSED UP in the head.

Fat raindrops started to fall as he walked home just before 1:00 a.m. Insult to injury. He briefly wondered where Marshall had ended up and whether he was facedown in the grass somewhere. The good news was that the dumbass hadn't had access to a car.

Alex had made it all the way to the redhead's—Allison's—living room. Nice, flirty girl, intelligent, unless you went by Taylor's standards. Definitely attractive. Sexy in a subtle way.

And he hadn't had any desire to make a move on her.

He'd kissed her several times, at the bar, on the way to her place, in her kitchen, hoping to get carried away by lust. But when he'd drawn away after

the last kiss and opened his eyes, he'd expected—
wanted—to see a different woman. And that realization had been like a bucket of ice water over
his head.

Escaping from her apartment was a more complex stunt than extracting a hostage from a Middle
Eastern cave, but he'd finally gotten out without
having anything thrown at him.

It wasn't that Taylor was the one for him. She
was top of mind, yes, but only because he'd been
around her so much lately. Just because he didn't
have any desire to follow a near stranger into her
bedroom and have wild monkey sex did not mean
he was hung up on anyone.

It just meant that next time he went out with the
intention of meeting a woman, he was going for a
blonde.

CHAPTER THIRTEEN

TAYLOR HAD DONE IT. She'd landed a date with a man she'd met in person who, at this early stage, appeared to have several qualities on her list. And no video-game obsessions to speak of.

Even more amazing, her date was Joel Cavelli, one of the "brainiest bachelors" in the business journal—the one Vienna had commented on because he seemed like the perfect guy for Taylor.

She walked up her driveway toward the back door after Vienna dropped her off from the Information Technology Professionals meeting. As she crossed the deck, she stopped at the planter she'd bought on a recent hardware-store visit and plucked off the biggest, pinkest daisy at the base of the stem. Setting her purse and satchel by the door, she wandered to the edge of the deck, noticing the brand-new wood in passing, and for once taking the chance to stop and enjoy the moment. She considered relaxing on the old wooden bench swing at the back of the yard, but didn't want to get her new clothes dirty. Next time.

Vienna was a goddess. Fashion goddess, hair

goddess, social goddess. Without her, Taylor would still be at the office, slaving over some brain-bending line of code, still dateless.

The Information Technology Professionals' happy-hour social at Mickey's Pub this evening had been Taylor and Vienna's second undertaking for Operation Checklist. The first had been on Wednesday. They'd gone to a Madison Mathematicians meeting. The math boys, as Vienna affectionately called them, were a tough crowd. More business—or numbers, rather—and less socializing, probably because they seemed to have fewer social skills overall. Date-wise, it'd been a bust, but Taylor had been enthralled with the formal discussion on multivariable calculus and had enthusiastically paid for a year's membership.

She never would've had the nerve to do any of this without Vienna's guidance. After they'd researched several local organizations Sunday night and chosen which ones to hit first, Taylor had made a panicked late-night call to Vienna regarding her ongoing wardrobe dilemma.

She'd never put much energy into buying clothes or keeping up on trends. Talk about monumentally overwhelming. Database development she could handle. Skirt lengths and hairstyles she could not, with the exception of the shoe passion she'd been blessed with. A few years ago, when she'd finished her master's degree and landed a real job, she'd been determined to demystify the world of style. She'd bought every magazine on the rack that had anything remotely to do with the subject and spent the week before she started her job poring over them. In the end she'd just been more confused and intimidated and had picked out a few classic, versatile—in other words, nontrendy and bland—pieces to build on. Unfortunately, she was still relying on those same basics today.

But having an expert to go with her, help her—okay, just about do it for her—that was enough to make Taylor take action.

Two marathon shopping trips and a small fortune later, she had a month's worth of clothes in her closet that actually had style, current style, plus a new look for her hair. She'd also dug out the contacts she rarely wore and was adjusting to using them every day. She had to admit, she didn't miss her glasses. Vienna complimented the changes Taylor had made repeatedly, until Taylor had had the confidence to set foot in the math meeting and tonight's computer geek get-together.

End result: a date for dinner and the symphony next Tuesday with a seemingly very nice man.

Taylor let herself inside, a little surprised to find the door unlocked. Alex must still be here working. She could never tell because he hadn't gotten around to buying a car, deciding it wasn't worth it when he'd only be around for a few months if his therapy went as he planned. He apparently either caught a ride, walked or jogged back and forth each day. She didn't really know because she hadn't seen him in over a week. Not since the Sunday-night Worth family dinner. Which suited her fine. He distracted her too much. Made her think about things she'd promised herself to forget, like…kissing him.

Joel Cavelli wasn't drop-dead gorgeous or dripping with raw masculinity the way Alex was. He didn't turn her into a tongue-twisted idiot just by looking at her. These were major points in his favor.

She took a slender vase down from the top shelf of the kitchen cabinets, filled it with water and added the daisy. It was just the right size to go on the windowsill over the sink. Listening for a hint to Alex's whereabouts, she opened the refrigerator, hoping something suitable for dinner had magically appeared while she was at work. No such luck on either count…the most appetizing thing in the fridge was half a cantaloupe. And if Alex was here, he was silent. Maybe he'd just forgotten to lock up when he left.

She poked her head around the corner to the basement stairs, listening, but the lights were all off. Shrugging, not allowing herself to acknowledge even a drop of disappointment, she locked the back door and headed to her bedroom to change out of her new clothes.

When she'd taken two steps into her room, her heart nearly jumped out of her chest. Alex lay diagonally across her double bed, sound asleep.

That was the raw masculinity she was talking about. *Lord above.*

He was sprawled on his belly, giving her all the time in the world to admire the way his black cargos fit over his perfect butt. Even more distracting was his lack of a shirt. Her mouth went desert-dry as she studied the bulge of biceps disappearing beneath the pillow—her pillow—and the ridges and valleys of endless, beautiful back muscles.

So much for not thinking about kissing him. The temperature seemed to climb twenty degrees and a small part of her wanted nothing more than to shed her clothes and climb in next to him. Maybe in a different lifetime…if she was a different person.

ALEX KNEW THE SECOND Taylor entered the room. He'd been sleeping but he never slept deeply, especially when he was not in his own bed.

He hadn't intended to drift off in here but his PT session yesterday had been harsh and he'd busted his butt getting the deck repaired today in spite of screaming muscles. The coolness of the air-conditioned house and particularly her bedroom, as well as the hint of Taylor's scent, had lulled him to sleep.

Damn her sweet scent of apples and innocence. She'd been in his dreams the whole time, preventing him from getting any true rest. Consequently, he was rock-hard and uncomfortable as hell. He debated rolling over and allowing her to see just what she'd done to him. Best to keep it to himself, though...he couldn't promise what would happen if he got any more turned on.

He opened his eyes and looked over his shoulder. Taylor had her back to him as she took her earrings off and set them in the jewelry box on her dresser. His eyes widened. Her pants were... sexy, outlining her body. Her clothes had never done that in the past. Same with her shirt. Instead of her usual frumpy blouse, suitable for a senior citizen, the shirt hugged her, showed off her slenderness. And her hair...the boring ponytail was gone. Instead, silky locks hung freely, just like his brain had conjured her in his steamy dreams.

"You're home early," he said, his voice gravelly.

She startled and whipped around toward him. Stared at him for a moment as if lost in thought, and he realized she'd done away with the glasses, as well. "It's interesting to come home and find Goldilocks still in my bed."

"Not bad," he said. "Kind of flirty."

Her eyes got big and darted to the nightstand by his head. Mortification washed over her face as she realized he'd found her *Flirting Basics* book.

"Your secret's safe with me, Scarlet."

"Why are you in my room?"

He pointed at the new closet doors. "Just doing my job, ma'am."

Her shoulders relaxed and she walked to the closet. Opened and closed the accordion-style doors a few times. "So much better. Thank you."

"At your service." He finally rolled over and sat up. "You look…different."

She headed back to the dresser and rearranged the already organized things on top of it. Okay. Apparently that topic was off-limits.

"What brings you home so early?" he asked, massaging his left thigh.

"Let's see, how would you put this? Vienna and I went 'trolling for geeks' at the local Geeks' Anonymous meeting."

He looked down at the floor. "I come across like a bastard, don't I?"

"Those aren't the *exact* words I'd choose…"

Alex shook his head, half grinning at her attempt to soften the truth. "I'm sorry." He stood and walked over to her. "Here's the thing, Scarlet. I want you to be happy."

"If that's true, then you'll be thrilled to hear that I met someone this evening. He asked me out."

He wasn't thrilled.

He beat down the jealous jerk that reared its head like a rutting caveman. Reminded himself he was not the man for Taylor. He was attracted to her, yes. He wanted to go to bed with her. But he was not her long-term man, not her list guy.

He lived with demons that prevented him from being the man who could let himself love her.

"What's he like? Is he a decent guy?"

She stared at him, narrowed her eyes. "I think what you mean is, 'That's great, Taylor. I'm happy for you.'"

"I'm happy for you as long as he doesn't turn out to be a douche bag."

She smiled. Sort of. "That's almost sweet of you. He seems perfect for me so far. He's the IT manager at Kohl Enterprises. Enjoys the History Channel, photography and baseball. No video-game obsessions, and yes, I asked."

Alex nodded, biting his tongue on anything negative. She was right. This guy could be the one for her. It was a long shot but he'd give him a chance. His decision must not have shown on his face, though.

"I know you don't have any concept of what it's like to have trouble getting a date."

"That's not true—"

"Stop." She shook her head resolutely. "You have no idea what it's like to come home to an empty house every single night. To go to movies by yourself just to get away from the mocking quiet..." She glanced at the tidy stack of mail on the dresser behind her. "To always be the single, dateless girl at every office party, every business function." She picked up the top item from the pile. "This wedding? One of my coworkers? Maybe I'll have a date. I'm sure that sounds like no big sappy deal to you, but just once I'd like to have someone to sit with. Someone to dance with."

Her hair had fallen across her cheek during her impassioned minispeech and he checked himself from brushing it out of the way. "Fair enough. I hope this guy works out."

"Thank you." Her words were forceful, still carrying the momentum of her diatribe.

"You don't seem so nervous around me anymore."

She opened her mouth then looked away. Her cheeks reddened and he held back a smile.

"As much as you've been hanging around, it took too much energy," she finally said with a hint of defiance.

That made him laugh. "When are you going out with List Guy?"

"Next Tuesday." She regretted telling him. He could see it on her face the second she got the words out. "That's all you need to know."

"Always did catch on quick."

Showing up on her date again would be too much. He wouldn't blame her for blowing up at him if he did that. He'd have to do his recon some other way, because he fully intended to make sure the guy would pass a brother's approval.

Brother's.

He looked across the narrow hallway to the bedroom that had been Quinn's. Ugly black curtains that Quinn had chosen during his high-school tough-guy phase still hung at the window, blocking out the last traces of evening sun.

Alex let the pain hit him. Forced himself to stand there and stare at the familiar room where Taylor's brother would never set foot again. Didn't try to brush it to the side or ignore it.

Grief closed his throat, nearly blocked his airway. Throbbed in his chest and made every breath hurt as his half-destroyed leg never had.

This was what he deserved. Not something as good as Taylor.

CHAPTER FOURTEEN

ALEX MADE RECORD time running home from Taylor's. He could tell even before he looked at his watch—his muscles were screaming at him. Sure enough, his best post-accident time yet. And he was closing in on where he'd been pre-injury. He winced at the stab of pain through his leg, allowing it to drown out everything else in his mind.

His muscles shook as he let himself in the house through the garage entrance. He'd hoped to come in unnoticed, grab a bag of chips and disappear upstairs to his room, but, of course, that was too much to ask in this house, at least when the two females were home.

"Army guy's home," Vienna called out as he shut the door. "Just in time for Mom's spaghetti."

Damn. He couldn't resist his mom's spaghetti even on a full stomach. As it was, it'd been hours since he'd eaten lunch. He didn't stand a chance. He took a right turn into the kitchen instead of going left toward the stairs and his refuge.

"Look who it is," his mom said.

"Smell who it is." Vienna wrinkled her nose. "Why didn't you call for a ride?"

"Didn't want a ride." He said it more harshly than he'd intended but he really wasn't in the mood for the feel-good feminine yammer. "Where's Marshall?"

"I wish I knew," their mom said, sounding concerned. "He hasn't been home since yesterday afternoon as far as I can tell."

"He's a big boy," he said automatically. *A big boy going down a bad road.* Alex was starting to suspect alcohol was the easy way out from a shitty place.

"Your leg must be doing pretty well as much as you're exercising lately," his mom said.

"Yeah, how's therapy going?" Vienna asked as she poured milk for all of them.

"Making progress."

Not fast enough for his taste but Helen refused to let him increase PT to four times a week. She insisted he was doing extraordinarily well. Admitted he'd surpassed her expectations.

"You're still determined to go back to the army, huh?" his mom asked quietly. She spooned the garlic-laden sauce into a serving bowl then carried it to the table.

"It's my career, Mom. I'm going back to it." He finished washing his hands and caught the concern in his mother's eyes. "I'll miss you and your cooking, of course."

"Nice catch," Vienna said. She meant well, he was sure, but the cheeriness grated on his nerves tonight.

He took the bowl of pasta from his mom and set it on a trivet.

"This is it, kids," their mom said. "Let's eat."

The three of them sat in the places they'd claimed years ago—Cheryl closest to the stove, Vienna to her left and Alex across from her. They passed the food around, the clinking of silverware on dishes the only sound.

"Were you at Taylor's all this time?" Vienna never had done well with quiet.

"Yes, ma'am."

"Did she tell you the good news?"

He grunted as he shoved a fork full of pasta in his mouth.

"What good news is that?" their mom asked.

"Operation Checklist was a success tonight!"

"You've got to be kidding me." Alex's food went down wrong and he nearly choked. "Operation Checklist? You have a name for the nonsense?"

"Maybe not as far-reaching as Operation Enduring Freedom or whatever the heck the current war is called, but pretty exciting for Taylor, nonetheless."

"Good for her," their mom said. "She deserves a nice man. She's been through so much lately."

"You know you're just setting her up to get hurt with this ridiculous list thing, don't you?" he said to Vienna. "Maybe not today or next week but sometime."

"Aren't you Mr. Positive?"

"Really, Alex, when did you become such a nay-sayer?" their mom asked.

"You try to force this whole dating thing, measure every guy up to that damn list, it's going to end badly. It's not realistic and relationships aren't nice and neat like that."

"Maybe," Vienna said, taking another bite. "Maybe not. Why are you so concerned?"

It was a damn good question. Maybe he wasn't that concerned after all. Maybe he was just in a foul mood and needed to take it out on the closest cheerful person.

Vienna dropped her fork on her plate and stared at him, her mouth open. "Oh, my God."

Alex made the mistake of eye contact and immediately looked back down.

"You want her for yourself," Vienna said.

Without looking up, he sensed that his mom was staring at him, too, her fork halfway to her mouth.

"That's not true." Not exactly.

"It explains why you're doing all that work for her. Why you're over there so much…"

"She's paying me for the work."

"Alex, do you think that's wise?" Their mom finally lowered her fork. "You're leaving in the near future. I would hate to see her get hurt…"

"Mom. I'm fixing up her house. She's paying me. End of story."

"Except it's not," Vienna said. "That's why you showed up at Ian's when she was there on a blind date. And why you're so grumpy tonight. It all makes sense now."

Every muscle in his body, depleted or not, coiled with the need to jump out of the chair and protest. He fought it hard, knowing full well that would convince his busybody sister she was right. Anything he said right now to set her straight would have that effect.

"Think what you want but I have no intention of getting involved with Taylor. Or anyone else, for that matter."

His sister stared at him, deep in thought. He hated that look.

"I can't help but think she could do a lot worse," Vienna said.

He couldn't help but disagree completely, but he was done with this conversation. He shoved back from the table.

"I'm taking your car, Mom. Going out to find Marshall."

And if he found him keeping company with a bottle, Alex was giving serious thought to joining him.

"YOU'RE DOING *WHAT?*" Karen Fleming, the receptionist in Taylor's office, uttered the question loudly enough that surely everyone in the nearby cubicles and offices could hear.

"I'm leaving for the day," Taylor said softly, strongly considering returning the wedding gift she'd bought for this woman whom she'd liked up until this very moment.

"It's quarter till five, Taylor. Isn't that about when you usually break for lunch?"

Maury Peterson walked toward the mail room. "What's the occasion, Taylor?" he asked as he passed.

"I have an appointment to plan Karen's funeral," Taylor muttered, her face undoubtedly bright pink. Thank goodness she hadn't confided to anyone here about her date. She'd never hear the end of it, and that was saying a lot for an office full of relatively antisocial computer geeks.

"You're not going to tell me what's going on, are you?" Karen said at a more reasonable volume.

"You're perceptive." Taylor smiled and slid

her magnet to Out on the big white status board. "Have a good evening."

"Oh, you, too, Taylor." Karen's voice overflowed with conspiratorial excitement. "I'll expect details tomorrow, whatever it is."

"Goodbye," Taylor singsonged as she escaped.

Most people with a dinner date would leave work fifteen minutes early in order to go home and take their time getting ready for the outing. Taylor's reasoning had more to do with A) avoiding vomiting in the workplace, and B) giving herself time to defrag before Joel showed up so she wouldn't embarrass herself more than usual on a social outing.

She hurried out of the building and across the parking lot to her car. Once inside, she started the engine, blasted the cool air and noticed she was shaking. Over an hour to go before Joel had said he'd pick her up and she was already at this advanced stage of panic.

She'd never make it at this rate.

Practical matters, she coached herself. Focus on practical matters. She pulled out her phone and clicked on the pre-date to-do/consider list she'd made. Setting her phone on her thigh, she backed up and headed home, making a conscious effort to breathe slowly, deeply.

Number one: choose outfit. Check. Thanks one

hundred percent to Vienna, she planned to wear her long black dress with the empire waist. She was going conservative on her shoes with simple black three-inch heeled sandals—one of her favorite pairs. Security, in a twisted way, and lord knew she needed security of some kind.

Number two: jewelry. Check, again due to Vienna's assistance. Or rather, Vienna's *doing*. She'd picked out a delicate silver chain with a dangling purple stone and silver earrings that coordinated.

Number three: conversation topics. Sub-lists for car ride, dinner and waiting for the symphony to begin. Check…

As she turned down her street, the nausea had subsided marginally.

When she pulled into her driveway and saw Alex through the window—shirtless—painting her living-room walls, the intense need to hurl increased tenfold.

CHAPTER FIFTEEN

A DATE WITH MR. WONDERFUL must be the only thing that could get Taylor home before five.

Alex was relieved to hear her car in the driveway, though. Both she and his sister had been tight-lipped about the details of tonight's date, so his only option was to stay late himself and see if the guy picked her up at home.

The back door closed. The shyer cat, who'd been watching him suspiciously from the doorway all afternoon, darted in to greet its mistress, and Alex heard Taylor set her bags down on the table as she always did. He dipped his roller in the pan and sloshed more paint on the wall. Waited.

And waited.

He stopped rolling paint to listen for a clue as to what she was doing.

Nothing.

Thinking maybe she'd gone back outside or down to the basement for something, he added one more roller-full of paint to the wall. When the roller was empty, he'd still heard nothing so he set it down on the edge of the pan and went to the kitchen doorway.

Taylor's back was to him. She leaned on the counter, supporting her weight with her elbows, her hands over her face, feline at her feet.

"Taylor? Are you okay?"

She shook her head.

Alex shot forward. "What's wrong?" He leaned over the counter next to her, his hand on her back.

She expelled a long, shaky breath. Straightened, but avoided looking at him. "I'm not going. I can't do this."

And here he'd been expecting her to march inside and rake him over the coals for hanging around. She'd done so well at keeping her insecurities hidden lately, he hadn't anticipated this at all.

He'd done his best to harden himself toward her when he'd gone out last Friday night. He'd attempted to purge her from his system with help from his three-sheets-to-the-wind brother and a bottle of bourbon. He'd steeled himself to watch her walk off with the geek of her choosing tonight.

Reality found him floundering in the face of her vulnerable side.

"You're going," he said, facing her.

Her lids remained lowered, her jaw firm. "I

can't do it." She turned away from him again. "This must seem so stupid to you."

"Not stupid, no. Waste of your energy, yes. Because you're going. It'll be okay."

She narrowed her eyes at him. "Who are you and what have you done with Alex?"

"Paint fumes. Come on." He grabbed her hand without waiting for her acquiescence and pulled her through the kitchen, down the hall. To her room.

"*What* are you doing?" she asked.

He went for the closet door. There was a dress hanging on the outside of it. "This what you're wearing?"

"That's what I'd planned." Uncertainty filled her voice.

He took it down from the door. Slid the dress off the hanger and tossed it at her. Spotting the black heels lined up precisely square to the front of the closet door, he smiled to himself. "I see you have your shoes ready, too."

She almost grinned back. "My jewelry's laid out on the dresser."

He liked a woman who could embrace her crazy.

"That's as much as I can do, Scarlet. If you need help getting that on, I'll have to call Vienna."

"I can dress myself, thanks."

She didn't sound entirely committed to the

cause, but he headed for the door, pulling it closed behind him. He paused and stuck his head back in. "Five minutes. Dress, shoes, jewelry. No dithering around in here about 'I'm not going.'"

She stared at him as if he'd grown a second head, and he pulled the door all the way closed.

He went to the kitchen. Maybe the three bottles of wine in the minirack on the counter were meant to be a decoration—he'd never seen Taylor drink anything alcoholic at home—but he grabbed the red in the middle, easily worked the cork off and hunted for a wineglass. After a futile search, he pulled a juice glass out and filled it halfway with merlot. Etiquette or tradition or whatever be damned.

The door was still closed when he returned, so he leaned against the wall and waited. Ten minutes had passed. Eleven. He knocked.

She opened it a foot and shielded her body with it. He could tell she'd changed clothes, though, because she'd grown by several inches thanks to those stilts she'd set out.

He wordlessly motioned with his head for her to come all the way out.

"Maybe I should change to black slacks," she said as she emerged.

Alex swallowed hard and bit the inside of his mouth. "You shouldn't change to black pants."

The dress accentuated her slender waist, gathering under her breasts and making them damn tough to ignore. The neckline was modest but the creamy skin that Taylor didn't normally expose got his pulse and his imagination working double-time. The delicate pendant around her neck gave him a new fascination with collarbones.

She nervously grasped the loose material at her sides. "I don't wear dresses often...."

He waited for her to meet his gaze, and when she finally did, the doubt in her pretty green eyes faltered. For a moment, a mutual need seemed to stretch palpably between them.

"You look...good, Taylor."

Damn he hated that.

"Thanks." The moment passed as she looked at the floor and fidgeted. Checked her watch.

"What else?" He crossed his arms, careful not to spill the wine, and tried to keep from staring at her.

"What else?"

"What's left to do? There's no way a woman could be ready in less than fifteen minutes."

"Oh. Yeah. Hair. Makeup. Told you I'm not good at this."

"Get in there," he said. He held the glass of wine out to her as an afterthought. "Drink this while you get gorgeous. I'm going back out there to paint." Or break something.

"Alex."

"Yeah?"

"Thanks for…whatever this is you're trying to do, but you can go home. Really."

"Nice try," he said. "Paint fumes wearing off, though."

He expected her to argue—she was nothing if not persistent—but she looked at her watch and shook her head, distracted, before brushing past him toward the bathroom.

"WANT ME TO GET THAT?" Alex called when the doorbell rang half an hour later.

"No!" Taylor came rushing out to the living room and he wondered how she avoided twisting an ankle in those shoes. "I want you to disappear," she hissed as she headed toward the door.

"Just tell him I'm the hired help."

She stopped at the door and stared at him. Alex smiled, trying to act as though he didn't have the overpowering urge to knock the guy's teeth down his throat before he even met him.

"Please behave yourself," she whispered. She didn't wait for him to respond—just as well because he couldn't make any promises. She turned away, stood two inches from the door with her forehead pressed against it, and inhaled deeply before opening it.

"Taylor," a faceless, unimpressive voice said from the front stoop. "You look beautiful."

Alex clenched his jaw harder and dipped the roller.

"Thank you, Joel," she said, stepping back to let him inside.

Alex didn't have to look to know she was smiling widely at the flattery. Beautiful? Was that the best the guy could do?

"I made reservations at a new place downtown that specializes in local organic food. I hope that's okay."

And there was the health-conscious from her list. Suck-up.

"It's perfect. Joel, this is my friend Alex Worth. He's doing some work around the house for me. Alex, Joel Cavelli."

Alex finally turned and got a look at the guy. He was three or four inches shorter than Alex and as scrawny as a teenager. His hair was thinning—he'd be half-bald in two years, max. In his favor, he didn't have a pocket protector or tape on his glasses. His wardrobe was nondescript but neat… wasn't that another criterion on the holy list?

"I just need to grab my purse," Taylor said, apparently convinced the two men could play nicely for sixty seconds. She walked out to the kitchen, her death-wish shoes clicking on the hard floors.

The guy was a little overzealous as he took three steps toward Alex, hand extended.

Alex nodded in an attempt to be polite. "Hands are covered with paint," he said.

"Have you known Taylor long?" Joel asked.

"Most of her life."

"So you're...a handyman by trade?"

"I fly helicopters and blow up al-Qaeda by trade."

Joel's eyes widened as Taylor came back in. She smiled at her date, oblivious to the tension that buzzed between the men.

"It was nice to meet you, Alex," Joel said.

"Likewise," he lied.

The computer dude held the screen door open for Taylor. As she stepped outside, she turned toward Joel to thank him. Alex happened to look at just the right moment to see it—her eyes came alive as they hadn't in...forever.

He sat down hard on the second step of the ladder, realizing what a jackass he was.

He'd been so self-involved, he'd disregarded the most important thing: what made Taylor happy. Judging by that look just now, it had nothing to do with him and everything to do with Joel what's-his-name.

CHAPTER SIXTEEN

WHEN YOU SPENT AS MUCH time alone as Taylor did, you tended to get pretty skilled at keeping the bad stuff to yourself. Embarrassments. Disappointments. This time, however, it was a struggle to act as if nothing was wrong in front of Alex.

The past two weeks had flown by in an exciting blur—until yesterday. She shook her head against the thought of it.

This morning, Taylor had deliberately had the car stereo on from the moment she'd picked Alex up. It had worked to keep conversation between them to a minimum for the entire ride to the home-improvement store. Now, as they entered the store, she made a beeline to the bath department, dodging around the Saturday-morning throngs, just wanting this errand—the day, as a matter of fact—over with.

"Yo, Scarlet," Alex hollered after her. "What's with the woman-on-a-mission drill?"

"Sorry." She slowed but didn't look at him. "I guess I'm just over the romance of the home projects."

Alex had been chipping away at the list for several weeks and she could no longer avoid the looming prospect of putting her house up for sale and hunting for a new one.

Of course, she'd been quite happily otherwise occupied lately and it'd been easy to procrastinate. She and Joel had seen each other a couple of times for dinner or drinks on weeknights, then gone out on the weekends to movies, to farmers' markets. They'd emailed daily, slowly getting to know each other better.

Taylor wouldn't call it a hot, passionate affair, but that wasn't what she was looking for. He'd kissed her a few times and it had been nice. But she wasn't in a hurry to take it any further right now, and neither was he.

He was perfect for her.

She ran through the list in her head—again. Because it satisfied her to revisit just how ideal Joel was. There wasn't a single criterion that he didn't meet.

This current thing—it was just a small bump in the road. Nothing to get upset about, and really, she wasn't upset. Just disappointed.

"Countertops first?" Alex asked, thankfully not seeming to notice her preoccupation. "Flooring? Tubs?"

"Whichever," she said, unable to care much about any of it.

"Let's get the shower taken care of first. They're this way." He pointed to an aisle in the back and they walked toward it.

Halfway there, as they crossed the wide perpendicular aisle, Taylor glanced to her left and froze.

Her head felt light—and not in a good way—and her chest seemed as if it was filling up with water, taking away her ability to breathe.

Joel stood three rows away at one of the end-cap displays, with a short, slightly chunky brunette. His arm rested at her waist and his lips brushed her ear.

At once panicked and heartbroken, Taylor rushed forward to the safety of the shower aisle before Alex could figure out her world had just come crashing down around her. Unfortunately, Joel looked her way just before she was home safe.

Bile burned her throat and she truly thought she might empty her stomach right there in one of the display tubs. Air. She needed oxygen. She held on to the edge of the closest tub, which stood on end, and concentrated on inhaling deeply and evenly. Alex was about two models down, inspecting the shower as if the world depended on this decision.

Taylor couldn't care less about a shower.

A clerk approached Alex then and they began discussing options, installation, who knew what else.

As soon as she was sure she could make it to the front of the store without embarrassing herself, she caught Alex's eye. "I'm going to the car. Don't feel well. Take your time."

It was probably crappy to leave him to do her job, but she had to get out of there. Immediately.

She made the monumental but unavoidable mistake of checking the end display again on her way past. And again, Joel noticed her. She rushed away without acknowledging him.

The bright sun nearly blinded her as she exited the store, but the fresh air helped marginally. Until she heard Joel call her name right behind her.

No. Not here. She didn't want to face up to him in the parking lot, with cars driving by and people gawking. Without conscious thought, she took a left turn down the sidewalk, toward the lawn and garden department.

"Taylor, wait up." Joel's footsteps weren't far behind her.

She had no escape, so she stopped at the first patio table on display. Held on to it to steady herself.

"Taylor, I'm sorry," Joel said, coming up beside her.

She moved to the side, away from him, keeping her hands on the tabletop.

"I need to explain to you," he said.

"It didn't look like there's much to explain." Vaguely conscious of other shoppers nearby, she lowered herself to one of the patio chairs as if to test its comfort.

"That's Sheila," he said, taking the chair across from her. "My ex. The one I told you about."

Wasn't this cozy? Just two people sitting out in the Saturday-morning sun, discussing this man's ex-girlfriend as if it were nothing more than the color of seat cushions and umbrellas.

"You said you couldn't come with me to the wedding tonight because you were going out of town. Last I checked, this is part of the metro area."

He looked down. Leaned forward nervously. "I'm sorry I said that, Taylor. What happened is that Sheila and I started talking this week. Tentatively. We talked about maybe getting back together but it was nothing concrete."

"That's nice. Congratulations." Her chest felt as though something was compressing it.

"I didn't hide that she was still important to me."

But she'd blown it off because the relationship was over. Or so he'd said.

"She saw us at the symphony that night of our first date," he continued, even though Taylor didn't really want to hear. There was no way she could stand up and walk away at this moment, though. "I guess that got to her..."

She registered what he was saying. "You knew she was there, didn't you? That's who you kept staring at."

He nodded. "I never meant to hurt you, Taylor. I like you..."

A new wave of nausea staggered her, would've knocked her on her butt if she wasn't already sitting down. A particularly painful idea occurred to her. "Tell me one thing, Joel. Be honest. Did you ask me out hoping to make her jealous? Is that why you took me to the symphony?"

His gaze flitted away. Wouldn't meet hers no matter how long she stared at him.

"I asked you out because I liked talking to you."

"And the symphony? Did you know ahead of time she'd be there?"

"Yes. But I..." He didn't finish the sentence and he didn't look at her.

Taylor realized a gaping oversight at that moment—she'd neglected to add *honesty* to her list.

She stood, unseeing, blinded by tears and humiliation. "Better get back to her," she managed to say before she walked off to her car.

She'd no sooner closed the passenger door— no way was she capable of driving in this condition—than Alex opened the driver's side.

"What the hell?" he said as he got in. Then she felt his gaze on her. His confusion was tangible. "Taylor, what happened? I saw what's-his-name out there. What did he do to you?"

That's all it took—Alex's concern, the way he was automatically, unquestioningly on her side without knowing what had happened—and the tears started falling. She shook her head and covered her burning face.

"Can we just go?" she asked when she could get the words out.

He stared at her for another few seconds. Touched her thigh lightly. "You have the keys."

Taylor squeezed her eyes shut and dried her face. Nodded. She took her purse from beside her on the seat and dug the keys out.

Alex started the car without further question and drove to her house in silence. She would've preferred for him to drive to his house and get out, but she didn't think of that until the car was in her driveway.

She climbed out before he could question her again and headed inside. She went to her room to take her shoes off. Hide. Hope like crazy Alex didn't follow her. Maybe he just wanted to run home for some exercise.

Or maybe not.

She heard the back door shut and decided action was the best thing. The house could use a good cleaning. Another one. If that scared Alex off, so much the better.

She slipped out to the hall linen closet where she kept some of her cleaning supplies and picked up a dust cloth and the bottle of wood cleaner. Before Alex appeared, she ducked back into her room and cleared off her dresser to dust it.

When Alex sauntered in and plunked himself down on the decorative antique chair in the corner, she ignored the need to tell him the chair wasn't very sturdy. Managed to ignore *him*, as well. She went over the entire surface of the dresser twice. She took her time rearranging everything once she was satisfied.

"You about done?" Alex said.

"Done with what?" Stretching out the chores for several hours was a distinct possibility. An appealing one.

"Avoiding." He shifted and the chair creaked. "Talk to me, Scarlet. I'm not leaving until you tell me whether you need someone to go beat him up."

He was attempting to get her to lighten up but it wasn't working.

She went around the bed on the opposite side of the room from him and attacked the nightstand.

Before she was even halfway done, she sat heavily on the mattress. Alex wasn't going to let it go. Wouldn't walk away until she told him what had happened.

"Yesterday Joel canceled on me for the wedding tonight. He said he was going out of town."

"He didn't look very out of town," Alex said. Her back was to him but she heard him lean forward in the squeaky, delicate chair.

"Apparently his definition of *out of town* is something similar to *getting back together with his ex*."

Alex let loose a crude but poetic stream of swear words in Joel's honor. In a twisted way, it tugged at something inside Taylor, made her feel less alone. He stood and came around to her side, sat on the bed a few inches away from her.

"He's a jerk, Taylor. He doesn't deserve you."

"I don't think he's quite seeing what a prize I am," she said sadly.

"That's the first clue he isn't good enough."

"Something like that." She was far from convinced of anything of the sort.

"I'm okay, Alex." She stood and put space between them. "We weren't really exclusively dating or anything. I was just…surprised. Don't feel like you need to babysit me."

"I was going to work on your bathroom."

"Yeah. I guess we'll do that another day. Sorry to waste your time." She walked over to the window and adjusted the curtains so they were symmetrical, waiting for him to leave.

"What time's the wedding?"

The curtain on the left wouldn't fall quite right so she fought with it. "Six-thirty."

"I'll pick you up at six," he said, standing.

Taylor whirled around to search his face and gauge his sincerity. "No. Absolutely not."

"I'll clean up," he said, acting insulted.

"It's a big formal to-do, Alex. You'd hate it."

"Pretty sure I have a suit in my closet. It should fit fine."

She ran out of arguments because, lord, the thought of him in a suit, and of being the lucky one holding on to his arm, was impossible to resist. Even knowing it would only be for one night.

"Why would you do that?" She couldn't help asking him.

He studied her for several seconds, and her heart pounded so hard she swore he could hear it. "Because I know how much you want to go to a wedding with a date."

Taylor blinked. Forced a grin.

She hadn't truly thought it was because he'd wanted to be with her, and after the morning she'd already had, she figured this should just bounce right off her. It didn't, though. It stung.

That was okay, she told herself. She decided then and there she would take what he offered and pretend for one night she wasn't someone's obligation.

CHAPTER SEVENTEEN

DANCING WITH TAYLOR all night had been hell.

Touching her. Breathing her. Catching private glimpses of creamy skin beneath the neckline of her gown.

He'd tried to tell himself he was only there to do Taylor a favor, tried to twist it into some way to honor Quinn, but he knew better. Quinn didn't have a damn thing to do with the reason Alex had catered to her all night, spoiled her. Quinn did, however, have everything to do with why he was trying like the devil to keep her at arm's length.

Following her inside her house now at—he checked his watch—quarter after midnight was probably a dumb idea. But they'd ordered pizza within five minutes of driving away from the wedding reception, both of them starving after picking at strange, unidentifiable "gourmet" creations all evening. Alex was pretty adventurous when it came to food but he hadn't seen anything quite like the stuff that had been served tonight. Some of the dishes had made him long for MREs, the military's version of combat-ready TV dinners.

At the back door, he held out his hand for her key and unlocked it. "Pizza should be here within five."

"I'm going to change clothes before I move the wrong way and split this thing open," Taylor said.

This thing was a long midnight-blue dress with thick straps and a modest neckline in front, but that dipped to the middle of her back and looked amazing on her. Hell yes, it was time for her to change, preferably into something frumpy and old.

When she disappeared into her room, Alex removed his tie and tossed it on the counter.

Taylor padded back into the kitchen a few minutes later, still in the dress but minus the stilts. "Good thing you came inside, otherwise I'd be stuck sleeping in this. Would you mind?"

She turned her back to him and Alex's mouth went dry. Holding her hair out of the way, she backed a step closer and waited. He pushed aside the material that hid the tiny zipper pull and fumbled around, his fingers suddenly clumsy. At last he managed to grasp the sliver of metal and ease it down. And down. His eyes widened and he wondered where the zipper was going to stop.

Right in the middle of her ass, as it turned out. If he was a gentleman, he would've tried harder not to get a glimpse of the white silk with pink polka dots beneath. But he'd never once been accused of being a gentleman.

"There." His voice didn't quite work right.

"Thank you," she said demurely as she walked away again. That was Taylor, prim and proper to the end, even after flashing him her panties.

Alex had abstained from drinking all evening so Taylor could enjoy the wedding without worrying about driving home. Now, though, he went straight to the fridge and took out one of the beers he'd left there. He took the cap off and downed half of it at once.

Pizza and home. That was the plan.

Taylor had drunk only enough wine and champagne to keep her confidence up throughout the evening. Her senses were fully functioning and the cool air that hit her backside when Alex unzipped her made her shiver, but not because of the lowered temperature. It was more due to the fantasies—delusions, really—she'd allowed herself all night. That Alex was hers. That he was with her because he wanted to be. That they would come home together and do more than eat pizza.

Now that they were at her house, she felt like Cinderella after midnight. Back to her insecure self. Or perhaps she was even more insecure than usual because of the direction she'd allowed her thoughts to go throughout the evening.

She brushed her hair, washed off the god-forsaken makeup that made her feel slimy, and changed into yoga pants and a tank top. Comfy but not too revealing.

When she returned to the kitchen, Alex was standing with his back to the counter, leaning against it. Shirtsleeves rolled up, top buttons undone, he belonged in a magazine advertisement. He'd shaved tonight, and though she liked his often shadowed chin, she was transfixed by his smooth skin. Wondered what it would be like to touch it. His eyes were on her as she crossed the room to the pizza box on the counter. She tried to concentrate on serving herself but he kept staring.

"What?" she asked, wondering if she'd missed a blotch of mascara or something.

He shook his head, nearly smiled and took a swig of his beer. He'd been busy while she was changing—there was already an empty bottle by the sink. A drink seemed like an excellent idea to her, but likely for different reasons. God knew Alex wasn't nervous around her. Wasn't having the same R-rated thoughts she was.

She pulled out the bottle of red wine he'd opened before her first date with Joel and poured herself a glass. They both helped themselves to slices of pizza. Taylor hoisted herself up onto the counter to eat. Maybe the evening's alcohol was affecting her more than she'd thought because she'd always been the sit-at-the-table type.

They ate without speaking at first, both of them shoving in the pizza as fast as possible, then they graduated to small talk about the wedding, the bride, a little about the dynamics of Taylor's office. When she was done eating, she set her plate aside, knowing he'd be leaving soon. Wishing he wanted to stay. The idea of being in this empty house after a nearly perfect night in Alex's company depressed her.

"Alex," she said, taking a sip of merlot. "Thank you."

He stuffed the last bite of pizza in his mouth and wrinkled his forehead. "For what?" he asked when he'd swallowed.

"For going tonight. Dancing with me, even the goofy songs. Being okay with being stuck with me when there were plenty of pretty single girls around."

He wiped his hands on a napkin and tossed it in the trash. "I wasn't stuck with you, Scarlet."

She stared at her hands as she folded and unfolded them repeatedly. "I know it wasn't the way you wanted to spend your Saturday night."

He set his bottle down hard on the counter. "Why do you do that?"

The harshness in his voice made her snap her head up and look at him. "Do what?"

"You're so damn hard on yourself."

"I like to think of it as being realistic."

"No." He pushed himself away from the counter. "Realistic is that you're a hell of a person."

Taylor inhaled deeply. Her throat felt as if a tennis ball was stuck in it. "Thanks. Tell that to Joel."

"I wouldn't waste my breath. He may be intelligent but the guy's dumber than a Marine. How can I get you to see his opinion is worthless?"

"Maybe if it was just him you could, but it's been kind of ingrained for most of my life." She lowered herself from the counter and set her plate in the sink. "I'm going outside to get some air."

THE SADNESS IN TAYLOR'S EYES as she slid down from the counter fueled the storm inside Alex. He'd like nothing better than to track down the loser who'd screwed her over and shove his fist down the guy's throat. The only thing the jerk was good for was proving her list completely useless.

Battling with the violent urge was his soft spot for the woman who'd just walked out the back door with her shoulders sagging. He knew without a doubt she didn't believe what he'd said, but what the hell could he do to change her mind? And he was in no position to do so even if he did know how.

He put the leftover pizza in the refrigerator and cleaned the rest of their mess. Turned out the overhead kitchen light. Thought about starting the walk home.

Shaking his head, he went out the back door to find Taylor.

The deck was empty. He checked to see that her car was still in the garage and it was. Then he saw motion at the far end of the yard. Without hesitation, he headed down the steps toward the bench swing on the lawn.

Taylor was lying on it on her back, her knees pointing to the sky. The swing rocked slightly, almost imperceptibly, as if the breeze carried it. Alex lowered himself to the grass and stretched out. Stared through the dark tree branches above to the few stars visible from the middle of the city.

"You'll get grass stains on your white shirt," she said.

"If that's the worst thing that happens today, I'll count myself lucky." He silently swore at himself, remembering she'd had an all-around shitty morning when she'd found her guy with another woman.

Minutes passed and neither of them spoke. The

swing rocked, the crickets chirped. Alex began to wonder if she'd drifted off to sleep.

"I know you think I'm hypersensitive," she said out of nowhere. "It's kind of a *thing* with me. Feeling like I've never been good enough."

"You've always been the best of the best. Brains. A list of achievements a mile long. You have a killer career—"

"I'm not talking about that stuff," she interrupted. "I love my job. Know I have a decent brain. It's...I don't know...overall, I guess. Whole person."

Her use of *decent* to describe her mind made him smile in spite of the seriousness of the conversation. She had a decent brain like Africa had a decent desert.

"You know my dad left us when I was little. Yours did, too, didn't he?" she asked.

"When I was eleven."

"Did you ever wonder if it was because you weren't good enough? Like, if you'd been a little smarter or a little more helpful around the house, he would've liked it enough to stick around?"

He nodded even though she couldn't see him, her words hitting an insecurity he'd buried deep.

"Between that and the way I was treated at school...I would've done anything to have a less super brain and be a more normal kid."

"Kids are harsh." That was an understatement for the teasing and bullying she'd undergone. Kids had been downright ugly.

"Maybe I should've been smart enough to know things would be okay but I never once in my childhood felt *okay*."

He sat up and rested his arms on his bent knees. "You're an adult now. A damn successful one."

"In some ways."

It was what she left unsaid that hung powerfully between them. Taylor believed everything she was saying, regardless of what he or others thought of her.

She sat up, too, the swing creaking softly with her movement.

"I've never told anybody this…" she hesitated "…not even Quinn. Every time our mom left on one of her research trips, I went through this horrible anxiety thing. I knew there was always some danger involved, and it scared me to death that she'd be like my dad and never come back."

He'd been well aware that Mrs. McCabe's, a professor at the university, frequently traveled out of the country, usually to South America, to do research in the field of women's studies. She'd usually go for a couple of weeks at a time, leaving Quinn and Taylor with a random college-aged babysitter. When he and Quinn had been in their early teens, their only interest was whether the sitter was a female, and if so, how good-looking she was. There'd never been a hint that Taylor had so much awful stuff going on inside her.

"That was proven a legitimate fear, I'd say." Judy McCabe, had been killed in Colombia or Brazil or some tension-filled place down there. It'd been after he and Quinn joined the military, after Taylor had been at MIT for a couple of years. After she'd turned eighteen, he remembered, because Quinn had been concerned about her and she'd reassured him she was legally an adult and could take care of herself.

"I always wondered how I could be enough to her to make her stay home."

He moved up to the swing next to her, took her hand in his. "Your mom loved you. There's no question in my mind."

"Oh, I know. Now, anyway."

It killed him to imagine what she must have gone through all those years. The bullying and the school thing had been bad enough, and he and Quinn had made it their mission to shield her from it as much as they could.

He and Quinn had met in seventh grade, when they'd hit junior high. Every day after school, Quinn had beaten a path to the elementary school to walk his sister home. Being a typical preteen jerk, Alex had ribbed Quinn about it. Once. Quinn had hauled off and punched him. In Alex's warped twelve-year-old existence, that had generated respect and they'd been best friends ever after. Instead of razzing his buddy for looking out for his little sister, he'd adopted the cause himself.

They'd thought they were all kinds of heroic for setting the little grade-school creeps—and later the junior high ones—straight when it came to Taylor, and yet, they'd barely scratched the surface of what she'd gone through.

Her revelation now nearly burned his insides out with regret. Imagining what had been going on in Taylor's mind made him want to hold her until her demons were gone, but he settled for just continuing to hold on to her hand. He knew her well enough to realize sympathy would do nothing but push her away. Probably cause a cleaning frenzy at two in the morning.

"That's some heavy shit going on inside of you," he said.

She made a noise in response, half laugh, half scoff, and removed her hand from his.

"I don't know why I told you all of that." Now she sounded embarrassed.

"Wish I knew how to make you see what a cool chick you are." He kept his tone light, but damn, there was nothing he wanted more than to do exactly that.

She laughed quietly again, and this time it sounded a little more real. "I wish kicking Joel's butt would actually solve my problems."

"You sure it won't?" He stood abruptly, causing the swing to sway unevenly, and took several steps away from her. The thought of the scrawny loser had Alex clenching his fist. The good-for-nothing jackwad deserved it for what he'd done to Taylor. She should be treated like a princess, not lied to.

He stared off into the neighbor's yard, into the dark night, torn. He wanted to show Taylor how amazing she was, to make her see herself the way he saw her. To hold her, make her forget everything else, everyone else. But he would ultimately end up just like the computer dork because Alex couldn't be what she needed. He wasn't her long-term kind of guy. Hell, who was he kidding? Wasn't her kind of guy at all.

When he turned back around, he found her inches away from him, and he momentarily wondered how rusty he'd gotten that she could approach without him hearing her. All rational thoughts slipped away as she took a hesitant step even closer. Tentatively touched his chest and ran her hands upward, around his neck. She pressed her cheek into his chest and his arms instinctively came up and around her. Holding Taylor felt like the most natural thing in the universe. He pulled her closer and his body went where he'd tried to keep his mind from going.

He wanted this woman. Wanted to hold her, protect her. Make all the bad stuff go away, if only for a night. He wanted to make her believe she was sexy, beautiful, inside and out.

And he could acknowledge that a good fifty percent of that was selfish, as well. Which was why he would've put space between them—if she hadn't peered up at him and clumsily risen on her toes with the very clear intention of kissing him.

He was toast.

He met her halfway, all traces of sympathy and sadness imploding when their lips touched. There was only heat, like fire, arcing between them. Heat and too much space.

He wound his hands around her, over her, up and down her back. Slid them farther down to the softness of her ass and drew her even closer, leaving no question about what she did to him.

Again, she surprised him with the depth of her response, her hands in his hair, her slender body pressed into him. The little sounds that came from her throat, needy gasps for air, turned him inside out.

His hands were all over her, under her tank, on her baby-soft skin. Her apple scent enveloped him.

He lost his mind a little bit, let all thoughts disappear and matched her intensity. This wasn't the lonely little girl who'd twisted his heart up minutes earlier, wasn't the insecure woman who'd evoked his sympathy or his protective urges. It was just Taylor. And right now, she was everything.

Alex slipped his hands back to her ass and lifted her up his body. She wrapped her legs around him, sliding into him and fitting like the last piece in a puzzle. Need pounded through him. He was on the verge of losing every last shred of control. He broke the contact of their lips, forced himself to breathe in the cool air and attempted to grasp on to any hint of reasoning he had left in him. There wasn't much.

"Taylor," he said, his voice husky. "We can't do this."

CHAPTER EIGHTEEN

TAYLOR NIPPED NEEDILY at his lips, each touch killing him. "It's one night." She breathed the words into his ear, the whisper of her breath having a crazy erotic effect on him. "I know. I want one night with you, Alex."

Maybe a saint could have walked away from her, but he was about as far from a saint as a guy could get.

"You sure?" he forced out.

She answered by kissing her way along his jaw back to his lips, teasing them briefly before kissing him full on. She pressed her tongue inside his mouth confidently, as if knowing she was about two seconds from being able to get anything and everything she wanted from him. "Absolutely sure," she said between kisses.

That was all the confirmation he needed and then some. He walked toward the deck with her wrapped around him, kissing her, nearly stumbling over a bump in the ground. Laughing with her, their breath mixing, their bodies twisting together. He made his way up the deck steps, oblivious to any pain in his leg—the last body part he was concerned with just now.

He carried her to her room, to her bed, set her down as he eased on top of her. Something moved on the mattress to the left of them, startling the crap out of him.

"Elanor," Taylor said, laughing.

He heard the feline race out of the room and down the hall then quickly forgot about it.

Taylor insistently pulled him to her by the neck. Devoured his lips with hers. God, this woman made him wild with need.

She pulled his shirt out of his pants, unbuttoned it. Slid it off him one arm at a time. She ran her hands over his bare chest, then wound them around him and again pulled him to her.

He needed to feel her flesh, taste her skin. He sat up in an awkward straddle, his left leg angled out slightly since he still couldn't support a lot of weight in that position. His concern was fleeting, though, as he took Taylor's tank off her. She arched upward so he could unfasten her bra and she tossed it over the side of the bed.

Faint light came in around the edges of the curtains, and he feasted his eyes on her milky skin, her perfect breasts. He ran his hands over every inch of her before readjusting his leg and bending over her to taste her.

He took her breast into his mouth, suckled her, teased her. First one, then the other, until Taylor pressed her lower body insistently into him. He peeled her pants and panties down her legs as one and threw them aside.

The sight of her, naked in the moonlight, her dark red hair splayed on her pillow—holy hell, he could never get enough of her. He pressed his lips to her navel and kissed his way slowly up her body, then shifted slightly to the side, brushing his fingers along her inner thigh. When he grazed her core, she eagerly lifted into his touch and moaned.

"You blow my mind," he whispered, nipping and kissing her ear, all the while still exploring her. Learning what drove her wild. He watched her eyes meet his, then flutter shut as she let his name slip out.

TAYLOR HAD NEVER RESPONDED so wildly to a man's touch. Not that she had much experience, but instinct told her that had nothing to do with her reaction.

She should feel shyer, try to hold herself back, but this was Alex. He did amazing things to her and she was just going to go with it. As if she had any choice—in a good way. He touched her body as if he knew all the secrets of it, ones she'd never realized herself.

When he kissed his way down, to her navel

and then farther still, her eyes popped open. The instant his tongue took the place of his fingers, heat shot through her, had her dropping every last ounce of inhibition. She clung to him, encouraged him, begged him with her movements and her words. She didn't know this woman he'd unleashed and could no longer find her inner shy girl. No longer cared. Just needed.

He carried her to the edge with his tongue, repeatedly, until she thought she would die. Then at last, release. Her body exploded and she couldn't hold on to a single thought.

Slowly she regained the use of her brain, aware of Alex caressing her everywhere, his hands and mouth feasting on every inch of her skin. It occurred to her she'd been nothing but selfish. He'd made her crave him so much, need him more than air, and he hadn't even gotten his pants off yet.

With a self-conscious grin, Taylor reached for his fly.

"These are supposed to be off," she said apologetically, unzipping his pants, sliding them down.

She rose partway to better reach him, but instead of helping her, he took her nipple in his mouth again. "You have this way of distracting me."

A sexy deep laugh came from his throat, vibrated on her breast. "Good."

She couldn't reach any farther to get his pants off and he made no move to help her.

"Don't you want…?"

"Taylor, I want. Like you wouldn't believe." He worked his way to her other breast. "I'm a patient man."

He finally shifted to the side and quickly dispensed with his pants, then resumed where he'd left off. His hardness jutted heavily against her leg. She touched him and he sucked in his breath, making her savor this unfamiliar power.

A few seconds later, he reached for her hand. "Going to make me lose it." He wove their fingers together and kissed her gently, as if it was their first kiss.

"Taylor…" His voice sounded strained.

"Yes?" Had she messed something up?

"I don't have protection…"

She grinned, relieved. "It's okay. I'm on the pill. For medical reasons." She didn't know why she felt the need to explain that now.

"I don't care what reasons," he said, kissing her urgently again. "I'm just thankful."

He wasted no time in showing her exactly that.

ALEX ACKNOWLEDGED THAT NOT being with a woman for going on a year meant that almost any sex would be good. But though he made a point of not thinking too much, a nagging alarm in the far reaches of his mind told him this was more than simply a physical release. This was Taylor.

The thought disappeared as the incredible things this woman was making him feel took over. He'd said just one night, but love of God, he never wanted this to stop. He couldn't get enough of her lips, her breasts, her skin. The sounds she made, the little things she said drove him wild.

Yet again, her uninhibited passion blew his mind. Well, okay, everything about her was blowing his mind. She was every bit right there with him, as if they'd had years of being together.

He held on for as long as he could, but she did him in when she uttered his name repeatedly, and he came along with her.

He kissed the side of her porcelain face, their hearts thundering together. He tried to catch his breath. Eventually, he registered the coolness of the air on their sweaty bodies. They hadn't even managed to pull back the covers.

"I had no idea you were capable of that, Taylor."

"Neither did I." She sounded genuinely surprised and a little self-conscious.

Chuckling, he shifted to the side, pulling her with him. He caressed her tousled hair. Drank in her scent. It took several minutes for him to register the throbbing in his bad leg, but he didn't give it a second thought. Thinking was overrated. Dangerous, in fact. Because he knew if he thought too hard about anything right now, it could ruin the moment. And this moment was too damn good to mess with.

TAYLOR KNEW BEFORE SHE opened her eyes the next morning, before she even stirred, that he was gone.

She lay without moving. Refused to open her eyes. Maybe she could go back to sleep. Put off the inevitable. Ignore reality.

If she tried hard enough, she could imagine his body beside her, so close she could feel his heat.

Who was she kidding?

She rolled onto her back, took inventory of her sore muscles as she stretched. Savored that soreness in seldom-used places because it proved it had been real. Alex had been here, in her bed, doing all kinds of lovely, wicked things to her body throughout the night. She'd practically had more orgasms in the past eight hours than she'd had in her entire life.

Warmth spread through her as she allowed herself to remember in slow, minute detail everything he'd done to her. Everything she'd brazenly done to him. Maybe she'd found the courage because she knew it was one night only, the single chance she had with him, and she'd needed it to be as spectacularly memorable as possible. Maybe she'd thought that by letting go of her inhibitions he'd find spending the night with her hard to resist, be tempted to pull a repeat.

Or maybe just because it was *him,* and that's how he affected her. Alex Worth made her lose her everloving mind.

The warmth morphed into an embarrassed flush as she shifted back to her side, away from where Alex had slept. She drew her knees into her chest, hugged the tangled blankets to her, pulling them securely around her chin. The motion did nothing to combat the sensation of utter nakedness. So much more than her body had been exposed.

She leaped out of bed, taking the top blanket with her and securing it at her chest with one hand while she picked out clean clothes to put on. In the bathroom, she turned the shower on and dropped the blanket. She stared at herself in the mirror, at her face, her body. Wondered what Alex had seen when he'd looked at her—and, oh, lord, he'd had ample opportunity to look. Her cheeks reddened as she studied herself. Had he seen her as a lover, as a woman who could fulfill his needs—at least for one night? Or had he seen Scarlet, his friend's younger sister, who needed protection, guidance?

How much of last night had been out of sympathy or some gallant attempt to build her self-esteem?

Shaking her head and turning away from the mirror, she clenched her jaw defiantly, battling her own doubts.

She'd known going into this that it was just sex. She was the idiot who was trying to bring feelings into it, trying to make it something it wasn't.

It was just sex.

Exceptional, toe-curling sex, granted.

Taylor distractedly stepped into the stream of hot water. The trick would be not to get more hung up because of the sex. She'd been with Alex. She'd adored every second of it. But it still came down to the fact that he was not her list man. Not even close.

The best way to stop thinking about Alex was to find someone else to occupy her time and her brain. That would never happen if she spent every evening in this mausoleum-like house.

It was time to step up the mission. Time for a social life, even if she had to fake it.

Crashing professional meetings, hitting happy hour with coworkers...at this point she'd resort to church and the grocery store if she had to.

All she needed was one decent man who didn't have a hang-up on an ex, didn't have a video-game obsession, and did meet her simple list of qualifications.

CHAPTER NINETEEN

FALLING ASLEEP ON the ancient, more-for-looks-than-comfort sofa in the living room was a bad move, but it had nothing on what he'd done last night.

Alex sat up and rubbed the sleep from his eyes, cussing up a storm. A damn cot on the army base was more comfortable.

He'd made the walk of shame home just before daybreak, wearing suit pants, a dress shirt and dress shoes so uncomfortable he'd been tempted to toss them in the trash upon arrival. His suit jacket was still in Taylor's car and could stay there for the next decade as far as he was concerned. He dreaded seeing her again.

She'd agreed to a one-night thing and that had sounded damn good at the time, when he had her in his arms, her hungry lips on his. But reality the morning after was a different story. Taylor wasn't a one-night type of woman, regardless of what she'd said, and he never should've treated her like one. But what the hell could he do now?

He'd blown it.

The door to the garage slammed shut and he heard whirlwind Vienna sweep into the kitchen. He stood, intending to escape to his bedroom, but his damn leg locked up and pain shot through it. Apparently dancing, sex and walking three miles in shoes with support slightly less than cardboard had taken a toll on his recuperating muscles.

He sat back down on the couch from hell, stretching his leg out in front of him and massaging his thigh.

"You're awake." Vienna poked her head around the arched doorway between the kitchen and dining room, which gave her a direct view of him. She disappeared for a second, then carried a fast-food sack into the living room. "I brought you lunch."

She sat across from him on an overstuffed chair, took out a cheeseburger and fries for herself, then passed the sack to him.

"Thanks," he said, taking out a double and fries. "What's the occasion?"

"Looked like you had a hard night. What time did you sneak in?"

"I didn't sneak in." Much.

"Alex, I was up till four-thirty studying. You weren't home when I went to bed."

"Last I checked I didn't have a curfew."

She eyed him knowingly, an annoying grin tugging at her mouth. "I hope it was good. You sure got decked out for her, whoever she is."

"What are you studying for?" He took a large bite of burger and chewed, not tasting it. Not listening to her answer.

His sister would have a field day if she found out where he'd spent the night. It was Taylor's choice whether she fessed up or not, but he wasn't about to discuss his mistake.

Hell of a mind-blowing "mistake" it was, too. But nope, not going down that road. Couldn't afford to recall details of Taylor, not now, not ever.

"...as if you're even paying attention," Vienna said, and damn if he couldn't recall a thing she'd been yammering on about.

"Sorry. I'm sure you'll ace your test." If she had a test. "Have you talked to Taylor lately?"

"Not for a few days. She's been preoccupied with Joel. Seems like he makes her happy."

"Yeah, uh, you should call her today. She could probably use a friend."

"What's wrong?" Vienna scowled. "Did something happen with him?"

"I'll let her tell you."

"If he turns out to be a louse..."

"That's a positive."

She swore and Alex nodded in agreement. The women in this family had always been able to hold their own when it came to foul language. He couldn't think of a more deserving recipient than that scrawny punk.

"I'll head over there in a few. When did you see her?" Vienna asked before shoving fries into her mouth.

"Went over to do some work yesterday morning." All true. All she was getting from him.

"Speaking of louses...lice? Whatever. Marshall needs a come-to-Jesus talk from you."

"What'd he do now?" He'd barely seen his brother for a week. They held different hours these days—Alex those of a working man, and Marshall a drunkard's. Twice last week Alex had managed to take his brother's car to Chicago and back for therapy without Marshall even realizing it.

"Have you been in the basement lately?"

"Haven't had any reason to." Marshall had turned the finished lower level into his domain since moving home.

"It smells like a distillery and looks even worse."

"So what are you waiting for? Tell him to clean it up."

"I tried. He won't listen to me. I'm his baby sister—what the hell do I know?"

"Good question."

She crumpled her burger wrapper and nailed him with it.

"Mom's tried to talk to him and he basically told her where to go."

"Classy." Alex stood, slowly this time, stuffed his trash into the sack and held out his hand for his sister's empty fry container. "I'll give it a go but he's got no reason to listen to me, either."

"Wrong. You're a good man, army guy." She grabbed the bag from him and headed to the kitchen. "See you later."

A good man. Like hell. A good man wouldn't be weak enough to give in to Taylor. He scoffed at himself. *Give in* made it sound as though she'd had to convince him to take her to bed.

Shaking his head, he paced toward the fireplace, braced his forearm on it and rested his head on his arm. Tried to figure out what he would say to Taylor when he saw her again. It'd be a lot easier if he didn't have to see her, but that would be the coward's way out. After their conversation in her backyard about her insecurity, he knew exactly how she would see it if he cut her off. She'd take it as confirmation that her self-doubt was justified. It'd be a challenge finding the right balance, though. He couldn't give her hope that they could be anything more than friends, but neither could he make her believe he regretted what had happened between them. Though sleeping with her had been a big-time screwup and he was a low-life for letting it happen, he couldn't honestly say he regretted it. How could a guy regret some of the best sex he'd ever had? Yep, he was a pathetic bastard through and through.

Jaw clenched so tight it ached, Alex lifted his head and stared at the cluster of framed photos his mom used to decorate the mantel. It took several seconds before he registered what was directly in front of his face. A picture of him and Quinn, taken the day before they'd left for basic training. They were skinny, young guys. Naive. Ready to take on the world.

So damn full of life.

The sudden tightening in his chest nearly choked him.

"So freaking sorry, man," he whispered.

He flipped the frame forward and set it face-down on the mantel, unable to look his best friend in the face.

TAYLOR'S MOTIVATION to put her house on the market had been lagging until now. Today, the longest day of her life, the house seemed to have come alive and actively taunted her with reminders of Alex at every turn.

Evidence of him and his work existed in almost every room. The trim and countertop in the kitchen. Ceiling and doors in the basement. Closet doors in her room and light fixtures in her bathroom. Et cetera, et cetera, et cetera. She couldn't find peace today, no matter where she tried to settle.

She'd ended up doing what she did best—starting a new list. A complex, multicolumned one that would take up a whole notebook page.

While the major work was just about done, with the exception of the hall bath, there was deep cleaning, decluttering, and prepacking to do before she called a Realtor. Lots of busywork.

Busywork was good.

A knock came at the door and she halted midword in her scrawling. Her first thought was Alex, but she realized before her heart even started beating again that he'd be the last person to show up on her front steps. He'd shown her exactly where he stood by sneaking out this morning.

She tossed her notebook on the kitchen table and went to the front door, relieved to see Vienna out the peephole.

"Hey, stranger," she said, letting her in.

"Long time no talk." Vienna smiled and breezed inside, as always, full of tangible energy. "Alex said I should check in with you. Not that I wouldn't have anyway. What's new?"

Between Alex and Joel, Taylor had managed to do quite a number on her love life in a mere twenty-four hours. None of it good. Then it hit her exactly what Vienna had said.

"What did Alex say?" Her stomach nosedived and the walls seemed to close in on her.

"Just that you might need a friend. So. Here I am. What's going on?"

Taylor turned away and escaped into the kitchen. Opened the refrigerator so Vienna wouldn't see her squeezing her eyes closed. She randomly grabbed two bottles of water, trying to regain control.

He sneaked out and then sent his sister to comfort me? He must think I'm terribly pathetic.

Vienna entered the kitchen as Taylor shut the fridge door. Taylor spun around wordlessly and handed her friend one of the bottles. She spotted her letter-perfect script, the precise columns of her to-do list sitting on the table. Vintage, tangible signs of her troubled mindset this afternoon.

Alex knows me and my weaknesses well.

For some reason, that ticked her off even more.

She marched into the living room on her way to the front door then realized Vienna must think she'd lost her mind, or at least her manners.

"I was just going to take a walk," she called over her shoulder.

Vienna followed her, taking a drink from her bottle. As she replaced the lid, she tilted her head and narrowed her eyes. "Let's go, then."

The words were barely out before Taylor shoved the screen door open and stormed outside, attempting to reel in her crazy, out-of-control emotions.

"Do you have a key?" Vienna asked.

Taylor shook her head. "Just leave it unlocked." She forced herself to wait while Vienna pulled the heavy door closed and let the screen door spring shut.

They set off down the sidewalk at a quick pace. Half a block later, Vienna jogged a few paces to catch up. "Tay, short legs here. Is this a walk or a drill?"

Taylor forced herself to slow down. "Sorry."

There was a small park up ahead that Taylor usually forgot about. She headed for it now, knowing if she kept walking, she would again inadvertently zoom off without Vienna. She went straight for the swings. Choosing the higher of the two, she sat in it, noticing these things weren't as wide as she remembered. She straightened and pushed herself backward, then pumped her legs to gain altitude. Vienna jumped on the swing next to hers.

You couldn't talk very well when you were swinging.

They slipped into an unspoken contest of who could go higher, and Taylor gradually breathed easier, released the emotional tension that had balled up inside her throat. Flying back and forth through the air, stomach dipping at each crest, had a way of changing a girl's perspective, even if only temporarily.

Ten minutes must have passed, the only sound between them a sporadic laugh or holler. Taylor was taken back to another time, a simpler time when a swing in the park was the objective, not an escape. A time when supporting her body weight hadn't made her arm muscles ache or her butt feel like it had been wedged into a too-small harness. Instead of letting herself slow down gradually, she went for the instant dismount and jumped off as she'd always done when she was six.

The landing was harder than she remembered and she ended up on her side, momentarily stunned into silence.

"Are you okay?" Vienna hollered from midair.

Taylor rolled onto her back, soaking up the sun and the smell of the recently cut grass...and started laughing. When Vienna landed with a clumsy thud and an "Oof" nearby, she laughed until her stomach started hurting. She heard Vienna do the same. Tears filled her eyes and Taylor gasped for air. When she finally looked at Vienna, that set them off even more.

At last Vienna let out a long, loud sigh. "The

landing isn't quite the same as when you weigh fifty pounds."

"I think I have bruises," Taylor said, cracking up again. "But I haven't laughed so hard in ages. I needed that." She rose to her elbows, glancing around, relieved to see the park was still deserted. She pushed up to a sitting position, supporting her weight on her hands behind her. "That's it, Vienna. Your ticket to the big time."

Vienna sat up next to her with a questioning look.

"You need to market swinging in the park as therapy. Trademark it, give it a fancy name. You'll make millions."

"You're a genius." Vienna crossed her legs and pointed her face at the clear sky. "Speaking of career stuff, I have news."

Taylor sat up straighter.

"Well, are you going to tell me or just sit there smugly?"

"I had an interview!"

"Yesss! Where? With whom? When?"

Vienna practically bounced. "With Hugh Samuels."

"*My* Hugh Samuels? You had an interview with one of the VPs of my company and you didn't warn me?"

"*Your* Hugh Samuels? Is there something I

should know?" Vienna giggled wickedly. "And more important, do you have any influence over this man?"

"You don't need any outside influence. I'm sure you did well on your own merits. And my relationship with him is purely professional. The last thing I need is more male drama in my personal life." She sobered at the reminder.

"It happened pretty fast, otherwise I would've told you. Or given you the third degree, more accurately. He called Wednesday afternoon and wanted to meet Friday. My Thursday was nuts and I remembered you were going out."

With Joel. My, how quickly things could change.

"How did it go? I want details." Taylor knew her company was on Vienna's list of dream jobs—with good reason. It was consistently ranked one of the top places to work, both locally and on national lists.

Vienna smiled widely. "*Really* well. I think that man gets me—we're on the same wavelength marketing-wise."

Taylor relaxed as Vienna went on and on about the interview. She let herself forget about her own misery for a few minutes.

"He said they expect to fill this position quickly so I hope to know more within a couple of weeks."

It was a new position. One of the assistant marketing managers. Not entry level, but there was no question Vienna was ideal for it. Taylor would have to see if she could get any inside information on Hugh's impression of Vienna. Put in another good word for her.

"So that's that, for now," Vienna said. "I noted that mention of male drama. Are you going to spill?"

Drat. The interview was a much better topic. Taylor closed her eyes.

"Alex hinted that Joel was in the doghouse."

Taylor lay back on the grass again and rolled to her stomach.

"*Doghouse* makes it sound like there's a chance he could redeem himself."

"That doesn't sound good." Vienna stretched out on her side, propping herself up on her elbow.

Taylor shook her head. "It's too embarrassing."

"Embarrassing, my butt. This is me. We're friends. It goes without saying that whatever happened was the guy's fault one thousand percent."

That almost made Taylor smile. She'd spent so many years keeping things to herself that this opening-up business was hard to get used to. Especially when it concerned her disastrous dating life.

"What did Alex tell you?" she said. A stall? More than likely.

"Absolutely nothing. Infuriating man."

Taylor chewed on the inside of her cheek, gathering her courage. "We were supposed to go to a wedding together."

"I remember. We picked out the blue dress."

"Friday afternoon he called to cancel. He said he was going out of town for the weekend, last-minute. Something about his dad needing him."

"No," Vienna said. "You were so looking forward to going with a date."

One of her many mistakes.

She recounted what had happened at the hardware store Saturday morning in painful detail, including the suspicion that the only reason he'd asked her out in the first place was so his ex would see them together.

"Unbelievable," Vienna said when she'd finished the story. "I don't care if he was using you to get his ex's attention or not, he's a creep. You deserve so much better, Tay."

Taylor pulled the grass up by the roots, one blade at a time.

"So did you go to the wedding anyway?"

Drat. It'd been hard enough to talk about Joel. No way could she bring herself to confide about Alex. "Yes. I had to. I had the dress." Maybe humor would sidetrack Vienna from further questions.

"Wait a second." Vienna sat up quickly. "Alex was wearing a suit last night. He took you, didn't he?"

"He was with me at the hardware store and felt sorry for me," Taylor explained quickly. "What else could he do? The wedding was beautiful. They had the reception at the botanical gardens."

Vienna wasn't so easily distracted. "Alex was out late last night, Taylor. Was he with you?"

"No." The lie came out before she could consider it, but it was just as well. No way could she admit what happened. None of it.

"Hmm," was all Vienna said, though Taylor knew her brain was spinning, probably trying to figure out who Alex had picked up at the wedding and how he'd managed to ditch her. Let her puzzle over it. It was preferable to having her figure out the truth. "So…are you done with Joel? Moving on?"

Did sleeping with your brother's best friend constitute moving on?

Taylor chuckled sarcastically. "I don't appear to have any say in that. Joel's done. But yes…my illusions have been suitably shattered. I wouldn't go out with him again if he got down on his knees and begged."

"Amen, sister." Vienna watched a large black ant crawl up her arm and they were both quiet for several minutes. "You'll find your guy soon, Taylor. I'm sure the right one is out there somewhere."

Though Taylor's confidence was lagging, she was sure he was, too. The only question in her mind was: Did she need to find the right guy so that she could stop thinking about Alex, or did she need to stop thinking about Alex so she could find the right guy?

CHAPTER TWENTY

ONE THING BEING IN THE ARMY had taught Alex was that if you had to do something you dreaded, the best way to handle it was to jump right in and get it over with.

Seeing Taylor again was not that big of a deal, not when you put it in army terms and compared it with some of the hellacious situations he'd found himself out there. No big deal at all.

So why the hell were his palms sweating and his heart beating erratically as he parked Vienna's shit-mobile at the curb and walked around to Taylor's back door?

Because Taylor was sensitive. It'd be too easy to damage her self-esteem if he didn't handle this just right, and that was the last thing he wanted to do. He needed to say the right things about Saturday night without saying too much or too little.

No pressure whatsoever.

He cared what she thought, about herself and about him. Cared how their night together had affected her. That was most important now.

His footsteps on her deck seemed loud, exaggerated against the background bird symphony at this butt-early hour. He'd had to hustle to get to the grocery store for donuts to make up for the coffee cake he'd devoured a couple weeks back. Then he'd rushed to her house to try to catch her before she left for work. Though he wasn't sure what insane hour that was, knowing her knack for being early everywhere she went, he figured he'd be lucky to see her if he got here as soon after dawn as possible.

He knocked on the door and scanned the surrounding backyards for signs of life. No one on the block seemed to be stirring yet. By the third knock, he was sure he'd missed Taylor. Crazy woman must start her work day before seven o'clock. Maybe he was going to get off easier than he'd expected—for now, anyway.

The pastries wouldn't be as fresh by tomorrow morning, so he would just let himself in and leave them on the counter before heading to Chicago for his PT appointment. After he unlocked the door, he listened for any sign of her, but the house was silent, obviously empty.

As he set the box down near the sink, one of the furballs sauntered in and rubbed up against his legs. It gazed up at him eagerly. He sidestepped it, shaking his head and searching for a piece of paper to leave a note. He was almost to the living room when he heard the sudden blare of pop music from the back of the house. An alarm clock? Taylor must have forgotten to turn it off. He followed the sound to her bedroom and nearly pissed himself when he saw her.

She was stretched out on her stomach, the covers thrown aside, giving him one hell of a view of her slender, sexy body. It was barely hidden by the shortest pajama bottoms he'd ever been lucky enough to see on a woman and a loose, matching peach-colored camisole top that had worked its way halfway up her back. Her hair splayed wildly on both sides of the pillow, hiding her face. The wide swath of creamy skin between shorts and top begged him to touch it.

Images of the other night, of her naked, on top of him, beneath him, in the moonlight, bombarded him. Kicked his pulse up to double speed. All the blood in his body seemed to head south.

Before he could move from his spot in the doorway—whether to approach the tempting woman in front of him or to back away and respect her privacy, he couldn't say—she stirred. Slowly rolled to her back and groaned sleepily as she flung her arm toward the still-blasting alarm on the nightstand. Her eyes remained closed as she felt around for it, hitting it several times until the music stopped.

Alex swallowed hard, unsure how to avoid scaring the daylights out of her. Unable to keep from feasting his eyes on this new, even more revealing view of her.

Her scream made him jump guiltily and he moved toward her. "Taylor, it's me."

She whipped her extra pillow against her body and clung to it as she sat up, two pink spots appearing on her cheeks beneath eyes that shot fire at him.

"What are you doing in here, Alex?" Her tone left no doubt that she was less happy to see him than he was to see so much of her.

To prevent her from noticing his blatant arousal, he took two large steps to the foot of her bed and sat down.

"It's okay," he said. "Sorry I startled you."

She scooted toward the head of the bed, leaning against one pillow and still covering her body with the other. "Startled? You're lucky I didn't go into cardiac arrest! Why are you here?"

Without thinking, he reached out and touched her ankle. "I brought you donuts to pay you back for the coffee cake I owed you. I tried to get here before you left and then thought I'd missed you when you didn't answer your door."

Her mouth hung open as she stared at him. "Did it not occur to you to check for my car?"

He stared back and fought a sheepish grin at his own stupidity. "In my defense, it's early."

She threw the pillow she'd been hugging at him, catching him in the head. He could tell she regretted getting rid of her cover as soon as she realized what she'd done, but instead of being chivalrous, he held on to the pillow and checked his watch.

"It's five after seven, Taylor. Aren't you late?"

"I start work at eight." She crossed her arms over her chest and raised her chin. "I'm not much of a morning person."

"Miss Early-for-everything? Not a morning person?" He couldn't wrap his head around it.

"Well, technically we don't have to be at work until eight-thirty, so…"

"That's more like it. Your late is their early."

"Alex?"

"Yeah?"

"Could you get out of my room so I can get up and shower?"

He studied her, allowed himself three seconds to consider what he'd rather do. Getting out of here was a wise idea.

He stood, tossing the pillow back to the bed and trying to hide how affected he was by the intimacy of being here with her first thing in the morning, with her all tousled and sexy.

"For the record, I've already seen everything,"

he said, nodding to her body. Before she could nail him with the pillow again, he escaped and shut the door behind him. Then he went to the kitchen to figure out how to reel himself in and establish some boundaries in his head.

ONCE HER BEDROOM DOOR CLOSED, Taylor grabbed the pillow again and squeezed it to her, burying her face in it.

She was burning up. Had she forgotten to turn the air conditioner on last night? But no, it had nothing to do with room temperature. She couldn't say whether it was embarrassment and self-consciousness or...

She lowered the pillow and exhaled loudly. Yeah, that. It was impossible to deny that a part of her had wanted him to crawl into bed and spend the day with her. A big part of her. Close to ninety-five percent of her if she had to quantify.

In the four years she'd worked at Halverson Systems, she'd taken exactly one sick day, two years ago when she'd gotten food poisoning so severe she'd been sure she was going to die. Today, if Alex had stripped down and joined her, she wouldn't have blinked an eye at playing hooky to be with him.

Which was pathetic. Their one night was over. Equally pathetic was the way she was still sitting here pining over him instead of getting ready for work.

She hopped out of bed and headed to her bathroom. Locked the door because she wouldn't be surprised if he was still lurking out there, waiting for her, and turned on the water. Avoided catching a glimpse of herself in the mirror as she slid her pajamas off, all too conscious of how her body had reacted to having Alex in her bedroom again.

He had to be totally aware of what he did to her, what she felt for him, after Saturday night. Had to know that agreeing to one-time-only sex wasn't typical behavior for her, whereas she was pretty certain it wasn't out of the ordinary for a man like Alex.

Why was he here, really? Did it amuse him that she'd let her lifelong crush take over on Saturday night and eagerly done what was unheard of for her? What had gone through his head this morning as he'd sat on her bed and seen her so flustered she could hardly breathe?

Enough of that. She couldn't change what had happened over the weekend, but she didn't have to yearn for a man who only hung around, only checked on her because he felt he owed it to her brother to make sure she was okay.

She *was* okay.

Taylor stood straighter in the shower, determined not to be insecure Scarlet anymore. At least not in Alex's presence.

He was not at all suitable for her, she reminded herself. An army guy steeping in self-recrimination was so far off from the clean-cut go-getter type she envisioned spending her life with. Saturday night had been fun and, well, naughty, but that wasn't who she was.

After a speedy shower, she took her clothes for the day, which she'd hung on the back of the bathroom door last night, and pulled them on. Hair combed but still damp, she reminded herself with every step toward the kitchen that Alex was not the man for her. He'd sneaked out before the sun had come out yesterday, obviously unable to own up to what he'd let himself do.

She smelled coffee before she reached the kitchen but she refused to acknowledge any softening toward him. She couldn't afford to. Biting the inside of her mouth, she blustered into the room, straight to the coffeemaker, without sparing him a glance.

"Taylor," he said from the table behind her. "About Saturday..."

Her back stiffened. She was *not* going to stand here while he gave her the I'm-sorry-about-what-happened speech and reminded her it wouldn't happen again.

"Yeah," she said, filling a travel mug with steaming coffee. "I'm sorry about that, Alex. I hope we can just call it my getting-over-Joel adventure and let it go at that. It didn't mean anything to either one of us. It's all good."

She took a sip. The coffee scalded her tongue and made her eyes water but she didn't move away from the counter. Didn't dare look at him. Couldn't let him discern that everything she'd said was a lie.

Alex was silent for several never-ending seconds. "Okay, then," he said slowly. "As long as we have that cleared up."

She heard him stand, bit her cheek again as he joined her at the counter. She forced herself to meet his gaze.

"Everything's cool?" he asked, his eyes, greenish-gray today, boring down into hers.

Taylor nodded once, emphatically.

"Good."

He placed his hand gently on the back of her neck and kissed her forehead. Released her as she fought not to let that simple gesture get to her. She couldn't help noticing his relief at being off the hook.

"We'll go back to the way things were."

"Right." She somehow managed to flip him an unconcerned smile.

The way things were. Fabulous.

She turned away from him and took her phone out of her pocket to check her schedule. Tonight was happy hour with Vienna and a group of grad students. Vienna had assured her there would be men there. Smart men. Driven, intellectual men. Though the odds were low that she'd meet the one for her, she'd at least have somewhere to go besides her empty, echoing house.

That was something.

ALEX HADN'T INTENDED to walk out of her house hard as a rock and rejected. Not that he'd expected or wanted anything to happen back there. But he sure as hell hadn't foreseen *her* giving *him* the blow-off line.

Didn't that just serve him right?

An hour-and-forty-minute car ride hadn't done a thing to ease his agitation. Nor did thirty minutes of intense physical therapy. Which only annoyed him further.

"I'd tell you to go harder, Alex, but I'm afraid you'd actually try." Helen wasn't known for showing any kind of a personality. The therapist was all business, all the time, so the attempt at sarcasm was somewhat remarkable.

He didn't answer, just channeled all his unrest

and frustration into his leg muscles and managed to lift the weight again.

"Is that it?" Helen asked. Despite the question, her tone said the session was over.

She was more motivating than she realized.

Alex went for one more rep, squeezing his eyes shut against the pain in his muscles. His legs shook like a Blackhawk's vibrations and he wasn't sure he could move them another millimeter.

Damn the helicopter that crashed. Damn the enemy that caused the crash and took Quinn away from them. Damn all of it.

He forced the weight upward, using the pain and the anger. Helen grabbed it and motioned for him to let go so she could lower it herself.

"We're done," she said abruptly.

He checked his watch and looked at her questioningly. "We've got ten more minutes."

"Not today," she said. "I'm all for pushing yourself, but you have a death wish today. You're going to end up reinjuring yourself. That kind of setback is not happening on my watch."

He paced over to the wall and picked up his sports drink. Poured some down his throat as he tried to settle himself. He mopped his face with a towel and sauntered back to Helen, who was making notes on a piece of paper.

"Wednesday?" he asked to verify their next meeting.

Helen nodded. "Take it easy, Alex. I don't know what's got you so bothered today, but I hope you can work it out."

He thanked her halfheartedly, got his stuff together and walked out. Normally he changed clothes before the trek home, but today he just needed to get out of these four walls.

Helen was right. He was tied up in knots and for what good reason? The visit to Taylor's house had gone better than he'd expected. The reasons he'd dreaded it hadn't panned out. So what the hell was his problem?

Whatever it was, it was time to get over it right damn now. The sooner he got back to active duty, the better off everyone would be.

CHAPTER TWENTY-ONE

IT'D BEEN NEARLY TWO WEEKS since Alex had seen Taylor.

After the blow-off Monday morning, he hadn't felt obligated to go out of his way to prove everything was fine in spite of their night together. If it was "no big deal," then there was no need. He hadn't specifically avoided her, but he hadn't stayed late to run into her on the days he worked at her house, either.

Frankly, it'd been too long for his liking. That was the protective part of him, wanting to check on her. At least that's the story he told himself.

As he strolled up the driveway between her car and the side of the house, he tried to ignore the subtle relief, bordering on anticipation, at the sight of her car.

Okay, damn it all, he'd never been one to tell himself stories. He wanted to see Taylor for the mere fact that he'd missed her and he liked looking at her. Liked *her,* period. Which was perfectly fine. They'd forged a strange sort of friendship over the past couple of months, and that was acceptable. Quinn would be happy to know his sister could count Alex as a friend, and Vienna, as well. That was his duty to his buddy, right?

Not a duty at all, he corrected. Making sure Taylor was okay was something he felt he owed Quinn, but nothing more. He was here by choice. Her...*friend* by choice. Which made it okay that he was looking forward to working on her bathroom all day alongside her.

He knocked and went on in since the door was open. One of the cats was right there in the entry, soaking up the sunlight. It raised its backside and looked eagerly up at him.

"Hey, furball." He reached down to scratch its ears. He'd learned to tolerate Taylor's felines after all the time he'd spent alone in her house with them. They'd never quite figured out they were enemies to start with, and something about their quiet persistence had worn away his resistance. They weren't so bad.

"Help yourself to coffee," Taylor called from the back of the house.

As he was pouring himself a mug full, she came bustling out to the kitchen. He turned to greet her and—she wasn't dressed for working around the house. Not unless she suddenly didn't mind dirtying the denim skirt that hit just above her knees or the tank and button-down shirt she wore over it. And as much as she supposedly adored those green flip-flops his sister had given her, he was sure working in them wasn't on her agenda.

"Did Vienna bring you over?" she asked, not meeting his eyes.

"Was she supposed to?"

Taylor shrugged. "She and I are going shopping. I just figured you might carpool."

Shopping?

"I thought…" He shook his head, silently calling himself an idiot. "Bathroom supplies get delivered?"

"In the garage." She grabbed a half-green banana from a bunch on the counter and peeled it. "Everything you'll need to replace the countertop and tile the floor." She took a bite and chewed. Looked startled by a thought. "It's just a one-person job, right? You don't need me to help?"

Need, no. "Go do your girl thing."

He'd stay here and do his man-fix-it thing. Alone. No big deal.

THE ONLY REASON ALEX perked up at the sound of his sister and Taylor thundering into the house louder than a herd of elephants was the hope that they might've picked up some dinner for him.

Yep, hunger was his only concern. Nothing to do with a certain redhead who apparently really was unaffected by the night they'd spent together. He'd be hard-pressed before he'd admit to a soul that that very redhead had infiltrated his dreams on a nightly basis. Usually naked.

If someone were to suggest it was getting to him that Taylor had so easily dismissed him after sleeping with him, well, he had nothing to say to that. People could think what they wanted.

The bathroom door opened about a foot until it hit his backside, and Taylor stuck her head in. "You're still here?"

"Tile's going slower than I expected," he said, ensuring the piece he'd just laid was square with the others. "I'll stick around and finish it."

"Oh." Her tone made him crane his neck to look at her.

"That a problem?"

"You can go home. You've been working a long time."

"I don't mind. Just as easy to finish it now as it is to come back tomorrow."

"Vienna would probably take you when she leaves."

"I don't need Vienna to take me."

His sister's head appeared next to Taylor's. "She's got a date, army guy. She wants you to vamoose."

He turned back to his tile and scrutinized it unnecessarily. The women twittered off down the hall toward Taylor's room, gabbing about how the shoes would look with the outfit or some other all-important matter. Alex clenched his jaw and concentrated on finishing the row.

When Taylor and Vienna came out of the bedroom a good while later, he was midway through the next row of tiles, close enough to the door that he was forced to work with it open all the way.

"Alex…" Taylor's tone left no question she wasn't thrilled that he was still there. "No. You're not doing that again."

"Doing what?"

"Hanging around so you can judge Brian. Please."

Brian? *Judge* wasn't the first verb that came to mind.

"I wasn't—"

"Come on, Alex, I've got a study group for my last test in twenty minutes. I'll drop you off at home on my way." Vienna stopped in the doorway again and dared him to argue with a look she'd picked up from their mother.

He stood and glared down at her.

"Give me five," he said and turned to clean up for the day.

Both women were in the kitchen when he emerged. "I closed the door and turned on the fan to get rid of the fumes. Keep the cats out and use the other bathroom."

Taylor nodded as she flitted around, tidying the already neat countertop, and he could tell, though she fought to hide it, she was once again scared as hell. Instinct made him want to soothe that fear as he had before. He had to remind himself that wasn't his role. It'd be twisted for someone who'd slept with her to calm her down before a date with another man. Besides, Vienna was here.

Alex went to the sink and scrubbed his hands with melon-scented soap. As he was drying them, Taylor came up behind him.

"Here," she said, handing him an envelope. "I meant to give you this when you got here but had to run to the bank first."

He was just the hired help.

He took the envelope with a tight nod and headed to Vienna's car without a word.

MARSHALL'S CAR WAS the only one in the garage when Vienna dropped Alex off at home ten minutes later. Their mom might have told him where she was going tonight but he couldn't recall. Didn't much care as long as she and his sister were out of the house and he'd have some peace.

He slammed the front door harder than necessary.

Marshall was in the kitchen, and Alex headed that way. Later, he'd realize that had been his first mistake upon returning home.

"Hey," Marshall said from his spot at the table. He bent over a grilled cheese sandwich and took an oversize bite.

Alex automatically scanned for liquor. Yep. His brother was using his manners tonight, drinking the brown stuff from a cocktail glass instead of straight from the bottle. He bit down any insulting comments. Might as well broach the subject of his drinking, as Vienna had repeatedly asked him to do.

"Make a sandwich for me?" Alex asked dryly.

"What do you think?"

"I think if it's not about meeting Marshall's immediate needs, it's not happening."

"What the hell's that supposed to mean?"

"Nothing." Maybe Alex wasn't in the right frame of mind for a serious discussion but what the hell. He slathered butter on two slices of bread and lined up the last two pieces of American cheese between them. The burner was still switched to high, and the hot skillet sizzled when he tossed the sandwich in. "You trying to burn the house down?"

Marshall grinned. "Not intentionally."

"Well, that makes it okay, then."

"What did you and Quinn's sister do all day?"

"I worked," Alex snapped. "Her name is Taylor."

"We a little testy?" Marshall asked.

"*I* am just damn fine. *You* are once again lit."

Alex turned the heat down a couple of notches. Something had to change because if he hadn't come home when he did, who knew how long the stove would've been left on.

"You and *Taylor* are getting pretty cozy now that Quinn's not around to stop it."

Alex lifted the pan, flipped the sandwich and slammed the skillet back down on the burner. He clamped his jaw shut. Blowing up wouldn't help Marshall see what he was doing to himself. This was for his mom and Vienna's sakes, Alex reminded himself.

He eyed the bottle on the table next to the near-empty cocktail glass. More than half-full. Maybe it was early enough he could get somewhere.

"What are you doing, Marshall?"

"Eating a grilled cheese. What's it look like I'm doing?"

"Looks to me…" Alex said as he turned the heat off, took a plate down and slid the sandwich onto it "…like you're pissing your life away."

"Cheers, bro." Marshall lifted his glass, a smirk on his face, eyes bloodshot.

Alex sat down heavily at the table, reining in his temper, though the urge to punch the stupid out of his brother just about made him twitch. "When are you going to find a job?"

Marshall finished off the whiskey in his glass and set it down hard. He pushed the glass aside and slid the bottle closer, obviously intending to do away with formalities. "That's my business," he said quietly.

"When you're living in Mom's house, it's her business, too."

"You her spokesman now?"

Alex stared at him. "Looks like it. The way I understand it, Mom and Vienna have both tried talking to you."

"The women don't get it, Alex. I did my best to be polite while they had their say, but they have no idea what it does to a man when he loses…" Marshall looked around the kitchen as if searching for the word he wanted "…damn near everything."

"It sucks. I get that." Alex's anger cooled slightly because he did understand. He was living the same thing, to an extent. "But you've got to pick yourself up. Move forward."

"There's nothing forward that I can see." Marshall swigged down several gulps of whiskey.

He couldn't even stop drinking long enough to discuss this.

"If you won't do it for yourself, do it for Mom and Vienna."

"What the hell do they have to do with anything?"

"They have to live with you." Alex's voice rose in volume. "You're ruining your own life and making them watch. That's not goddamn fair to them."

"Yeah, well, excuse me if I'm not too freaking concerned about them. They'll be fine." He shoved his chair out and stormed over to the counter, gripping his beloved bottle as though his life depended on it.

"Not if you burn down their house." Alex stood, set his plate in the sink with a clatter. "You think they'll be okay if you drink yourself to death?"

"Guess they wouldn't have to worry 'bout me burning their house down then, would they?" A sloppy, self-amused grin spread across Marshall's face before he took another long draw of whiskey.

Being in a shitty place was one thing, but not giving a damn about the two people who would do just about anything for him...

Something snapped in Alex. He whipped the bottle out of Marshall's hand before he could lower it from his mouth. Marshall swore at him as Alex spun toward the stainless-steel sink and purposely hit the bottle on the side of it as hard as he could. The glass broke, shards landing in the sink, and the vile liquid ran down the drain.

"What the hell are you doing?" Marshall yelled as he lunged for Alex.

Alex held him off, but as he turned to drop the neck of the bottle into the sink, Marshall landed an off-center punch on the side of his jaw. Alex shoved him away, sending Marshall, who was short on balance anyway, into the counter on the opposite side of the room.

Alex ran down the basement stairs to Marshall's bachelor cave. The stench, like that of a filthy bar, was so strong his eyes watered. Dirty dishes and take-out trash littered the living area, along with countless empty bottles and piles of wrinkled clothing.

He searched for any full bottles as Marshall thundered unevenly down the stairs after him. A single one stood on the end table, lid still sealed. Alex winged it with all his strength against the concrete wall six feet away as Marshall hit the foot of the stairs and rounded the corner toward him. The crash of glass shattering was minutely satisfying.

"You've lost your damn mind!" Marshall went for him again.

Alex easily sidestepped him and shoved him

onto the disgusting couch. "You have to qui
drinking, man! You're going to kill yourself. O.
someone else. Where the hell are your car keys?"

Marshall got up for another round as Alex
searched the clutter. Then he remembered Marshall's idiotic habit of leaving the keys in the ignition. He took off up the stairs to check for them
his brother railing at him the entire way, lumber-
ing more slowly behind him. Alex rushed out the
door into the garage, opened the Acura and, sure
enough, there were the keys. He yanked them ou
just as Marshall burst out the door and down the
two wooden steps toward him.

"You can have them when you're sober," Alex
said, slipping them into his front pocket.

Marshall leapt at Alex, a wild look in his red
eyes. He thrust all his weight on him, knocking
Alex into the side of the car.

"I don't know who the hell you think you are!"
Marshall yelled, catching him with a punch near
his eye.

Alex easily managed to throw his smaller
brother off him again, landing him on the hard
garage floor. That didn't faze Marshall. He moved
faster than Alex would've thought possible and
came up swinging. Alex clocked him under the
nose and Marshall grabbed his face, stumbling
to the other side of the garage. He leaned against

the wall and the air was filled with the sounds of both of them gasping for breath.

Marshall took his hand away from his nose. Blood poured down his face and over his hand. He called Alex a crude name. "That McCabe girl makes you crazy or something."

"That was all caused by you," Alex said in a deceptively calm voice. "Taylor had nothing to do with it."

"You need to stay the hell away from her."

"You get your damn life together, man. Until then, I'm not listening to a thing you have to say."

Alex strode past him, refusing to entertain the idea that his brother might have a valid point.

CHAPTER TWENTY-TWO

SATURDAY EVENING WAS PERFECT for a romantic dinner cruise on the lake. Not a cloud in the sky, enough heat left over from the day that the cooler air on the water was refreshing. Boat traffic had dwindled as sunset approached.

A jazz quartet filled the air with soothing music from the deck as a formally dressed waiter made his way around the enclosed lower level of the boat taking after-dinner drink orders. Taylor scooped the last bite of the richest, densest chocolate cake she'd ever tasted into her mouth.

Her date, Brian Paulsen, ordered each of them another glass of wine, then continued their friendly debate on the impact of cruises such as this on the lake and its environment.

Over the past two hours, since their date had begun, conversation had been ongoing, intelligent, provocative. Taylor hadn't been forced to dip into her reserve list of fill-the-awkward-silence topics once. Which was a relief. If anything, Brian talked too much. However, she could overlook that minor point in exchange for the security that this man did not play more than the occasional computer game, and he hadn't been seriously involved with anyone for almost a year.

As he'd humbly admitted that his dating life had been almost nonexistent of late, Taylor had smiled and nodded. She ignored the fleeting voice in her head—the one that sounded a lot like Alex—cautioning her to beware of a man who willingly admitted to having trouble getting a date. Until recently, she'd been in the same position, she reasoned.

Brian was a list guy, through and through. The chief operations officer at a national not-for-profit organization based here in Madison, he was driven and successful. She'd met him at a Chamber of Commerce happy-hour mixer she'd taken Vienna to early in the week—he'd nervously approached her during an uncomfortable moment when Vienna had been off introducing herself to someone in the public relations department of the city's baseball team, leaving Taylor by herself and feeling conspicuous.

After more than a half hour of the two of them sticking together in an unspoken alliance that saved them from having to mingle, Taylor had done something she'd never done before. Something she never would have believed she could do just months ago—she'd suggested they should go out sometime. Brian had enthusiastically agreed, and he'd called her the next day with the invitation to tonight's cruise.

As the waiter returned with their wine and began clearing the small table, she allowed herself to really observe the man sitting across from her. He was telling her a story from his childhood about his aunt and a boat she'd owned. Taylor was only half listening, absorbed as she was in her post-dinner assessment of her date.

He wore a jacket and tie, appropriate for this particular cruise, and she noted how precisely his tie was knotted, how it rested, perfectly straight, on the pin-striped dress shirt. An image of Alex after the wedding two weeks ago crowded into her head. She couldn't help remembering how he'd thrown his tie aside, rolled his sleeves up. How comfortable in his skin he'd looked. Dripping with blatant sex appeal.

But what kind of man did she want to spend her life with? The tie-thrown-on-the-counter type or the tie-in-perfect-position type?

And then there was the small matter that the choice wasn't hers to make. This was her very first date with Brian, so who knew where they would end up? And she wasn't any more Alex's type than he was hers.

She realized Brian was looking at her expectantly and gathered he'd asked her a question. Lord, she hadn't heard a thing he'd said for the past few minutes.

"I'm sorry, the wine must be getting to me." She felt her cheeks flushing. "I missed what you asked."

"No big deal. Shall we see about seats on the deck by the musicians?"

Relieved that he didn't make an issue of her inattention, she nodded and stood along with him. He grabbed her nearly full wineglass and held it out to her and, for an instant, she wondered if his plan was to get her tipsy, to lower her guard. Admittedly, the thought had no basis. He was just being polite.

Polite was on the list.

As she took the glass from him, she had a flash of Alex handing her a juice glass of merlot before her first date with...

None of that bore thinking of right now, when she was with a man who was so...ideal for her.

Brian led her through the doorway to the front deck. It was more crowded out here, but he managed to score them two stools at the narrow counter along the wall separating the deck from the dinner area. He sat on the one closest to the water and she settled next to him. Though he partially blocked it, she still caught the breeze coming off the water and shivered. Her sleeveless dress left her arms exposed, and now that the sun was falling fast toward the horizon, she wished she'd brought a wrap.

Brian rested his warm hand on her arm, which helped marginally. As they listened to the relaxing music, she studied his hand. It was white-collar all the way, nails neatly manicured, wisps of light hair on each thin finger. Gentle strength. Reassuring in a way. Unlike, say, Alex's hands, which were rough and calloused. Brimming with raw masculinity that could make her squirm.

What was wrong with her?

This was not the time to be thinking of Alex. It was just that she was more comfortable around him than Brian simply because she knew him better. It'd only taken seventeen years or so for her to relax with Alex.

Brian bent close and commented on the music, his warm breath brushing her cheek. Taylor glanced up at him and caught his gaze. He smiled down at her. He had a nice smile. He was a nice, considerate man.

For someone who was supposedly so smart, she was acting like quite the idiot. Brian Paulsen was a list man. So far, he hit every last one of her requirements. She leaned into him and vowed to banish Alex from her mind for the rest of the night.

SUNDAYS WERE THE WORST. They had been ever since Quinn's death. Well, before that, too, Taylor supposed. It didn't really make sense that losing Quinn had made the day lonelier—he'd been seven thousand miles away for years before the accident. But…it was the *knowing,* she guessed. Knowing she was totally alone, with no family, no real friends.

Now she was lucky to count Vienna as a friend, and she almost had what one might consider a social life. Half of one, at the very least. And yet Sundays still found her restless and lonely.

She wandered down the hallway, the closed bathroom door making her wonder why Alex hadn't shown up today to finish the floor. Confident he'd eventually do it, she moved on, went from room to room, looking for a cleaning project or something she'd missed in her preparation to call a Realtor. She was nothing if not thorough, though. Quinn would have a field day if he could see her now. She smiled sadly as Lorien followed her into her office and wove around her legs.

"You've been fed, beast," she said. "Which means you want love."

Didn't they all?

She picked up the cat and cuddled her close. The sound and vibration of either of her pets' purring was normally a source of comfort, but today nothing seemed to alleviate her discontent.

She carried Lorien to the kitchen, calling Elanor as she went and nearly getting trampled by the second cat. Once in the kitchen, she set the blue point on the floor and served up gourmet kitty treats, as they knew she would. While the two cats buried their faces in the mini piles, Taylor walked out, headed for the front door without a destination in mind. The house was closing in on her.

She grabbed her keys on the way and felt in her jeans pocket for her cell phone out of habit. Pulling the locked door shut behind her, she breathed in fresh air and felt marginally better. She had a long way to go to anything resembling contentment.

She ignored the nagging thought that it went beyond the day of the week.

Mr. Petrowski, her elderly neighbor across the street, was out in his front yard digging up dandelions one by one. He slowly straightened when her door closed, waved at her. Taylor waved back, conscious of her lack of purpose. She'd stormed outside and…what? Where was she going?

The park. She walked to the end of the driveway, noticing the weeds that had popped up in the pavement cracks. She took out her phone and started a fresh list of outdoor chores. She'd add to it later. As she took a right turn on the sidewalk, her phone vibrated in her hand, startling her. She rarely got texts on the weekends when she didn't have to keep in contact with her colleagues.

Last night was perfect. Thank you.
Brian.

She smiled. Maybe her grin was a little thin, but she was tired. They'd been out until close to eleven, taking a drive and talking once the dinner cruise had ended.

He was a good guy.

Having to remind herself of that repeatedly signified a problem.

Taylor stuck her phone back in her pocket as she turned in to the park and went for the swings. She'd think of a reply later. Maybe flying would help her state of mind.

Pumping her legs back and forth, she gained height. Got that funny feeling in her belly at the top of each swing. It wasn't nearly as much fun without a friend, though, and she let herself gradually decelerate until the swing lost all momentum.

Laughter and shouts of children drew her attention to the playground on the other side of the park. Two boys, maybe ten or eleven years old, played rowdily on the teeter-totter. She could tell from here they'd made a battle of it, each of them seeing who could land hard enough on the ground to make the other go airborne. With each bounce, they both hollered competitively. Up. Down. The effect was like watching a vertical Ping-Pong game.

She pushed out of the swing and walked to the fat trunk of an old, towering tree. Sitting against the rough bark was considerably more comfortable than being wedged in a plastic form-sucking swing. The boys were still in her sight, still bouncing up and down. Like her restless mind.

She pulled out her phone again and opened a blank notepad screen. Typed in *Brian* at the top and hit Return.

Yes, lists would always be her comfort zone, her little island of security whenever she felt out of control. Just adding the number 1 now calmed her slightly. She entered his attributes.

1. Meets 10/10 list criteria (or 9.5…jury's out on health-conscious.)
2. Good conversationalist.
3. Attractive.
4. Creative date idea.

5. Well-off. (Not that this is necessary!)
6. Easy to be with.
7. Safe, respectable career.
8. …

She stared at the boys in the distance, thinking, trying to come up with more positive points. But her mind kept getting sidelined. After several returns on the screen, she typed again.

Alex.
1. …

She picked at the grass, lost in thought. The boys ran off, the silence seemed to buzz in her ears. Tilting her head back against the trunk, she absently watched a bird flit around in the branches above. She tossed her phone into the grass beside her.

It was no use.

She could sit here and try to convince herself that Brian would make her happy until the leaves fell off the tree and the snow started falling. She could tell herself Alex was wrong for her on paper and in real life. She could repeat the words till her voice was hoarse, but it wouldn't change the truth that was staring her in the face.

She'd fallen in love with Alex.

Taylor closed her eyes, feeling none of the lightness that love should bring.

Denying it had gotten her by for only so long, and now there was no avoiding the truth. If she could choose who she fell in love with, she'd pick someone like Brian. Someone who made a good match with her. Someone who called their night together "perfect."

Not someone who, most days, couldn't stop feeling responsible for her due to a random tragic accident that he blamed himself for.

So now what?

So now…nothing.

Because it came down to the fact that, while Alex might not fit on her list or be her type of guy at all, the even bigger issue was that she wasn't Alex's type of girl. To him, she was his best friend's little sister. It didn't matter if he called her Scarlet or Taylor. He would never let himself love her.

CHAPTER TWENTY-THREE

SOMEWHAT APPROPRIATELY, Taylor said a prayer Monday evening on the way to Saint Patty's Tavern that Alex had already left.

She hadn't had enough time to get her everything's-fine-we're-just-friends face on yet. But he'd said Vienna needed her, so here she was.

She'd just gotten home from work, on time or close to it for once, exhausted after a sleepless night. When she'd seen his number on her caller ID, her heart had flipped out and then she'd told herself that was a pointless reaction. She was proud of how quickly she'd talked herself down.

Navigating the bar's crumbling front walk was tricky this time, as she hadn't had a chance to change out of her three-and-a-half-inch black-and-white leopard slings or her work clothes. Her white pencil skirt and black ruffled shell were definitely overkill for Saint Patty's.

When she opened the door, it took all of three seconds, while her eyes adjusted to the darker interior, to figure out her prayers hadn't been answered. Alex stood at the back of the room near the doorway between the bar and the kitchen, talking to the male bartender. Facing the front door. Staring at Taylor as he spoke. She couldn't hear his words over the jukebox but she could make out his voice. And identify his body from a mile away.

The Monday dinner crowd was bigger than the Friday-night one in these parts. Besides Vienna, who sat at a table in the opposite back corner from her brother, and who didn't immediately notice Taylor, two other tables were occupied, and three people sat at the counter.

Taylor made her way toward her friend. With every step she was aware of the weight of Alex's gaze on her. Ridiculously self-conscious, she felt as if she was just learning to walk in heels and feared she would end up on her face any second. She made it all the way to Vienna's table before she weakened and darted a glance in Alex's direction again. Attempted a nonchalant smile at him, as he still watched her. When she turned to Vienna, she found her friend gauging the exchange with too much interest.

"What are you doing here?" Vienna asked as Taylor pulled a chair out and sat down.

Vienna's usual cheerfulness was missing, though she was trying to hide it with a halfhearted smile of greeting. Two beer cans sat on the table in front of her, her hand on one of them as if daring someone to try to pry it from her.

"Alex said you were upset. I came right over."

She shot a glare at her brother. "When did you talk to Alex?"

"Fifteen minutes ago. He called me," Taylor explained. "What's going on, Vee?"

"You didn't have to call Taylor," Vienna said as Alex strode up to the table. "Must've done it when I was in the bathroom." She muttered the last to herself.

"If something's wrong, why didn't *you* call me?" Taylor asked. Clearly something was up.

"I figured you were at the IT Professionals mixer tonight. Why aren't you?"

Taylor avoided Alex's interested gaze as he took the chair next to her. "I...I'm taking a night off." At least one. The thought of forcing herself to go out and be social again was painful. She needed a break.

"How was Saturday night?" Vienna asked, perking up. "Everything go okay?"

Taylor should have called her yesterday to report. Then she wouldn't have Alex giving her that look right now, waiting for her to tell all.

"It went really well." She answered the question honestly. So maybe it was misleading, but she wasn't ready to confess that there had been no spark. Not yet to Vienna, and definitely not to Alex.

She made the mistake of glancing at Alex then and saw his jaw tighten. Or thought she did, anyway. Maybe he wasn't paying any attention to them.

"You know I need details," Vienna said.

"First you need to tell me what's wrong." Taylor frowned, fiddled with the napkin holder in the middle of the table. "I'll fill you in later."

Her friend exhaled. "It's not that big a deal. I just heard from Hugh Samuels that I didn't get the job with your company."

"What?" Taylor put her hand on Vienna's arm. "Nooo. I'm so sorry to hear that. What did he say?"

"Standard lines. Blah blah, impressed with you, someone with more experience this time, yada yada." Vienna picked up her beer and took a swallow. She stared at the can as she set it back in front of her. "I'm okay. Just disappointed. You didn't have to call Taylor," she repeated to Alex.

"I'm not good at handling this kind of thing. You know that."

"There's nothing to handle. You ordered me a beer. Two. That's all anyone can do." Vienna tried to make her voice light but it didn't really work.

"Where's the white chocolate martini?" Taylor asked.

"Patty's not here tonight. She won't tell anyone how she makes them. They all try but no one can do it right. Kind of a beer situation anyway." She took another unladylike swig. "Speaking of...you need a drink."

"What do you want?" Alex asked, standing.

Taylor allowed herself to look directly at him and noticed the bruising around his left eye. "What happened to you? Did you get in a fight?"

"Brotherly love."

"You should see the other guy," Vienna said. "Lucky me, I live with both of them."

"Beverage choice?" Alex clearly wasn't going to discuss more.

"Just tea."

One side of his mouth hitched upward in a half smirk. "Gingko blend?"

"Do they have one?"

"They have a jar of instant crystals."

She narrowed her eyes at him, taking a second to grasp that he was messing with her. His steel-colored gaze was amused, and she couldn't help thinking how she loved that look. For whatever good it did her...

"Do they have water?" she threw back at him.

Appreciation—approval?—flitted across his

gaze as he studied her for a moment. Or maybe she imagined it. Regardless, a surge of emotion hit her—one that he no doubt didn't share—and she glanced quickly at Vienna, hoping she'd missed the silent back-and-forth.

She hadn't. As Alex walked off to get Taylor's water, Vienna looked between them. Thankfully she said nothing.

"Another beer for me, please," Vienna called out after him.

"I can't believe they didn't hire you," Taylor said, itching to get the spotlight off herself, but also genuinely shocked. "I talked to Hugh. He raved about you."

"He's a man," Vienna said matter-of-factly. "Stupid men."

"You said it. I'd drink to that if I had a drink."

"What's up with water?"

"It's Monday night. I'm all over the support thing but I've got a meeting first thing tomorrow and I can't be fuzzy-brained."

"You could always just wash the drunk off in the shower," Alex said as he rejoined them.

"You have a point," Taylor conceded, keeping a straight face. She took the bottled water from him. "I'll be the designated driver tonight. You," she said to Vienna, "do what you have to do."

Vienna finished off beer number two and took

the next can from her brother. "I'm on it. Stupid men."

Taylor chuckled.

"This is why you needed Taylor," Alex said. "I'm not up for the man-bashing."

"You're too good to me, army guy. Have a seat."

He shook his head. "I'm taking off in a couple. I'm confident Scarlet here will look after you."

She was in love with him and he was back to Scarlet. Fabulous.

Pathetically, Taylor was disappointed when he didn't glance at her. Even more so when he headed back to the bar and picked up his conversation with the man behind it without another word to her.

What did she expect, though? Nothing had changed between them. This—having him call her to comfort his sister, running into him at a hole-in-the-wall bar—was as good as it got.

She tried to ignore his presence as she and Vienna hashed over Hugh's earlier phone call and then discussed the other companies Vienna had targeted. Taylor couldn't help herself—she made a list of them on her phone as her friend rattled them off.

"You've got a lot of excellent prospects," Taylor said, typing away.

"Thanks to you."

"I guess Operation Checklist was good for something."

Alex's voice rose as he called out a goodbye to the bartender and headed for the front door. No glance at her. Not that she was waiting for one. Much.

"Okay, spill it," Vienna said.

Drat. Taylor wasn't sure what Vienna wanted her to spill but she could easily guess it wasn't something she was comfortable talking about.

"I'm empty," she said, lifting the depleted water bottle, fully aware that playing stupid wouldn't distract her friend. She couldn't talk about Alex, though. To anyone.

"Tay, this is me here. What's going on between you and my brother?"

"Nothing." She took the cap off the empty bottle. Screwed it back on while Vienna stared at her.

"That wasn't 'nothing.' The teasing back and forth is one thing, but the looks between you two? I'm not blind."

Taylor felt the slow burn crawl up to her cheeks. She'd always been open with Vienna about the guys she'd gone out with, even though it was hard for her. But Alex... Vienna was too close to him. And Taylor's emotions were too raw. She was in uncharted territory and had no idea how to navigate it. She wouldn't even know what to say if she were able to start. A lump blocked her throat and she shook her head.

Vienna stared at her. Leaned back in her chair and crossed her arms. "If you're not going to talk to me, let's get out of here." Her tone left no doubt she was ticked off. She pushed her chair back and angled toward the bar, asking the guy behind it what she owed.

"Alex covered it," the bartender said. "You're good. Take care of yourself."

Hating that her friend was upset because of her, Taylor followed. When she cleared the building, she saw Vienna heading toward the sidewalk, obviously intending to walk home.

"Vienna, come back. I'll give you a ride. Please?"

Vienna tilted her head as if considering, then turned around and approached Taylor's car. "Can we get some food?"

"Sounds good. Your choice."

WHEN TAYLOR SAID Vienna could choose dinner, she hadn't guessed she'd find herself on the lakeshore at a mostly deserted public beach eating Chunky Monkey ice cream from the container with a plastic spoon. The bananas in it had to give it some health benefits, right?

They'd run into the grocery store and then

stopped at Taylor's so she could change clothes. Vienna hadn't spoken much, and Taylor wasn't sure if she was more upset about the job or annoyed with Taylor.

They sat on smooth gray boulders at the water's edge. Vienna had kicked off her flip-flops and dipped her toes in the water as she shoveled ice cream into her mouth. The evening sun still warmed the air and Taylor briefly considered that it was hot enough to burn her fair skin if they were out for more than a few minutes. She watched a lone goose swim gracefully past them a few feet out, leaving a tiny wake. The bird made going solo seem so peaceful, so easy.

"I'm not really used to having someone to confide my secrets to," Taylor said, her spoon lodged upright in her ice cream. "I'm sorry. I didn't mean to hurt your feelings."

Vienna shook her head, gazing out at a water skier in the middle of the lake. "It's your business, Tay. If you want to keep it to yourself, that's your decision." She scooped another spoonful. "Just know that I wouldn't tell anyone or make fun of whatever you say."

Taylor thought back to the first night Vienna and Alex had sat in her kitchen as she troubleshot Vienna's laptop. Alex had blurted out her goal of finding a date and Taylor had expected Vienna to be amused. She hadn't been. Not once in Taylor's whole summer pursuit of a list guy had Vienna violated that trust or made her feel ridiculous.

Logically, Taylor realized her fears were unfounded. Convincing herself to speak up was another matter entirely.

She played with her spoon, dragging it around in the partially empty pint container, digging out a valley in the middle. Realizing she'd lost her appetite, she leaned over and set the package on the ground. When she straightened, she followed Vienna's lead and stared directly ahead.

"I slept with your brother."

Vienna made a choking noise, her eyes popping wide open as she faced Taylor. She patted her chest. "Let me get past the ick factor of knowing anything about my brother's sex life...."

"Sorry."

"Don't be. I'm over it." She rotated on her rock and managed to cross her legs without falling off. "I knew something was going on between you two. I've suspected it for weeks."

"Weeks?" Taylor wondered just how transparent she'd been.

"I stopped buying the protective older brother routine from Alex long ago. He's easy to read."

Taylor stared at her friend, confused. "Um, Alex is pretty indifferent, actually."

Vienna shook her head. "Oh, honey, I don't think so. So tell me what's going on. I want details...without details, if you know what I mean."

Taylor balanced herself and pulled her knees up to her chest. "I guess I've pretty much always had a crush on him. He and Quinn were my knights in shining armor growing up." She went into detail about the times Alex had defended her. "Hero worship, I guess," she said, smiling wistfully. Though she wouldn't go back to those days for anything, they'd been somewhat simpler times.

"He's a good guy," Vienna said. "Deep down. Sometimes he covers it up pretty well."

"It was the night of my coworker's wedding..."

"Aha! I should have guessed that. I knew how late he was that night, and then you told me he took you to the wedding. Duh."

"You asked me, actually. Sorry I lied. I was just...it was too much."

"I don't know how I missed that. So you guys have been supersecret lovers ever since or what?"

Taylor shook her head. "No. Not at all. Just the one night."

"That's when you doubled your social efforts, right? Right after the wedding. You went kind of nuts about going out and meeting people."

Taylor filled her in on Brian and the "perfect"

date. How she couldn't stop comparing him to Alex. Couldn't get him out of her head.

"You've got it bad," Vienna said. There was too much excitement in her voice.

Taylor didn't say anything. She couldn't quite bring herself to admit to the L-word out loud. But judging by Vienna's animation, she didn't need to.

"What are you going to do about it?" her friend asked.

"Not a thing. He's not into it, Vee. I may be socially dense but I can spot that from a mile away."

Vienna shook her head, a scheming look on her face. "I think you're wrong. He cares about you."

"He doesn't love me. Won't love me."

"How do you know?"

"I just…do. Look at me, Vienna. I'm an awkward computer geek. He's…he could do so much better than me. And that's if he wasn't beating himself up daily about my brother."

Vienna hopped off her rock and started to pace. "You did not just say that bit about doing better than you. You're gorgeous, Tay. And Alex is way aware of that." She smiled conspiratorially. "This could be so much fun to watch."

Taylor wasn't feeling her glee. "There's nothing to see."

"Have you discussed any of this with him?"

"Lord, no."

"Why not?"

"Why would I?"

Vienna clutched at her short hair. "Taylor! What if you could have a future with him?"

I couldn't. She didn't say the words aloud but they rang through her head loud and clear.

"He'll be going back overseas soon," she said instead.

"So? That's not for sure, and even if he does, who knows when it will be." Vienna stopped pacing and settled back on her rock. "I understand that you're scared, Taylor. All of us go through that."

She doubted it, but kept silent.

"Okay." Vienna stood again. "Forget the future, since who knows what that will bring. What about the right now? Can't you have fun with him now, for as long as he's home?"

"Define *fun*."

"Go out with him. Take him to the next work picnic, a movie, the symphony. I don't know. Sleep with him. Take showers with him. Okay, have to stop there. He's still my brother."

Taylor smiled in spite of herself.

"I guess he must not think I'm repulsive if he spent the night once..."

"Of course he doesn't, dork. He likes you, Taylor. He chooses to spend more time at your house than at home, and I don't want to hear anything about you paying him to work."

"It's true."

"He doesn't need the money, honey. Trust me. He talked about paying cash for a new car when he first got back and I'm pretty sure that wasn't going to break him."

Taylor's mind was spinning. Vienna had a point about just trying to enjoy being with Alex while she could. It didn't mean he had to be the man she married. Maybe he wouldn't flat-out reject her for just spending time together. Low stakes. "The thing is…I don't know if I can initiate anything."

"You don't have to ask him out on a real date. Have a movie sitting on your kitchen counter. Ask him to watch it with you. Go out for burgers on the fly. You're coming to my graduation party this weekend, right?"

"Of course."

"Hang with Alex. Hang all over him if you want to." A wicked laughed escaped her.

That sounded doable. The hanging out with him part. Plus it would solve the problem of not knowing another soul at the party. "I might."

"Suit yourself," Vienna said, scooping a spoonful of melted ice cream into her mouth. "But stop being so absolute. Doesn't have to be all or nothing."

Relationships are gray, Alex had said. He frequently accused her of seeing everything as black and white and she acknowledged that's the way she was.

But maybe she could make an exception in this case. Learn to embrace the gray side in order to be with Alex. For now.

"I know you've got plenty on your plate to get ready for your party but I'll try hanging around Alex. *If* you help me find something to wear."

"In a heartbeat," Vienna said. "Let's go. You're going to knock that army guy dead."

CHAPTER TWENTY-FOUR

THE CONVENIENT THING about keeping an electronic list on her phone was that Taylor could delete the whole document with a single click as soon as she completed it—or decided it was a waste of virtual space.

Like now. Or almost now.

Decked out in a floral cream-and-peach sheath and five-inch platform heels with little bows on the front, she flipped through the various "notes" on her phone as she walked down the hardwood hallway. As she hit her home office, she found what she was looking for: *Top Ten Characteristics.*

She didn't bother to read them. She did, however, email the list to herself. Maybe she was going overboard, but this moment felt important somehow. It required a certain amount of...drama.

Flipping her computer on, she opened her email account, located the list that she'd just sent and hit *Print.* The multifunction laser printer on the side table clicked to life and spat out a copy.

Back on her phone, she clicked on the trash can

icon and said, "Bye-bye," as the digital list disappeared.

Lorien jumped on the office chair and peered up at her as though she'd lost her mind.

"I'm just getting started, kitty."

Both cats seemed to sense impending change, for good reason. The house had been on the market for three days. Several parties had been through it and one was drawing up an offer.

Things were suddenly moving superfast, and Taylor was determined to make some personal changes, too.

She grabbed the paper off the printer and set the phone aside. Her heels echoed down the hall to the kitchen and Elanor darted out of her way. Once in the kitchen, she opened the catch-all drawer next to the stove and hunted through it like a mad woman.

Aha. Matches.

Tonight called for fire.

She walked over to the kitchen sink. With the paper on the counter right next to her, she struck a match on the side of the matchbox. A flame shot upward and, hand shaking, she picked up the paper and held the match to one corner.

The paper caught immediately, curling into nothingness as the fire devoured it. She stared at the glow with fascination and a healthy measure of fear, thinking it was lucky she didn't have sleeves that could catch fire.

Bit by bit, the top ten characteristics disappeared and the flames grew. At the first hint of heat on her hand, she dropped the paper into the sink, ready to turn on the faucet if necessary. She fought the urge, though, empowered somehow by the sight of the list vanishing.

She stared at the ash in the sink after the paper was gone, the burning scent in the air giving her the oddest satisfaction. When Lorien jumped up on the counter, Taylor didn't even scold her.

"Well, kitty, here goes nothing."

VIENNA HAD A LOT OF FRIENDS. A lot of pretty friends, Alex thought as he looked around the Worth backyard from behind the rented bar counter they'd set up on the patio. The crowded gathering was a cross-sampling of her life, from people he remembered from kindergarten to those she'd introduced as grad-school buddies.

And yet the only one who really caught his attention was Taylor.

The dress she wore gave him an alluring view of the slender, sexy legs that had been imprinted in his memory—stretched out beside him and wrapped around him in the moonlight. Her heels were so high it was a wonder she could walk, but they did amazing things for her. The flowered dress was modest compared to some of the get-ups here, but he had trouble taking his eyes off the way it followed the curve around her hips, cinching in at the waist.

He itched to run his hand over that curve, in the dress if he had to, but he'd prefer a smooth expanse of pale skin beneath his fingers. Her hair was pulled up in a carefree, sexy style unlike anything he'd ever seen on her. Fortunately, he was stuck behind the bar doling out beer and wine.

Their mom had gone all out for her little girl, as Vee deserved, putting no cap on the guest list. The food and beverage spread was impressive, with three expansive tables positioned around the yard, each offering an assortment of appetizers supplied by a catering company. She'd sprung for an ungodly amount of wine and beer with the agreement that Alex and Marshall would serve as bartenders. Of course Marshall had yet to show his face. Everyone would be better off if he'd escaped to some bar far from the festivities.

Alex suspected this was, in addition to a celebration of Vienna's achievements, his mom's unofficial salute to the beginning of her empty-nest years. There was the small issue of her overgrown boys bunking with her, but Alex, for one, hoped to be out of there soon. Marshall—well, it might be best if he was kicked out.

Cheryl Worth was in her element. She'd added several of her own friends to the guest list—those who'd known Vienna since she was born. Neighbors, coworkers. Alex hadn't seen her pull out all the stops like this since Marshall had finished school, back when Alex was relatively new to the army and had made it home on leave for the party. Alex was the lone child who hadn't done her proud with a degree, advanced or otherwise. He had a hunch that their mother would throw a bash the day he resigned from the service.

As he was filling a red plastic cup with beer from the keg and gazing toward Taylor instead of the tap, his sister came up on the other side of him and bumped him with her hip.

"Guest of honor isn't supposed to be behind the bar," he said, bumping her back.

"Guest of honor can help herself. Especially when the bartender type is staring at one of the guests."

Alex feigned intense concentration on getting just the right head on the beer. He handed it to the guy on the other side of the tall, surprisingly sturdy counter, a bookworm-hippy-looking twentysomething who was no doubt from the grad-school camp. The guy said, "You're the beer master, man. Thanks."

"Anytime." Alex watched him walk off then turned to Vienna. "Friend of yours?"

"Of course," she said enthusiastically. "They all are." She giggled and he guessed she was already feeling the wine.

"More chardonnay, princess?" He took her glass and picked up the opened bottle of white.

Vienna nodded. "I like how you ignored the bit about my good friend Taylor."

"What bit was that?" He filled her glass three-quarters of the way full and handed it to her, then turned to the female partygoer holding out an empty wineglass.

He busied himself pouring the cabernet she requested, hoping Vienna would wander off any minute now.

"She looks hot tonight, doesn't she?" his sister said. He could tell her eyes were on Taylor, though he avoided looking at her himself.

"Something you need to tell me?" he asked. "Is this why you never go on dates?"

Vienna slapped him lightly on the arm. "I like boys. Just not now. I need to establish my career."

"Lots of them to choose from tonight."

"They're my friends, Alex. Quit diverting."

"Diverting? Is that a fancy marketing term?"

He laughed as he handed a short, curvy blonde a cold beer.

Vienna set her glass aside and served the next two people at the same time.

"Show off," Alex said.

"So." Vienna faced him now that there was no one waiting for a drink. "You and Taylor."

"This again?" He helped himself to an unused cup and carelessly filled it. Took a gulp and frowned at the amount of foam on top. He needed to be fired from this "job" if that was the best he could do. He flicked as much of the foam out of the cup as he could.

"It's obvious you're attracted to her, army guy."

He squeezed the plastic cup until it made cracking sounds and the beverage went to the top. "It's not that easy."

Vienna nonchalantly waved at a group across the patio who had just arrived. "You're making it more difficult than it has to be."

Two women came up to the bar, making no secret of the fact that they were eyeing Alex. He was relieved for the interruption.

"What can I do for you ladies?" he asked.

The brunette on his left leaned on the counter, giving him a front-row seat to her ample and exposed cleavage. She definitely knew how to accentuate her assets. He did his best to keep his eyes on her brown ones, thinking they were pretty eyes once you finally noticed them. "If you mean drink-wise, I'd like a glass of white wine." She left no question that she had other possibilities on her mind.

"Page, you girls are trolling for trouble tonight," Vienna said, amused. "I have to caution you, though, this is my *brother*." She waved toward the backyard. "Many other better-adjusted guys out there."

"You've been holding out on us, Vienna," the other woman said. She had short, spiky, two-toned hair and round cheeks. Though lacking the cleavage of her friend, her outfit, a tight-fitting, lacy camisole, commanded attention, as well.

"Pick your poison." Alex held a bottle of chardonnay and one of Riesling before Page. She pointed at the Riesling and shot him a flirty look. In another time and place, maybe she would have sparked his interest.

"You?" he asked her friend as he poured the first glass.

"I'm a beer girl." She walked to the side of the house and carried one of the bar stools they'd brought up from the basement back to the bar. She set it in front of the counter, off to the side, and climbed onto it. Extending her hand, she said, "Kylie. Nice to meet you…?"

"Alex," he said, because there was no way out of this. Yet. He was stuck on drink duty until Marshall showed up.

"We thought we'd keep you company, Alex."

A HALF HOUR LATER, the lovely ladies were still keeping Alex company. He'd played nice, flirted back here and there for the first ten or fifteen minutes.

All the while Page and Kylie tried to draw him into conversation, he'd subtly watched three men monopolize Taylor out near his mom's birdbath. They made her laugh. One of them had touched her damn arm.

And here he was.

He took a drink of his now-warm beer. Just as well that the Bobbsey Twins were camped out. It prevented him from storming over there and doing something impulsive.

If Vienna had invited the guys to her party, they were most likely not serial killers. So Taylor wasn't in any danger. Whom she decided to talk to was neither his business nor his problem.

He managed to continue to interact—albeit in a half-assed way—with his apparent fan club while making a game of privately rating the women who came up to the bar on a scale of one to ten. He probably would've given Page and Kylie a seven and a six and a half when they'd first approached, but they'd each had a point deducted for wearing out their welcome.

The sun had set and the yard was illuminated by tiki torches that doubled as bug repellent. Strings of outdoor lights in the shape of flip-flops were strung between trees and around the windows of the house. The laughter got louder as the level in the second keg got lower. The roar of the party would probably be bothersome for the surrounding neighbors, but, in a genius move, his mom had invited every last one of them.

Alex's top rating so far was an eight, awarded to a pretty woman with long blond hair, and, wouldn't you know it, she was with a skinny, academic-looking guy in Harry Potter spectacles. Not that it mattered. Alex wasn't on the hunt tonight, merely desperate for entertainment while he tended bar.

As he drew another two beers from the keg for the Mooneys, who lived two doors to the south, he felt a feminine arm trail across his back and around to his side. He briefly closed his eyes, guessing Kylie had disembarked from her stool.

"Hey, babe, I missed you."

Taylor?

Calling him babe?

Making a move on him in public?

He wondered who'd slipped a mickey into the beer he hadn't managed to finish. Or maybe into *her* drink.

Glancing around to confirm it was in fact Taylor and not an overactive imagination on his part, he finished pouring the beers and handed them to the guests. He turned and looked questioningly at her. Taylor widened her eyes meaningfully. Before he could grasp her scheme, she smiled sympathetically at Page.

She was rescuing him.

"There you are," he said warmly, finally playing along with her. He leaned down and kissed her. Added some tongue action to make it convincing. All part of the charade.

Like hell.

When he stopped to get his bearings and remind himself this was for show, Taylor surprised him again by pulling him back to her lips. Who was he to refuse her?

Page, who'd still been hanging over the bar, now latched on to Bill Copperfield, a neighbor with about twenty years on her, but single. Maybe they'd make each other happy.

"You didn't mention you had a girlfriend," Kylie said, starting to sound sloppy.

"You didn't ask." Alex barely spared her a glance as he sent Taylor a thank-you with his eyes.

Kylie pointedly looked Taylor up and down. "I wouldn't have pegged her for your type."

"You would've been wrong," he said, feeling Taylor stiffen at the cheerfully delivered insult. He pulled her close to his side and there was no charade involved in the protective move. It came without thought, just as naturally as kissing her had been.

Dangerous ground, he told himself.

"Would you mind grabbing me another beer?" Kylie spoke to Taylor as she handed over her empty cup.

Alex took it before Taylor could. "My pleasure."

Taylor narrowed her eyes momentarily, then smiled at him as she picked up the beer tap. She held it up, silently offering to fill the cup while he held it. He choked back a laugh. Who knew Taylor had such a wicked side to her?

When the cup was full, he handed it to Kylie, who had climbed down from her self-made throne.

"Thanks, sexy," she said, then turned on her stiletto and stalked off to find her next prey.

Alex turned to thank Taylor but found her taking drink requests. In the past five seconds, a line had appeared out of nowhere. He fell in beside her and refilled at least a dozen beer cups as fast as he could.

"You don't have to help," he said in Taylor's ear.

"I want to." She handed over a shiraz to one of his mom's friends. "I've pretty much exhausted my party-talk repertoire. Having a job is good."

They spent the next hour serving drinks almost without a pause. Taylor took care of pouring wine and Alex was the beer guy. He tapped the third and final keg.

"Vee hangs out with a bunch of drunks," Alex said as he wiped up the spilled beer from the counter.

Taylor shifted her weight from one foot to the other. Her gaze landed on the empty stool Kylie had occupied and she pulled it behind the counter and inched her way up on it. Crossing one leg over the other, she flexed her shoes. "They look a lot better than they feel."

He meant to respond. Maybe he nodded. But the view of her calf and lower thigh...

It wasn't a revealing glimpse. Just sexy skin and perfect leg. He had a heck of a time keeping his eyes off her as they were once again inundated with thirsty guests.

The cases of wine soon ran out, and not long after, the last keg was running low. Word spread quickly and there was talk of moving the party to a bar, which suited Alex fine. He leaned his back against the counter and pulled his shirt away from his chest to get it to stop sticking. "I'd say Vienna owes us both a big, expensive dinner."

"Sounds good to me," Taylor said, standing. "I'm beat. It's time for me to go home."

"Speaking of owing…" Alex touched her arm. "I owe you one for your heroic rescue."

"You looked sort of miserable."

"Scared for my life."

"You do kind of owe me," she said, grinning.

"Yeah?" He could think of some choice ways to make it up to her.…

"It appears your handyman work is top-notch. I've got a family interested in buying my house. I'm going house-hunting with a Realtor tomorrow." She bit her lip, her gutsy playfulness gone. "I've never bought a house before. I'd…love to have a male point of view. You know, fix-it stuff, opinions on furnaces and fireplaces and who knows what else."

That wasn't quite what he had in mind but, funny thing, he hadn't yet learned how to say no to her. Besides, house-hunting fitted securely into the role Quinn would expect of him.

"Sounds like you should make a checklist. Top ten characteristics you want in a house." He was only partially joking.

"No. I'm trying something new." She straightened and exhaled. "I'm going to pay attention to my gut instinct tomorrow. Going to try, anyway."

"In that case, you're on. What time?"

"Bright and early if you're up for it." His exact words when he'd stood her up for their first hardware-store trip. "Nine."

"You got it."

"I'll pick *you* up this time." She gave him a meaningful look.

"Yes, ma'am. The higher your heels, the scarier you are."

"I'll try to wear flip-flops tomorrow, just for you."

"S'there any more beer?" Kylie draped herself over the bar and held out her lipstick-stained cup.

"There's a little in there. Help yourself." He gestured toward the keg. "Bartender's officially off-duty and I have to walk my *girlfriend* to her car." He tried not to hesitate over the word *girlfriend,* but truth be told, Kylie was too far gone to notice if he did.

"Let me say goodbye to Vienna," Taylor said as she hurried to one of the patio tables where his sister sat with two of her friends from grade school who'd come back to Madison for the party.

Alex packed up the remaining empty bottles while Kylie fought to get a few last drops out of the tap. Before she could call it quits, Taylor was back, smiling at him.

He took her hand, weaving their fingers together as they headed toward the driveway. Neither of them spoke the whole way, as if they both knew they should acknowledge the ruse but preferred to hold on to the excuse to touch while they could. By the time they got to her car, parked halfway down the block, nervousness had overcome him.

Nervousness.

Him.

Bad sign. Bad, bad sign.

"See you in the morning," he said as she opened her door. It took steely willpower but he backed away from her. Waved. Went on his way. Nonchalantly, of course.

As he walked back to the house, hand in his front pocket, head down, he kicked a rock repeatedly, following its trail before blasting it forward again.

If there was a nagging voice in his head that was set on pointing out how cozy and domestic house-hunting was, he paid it no heed.

CHAPTER TWENTY-FIVE

TAYLOR DIDN'T HAVE a lot of practice trusting her instincts, but they were screaming at her right now. Or something was.

She stood on the back screened-in porch of a house she'd never expected to like. One that, on paper, wasn't the most practical. But she not only liked it...she was falling in love with it.

It was a seventy-year-old bungalow with so much curb appeal it'd make the perfect Christmas card. Thick columns supported a wide, welcoming front porch, and the current owner had filled long, handmade flower boxes that stretched along both sides with dozens of pink, purple and white blooms.

The inside was cute and well-maintained, and the kitchen and bathrooms had been remodeled recently. The first floor was full of windows. She could picture Elanor and Lorien perching on the sills, in feline heaven. The two bedrooms on the main floor were decent-size and one would make a cozy home office. But the crowning feature of the house was the master bedroom. The

suite stretched over the second floor and included
two walk-in closets and a bathroom with a claw-
foot tub. Dormer windows at the front and back
let in sunshine and fresh air, and Taylor adored
the cushioned window seats.

This was the ninth house they'd been in today.
Genevieve, the Realtor Karen at work had recommended, had the patience of an old, loyal dog.
She had a way of appearing whenever Taylor had
questions, but otherwise she let Taylor and Alex
wander around without feeling stalked.

Alex was doing exactly what she'd asked him
to—checking construction quality, plumbing
systems, heating and cooling and other details it
wouldn't occur to Taylor to inspect. He'd been a
big help, practically speaking, but that was all.

After their boyfriend-girlfriend game last night
at Vienna's party, and the chemistry that had sizzled between them on the walk to her car, Taylor
had let herself get swept away in fantasy. Again.
She'd wanted his help on the house search, sure,
but more than that, maybe a part of her was test-
ing him. Seeing how he reacted to the domestic,
personal quest of finding a home.

So far, he hadn't. At all.

While she raved about a vaulted ceiling or a
stone fireplace, the only input he gave her was,
well, black and white. Facts. The flue of the fire-

place was jammed. The concrete wall of the basement was cracked. The garage was sealed well and would stand up to Wisconsin winters.

It was more apparent than ever that this move toward the future was hers and hers alone. In truth, it always had been, but maybe she'd hoped.

The current owners had excellent taste in furniture, even here on the back porch. A sturdy white rattan love seat with cheery yellow cushions looked out over the backyard. Taylor couldn't resist sitting on it, imagining herself relaxing on a summer evening.

The backyard was surprisingly expansive for an old, residential neighborhood. A grand, picturesque tree—she wasn't sure what kind—sheltered the back half of the yard from the sun, and a vision of a wooden playset appeared in Taylor's mind. One with a yellow plastic slide, a rope ladder and a sandbox on one end. A swing, definitely a swing or two. She could imagine a boy and a girl playing, climbing, hollering. Laughing.

"What do you think?"

She startled at Alex's voice from behind her. The screen door creaked as he opened it. He walked six feet in front of her, gazing out at the yard as she just had, but now her attention was fully on him.

Such an easy, natural thing to add him to the

scene in her mind. Standing behind the swing, pushing the boy until he squealed in excitement. Or crouching at the side of the sandbox, steering a minibulldozer with the pigtailed girl. Rising when Taylor joined them. Kissing her.

"It's a sturdy, well-built house," he said, his back still to her. "I think it'd get your brother's okay."

The make-believe scenario in Taylor's head vanished with an almost-audible crash.

When had she become such a dreamer?

She shook her head. She hadn't and she wasn't.

She'd never been deluded enough to think there was a future for her and Alex. It was just easy to do because buying a house made the future so top-of-mind.

Not something she would let ruin her day.

She had Alex's company for the time being. Even though he'd been noncommittal so far, having him with her had made house-hunting fun.

They were definitely deeply immersed in the "gray area"—somewhere between friends and lovers.

Definitions weren't necessary, she reminded herself.

Taylor stood and walked up next to him, their arms not quite touching. "Beyond the nuts and bolts and practical issues," she said, "what do *you* think of it?"

"What I think shouldn't matter."

"Oh, it doesn't," she assured him, grinning when he frowned. "My opinion is already formed. I'm just curious."

He turned and perused the porch thoughtfully. "If I were going to settle down and buy a house, this one would be at the top of my list."

His assessment shouldn't have caused the lightness in her chest, the irrepressible grin. What he thought really didn't count, in theory. But she smiled at him anyway. Nodded. "For once, we're in agreement about something."

She went to find Genevieve to discuss how to move forward.

VIENNA WOULD BE PROUD.

So far Taylor had stretched "time with Alex" into an almost twelve-hour span. He'd been easily convinced to come back to her place with just three words: *home-cooked dinner.*

It turned out completely going on instinct without second-guessing herself would require a little practice. After touring two more houses on Genevieve's list, Taylor had wanted to see the bungalow one more time. By then it'd been well after 6:00 p.m.

They'd stopped at the grocery store on the way to her house and she'd made oven-baked pork chops, scalloped potatoes and fresh green beans. She was no gourmet chef but Alex had been sweetly enthusiastic about the food.

She'd forced him, in spite of his protests, out to the newly furnished deck to relax while she hastily cleaned up the kitchen. As she closed the refrigerator on the last of the leftovers, she surveyed the room. Not up to her usual standards, but there was a sexy man in her backyard. A girl had her priorities, and while tidiness had always been one of them, sometimes those priorities changed.

Taylor went outside, closing the door behind her to keep the cooled air in. She left the porch light off in an attempt to keep the bugs at bay. Alex had lit the citronella candle on the side table next to him, she noticed.

Though dusk was settling in, it was still uncharacteristically warm for Wisconsin in late August. Taylor tucked herself into one of her new teak patio chairs—with the most luxurious, comfortable outdoor cushions she'd ever come across—and hugged a throw pillow to her chest.

Alex had claimed the lounger, the focal piece of the admittedly extravagant purchase. When she'd listed Taylor's house last week, Genevieve had suggested creating a cozy, welcoming atmosphere on the newly repaired deck as part of the staging. Taylor had had no intention of going overboard when she'd hit a nearby home and garden store, but once she'd laid eyes on this set, on the lounger specifically, she'd wanted it to be part of her new home—wherever that might be. She had visions of getting Vienna to create a haven similar to the one at the Worth house for her, and this furniture would serve as the inspiration.

"You might never get me to leave," Alex said, his head back against the cushion, eyes closed. "This thing makes my bed feel like a wooden crate."

Taylor watched him with a smile, thinking it'd suit her fine if he never left.

One night at a time, she chided herself.

"The plants add to the experience," she said.

Two giant potted palms and a ficus filled the corner behind him. Gave the spot a sheltered feel.

"Definite jungle vibe." He raised his arms and cradled them behind his head. "Dinner was killer. If I didn't know better I'd think you were trying to get me to move in."

The comment was meant to be funny but it hit strangely close to the truth. He didn't seem disgusted or threatened by the idea.

That was something.

Something that, combined with the single glass of wine she'd had with dinner, gave her courage. She stood and noiselessly crossed the deck to the lounger. By the time he sensed her close by and opened his eyes, she'd jumped over an imaginary line and was lowering herself to straddle his lap.

"Always good to have a handy fix-it type around," she said nervously.

"Hel-lo."

Hel-lo was right. She hadn't thought about the effect of her long, loose gypsy skirt in this particular position. Now she couldn't think of anything else. There was a lot more breeze than material between her legs and his cargos.

"If you wanted the lounger, all you had to do was ask," he said with a sexy, all-knowing smile.

She swallowed and met his blue-gray eyes. "It's not the chair I'm after."

"What, exactly, are you after?" The smile faded, his manner became serious, and she knew her answer would dictate what happened next. What happened for the rest of the night.

"Well…" The rough growth of hair on his chin held her attention. She traced her finger up his jaw and back down again. "Our one-night thing? In my opinion it was a very nice way to spend a night. And I was thinking we could maybe…have another 'one night.'"

She was no expert on desire but she could swear his eyes went hot.

"I don't possess your mad math skills," he said

in a husky, alluring voice, "but I'm pretty sure that would make it *two* nights."

"You're thinking too hard."

He chuckled. "That's not something I'm often accused of. Sounds more up your alley." He caressed her bare upper arm gently with one hand, giving her shivers, and rested his other at her waist.

"I'm taking the evening off." Her shyness and fear were slowly being replaced by the need to get closer to him. She looked at his lips, touched them with her finger. Leaned forward without thought.

Alex's hand came up to her nape and he pulled her to him. The contact of their lips shot heat through her all the way to her middle, then lower. She breathed him in. Tasted him. Was overcome by the sensual overload of kissing him again. Just as before, it took mere seconds for him to drive her over a line from tentative to voracious.

Maybe this was only for one night, or one *more* night, but he was into it. Alex wanted her. Taylor had never been sure about that before with any other man, but there was little left to doubt given the hardness that pressed between her legs and the growl that rumbled from his chest.

He pulled her skirt from where it'd been serving as a semi-barrier between them and adjusted her body, centering her on him. The thin strip of her panties allowed her to feel every contour of his cargos, every shift of him below her. Made her burn for more contact. She rubbed her body against his, shooting electric need through her, making her gasp.

She eased away enough to access his zipper.

"Taylor." His voice had gone lower. Rougher.

"Yes?"

"We're outside."

She laughed into his mouth as she kissed him again. "We are. In my backyard."

"Are you okay with…? You go much further and that's it, baby. Outside it is."

Sitting back on his thighs, feeling flushed and not giving a flying fig about where they were, she undid his zipper with shaking fingers. "Well, I could stop and compose a list. Pros and cons of intimate relations on the back deck… But it might take a few minutes."

She reached inside his boxers and touched the silky hardness she ached for.

"A few minutes isn't an option," he said, leaning forward to kiss her again.

"It's dark," she whispered. "Most of my neighbors are elderly. They go to sleep not long after *Wheel of Fortune*."

"Shh. I stopped arguing minutes ago. Get over here."

Alex brushed her hair off her cheek, ran his fingers through her long, tousled locks. Their tongues met again, hungrily. As he kissed her senseless, she felt his rough, strong fingers under her skirt, inching up the backs of her thighs. Over her rear. They dipped inside her panties from the top, eased them down over her hips. Taylor leaned to the side to help him remove them and threw them toward the back door.

Before she could settle back on top of him, he removed his wallet from the back pocket of his pants and took out a square packet.

"Just like an army guy," she said breathily. "Always ready."

"Preparedness is one of my many virtues."

He ripped open the condom and she leaned down to kiss him. The package flew to the deck next to them. He slipped his hands under her shirt and guided her back on top of him until he filled her, taking her breath away.

"You feel amazing, Taylor."

"So you're saying the one-more-night thing was a good idea?" It was difficult to talk as she moved, grinding into him, teasing him.

"One of your best."

He made his way up her rib cage with his large hands, slid his fingers under her bra, over her breasts, her nipples. She gave up talking and lost control of her thoughts. Let instinct and need take over. Working his shirt upward, she ran her hands over his tight abs, his hard chest. She lifted the shirt off and tossed it aside. The sight of his dog tags on his toned, tanned body, while he was doing wicked things to her body... Sex would be ruined for her after this. It could never be as amazing as it was with Alex.

She clung to him, kissed him, breathed him. Promised herself she wouldn't let him leave until morning, would barely let him sleep. She'd take the day off and they could extend one night into a twenty-four-hour period. Whatever, as long as this didn't have to end....

Alex whispered things into her ear, drove her higher when she already thought she was going to die. Seeming to sense the moment he pushed her over, he kissed her hard, quieting the moans she couldn't hold back. He gripped her rear under her skirt and arched into her, not releasing her mouth.

Gradually their kisses gentled. They exhaled shakily as one. Spent. Sated. So amazingly sated.

Taylor curled into him, still intimately joined to him. His arms were around her, holding her to his chest. Cricket chirps eventually worked their way into her consciousness, adding to her feeling of contentment. She ran her finger over the metal rectangles hanging from his neck, not allowing herself to consider what they represented.

"That wasn't what I had in mind when I bought the patio furniture, but I'm trying to embrace the less-planned lifestyle," Taylor said several minutes later.

A low laugh rumbled from Alex's chest, vibrated beneath her cheek. "I heartily approve of the less-planned lifestyle."

He kissed the top of her head. Caressed her back. A breeze rustled through the leaves of the trees, and the sheen of perspiration on Taylor's skin made her shiver.

"Is there room for two in your shower?" he asked.

"You tell me. You installed one of them."

"Do you think we should conduct an experiment?"

She could tell he was grinning by the sound of his voice. "You do know the way to get a science girl to say yes."

Taylor crawled off him and picked up the clothing from the deck. He was slow standing and putting himself back together, but once he did, she let him sweep her off her feet. Literally and figuratively.

CHAPTER TWENTY-SIX

ALEX COULDN'T SAY exactly what made him cancel his Monday PT appointment. Spending the night with an amazing, willing woman in his arms made a man do crazy things, to be sure, but his therapy time was sacred. He didn't skip it, period. Not even when Marshall had flaked on the deal they'd made that gave Alex access to his Acura three times a week. Alex had ended up paying a cab so much to get to his appointment that buying a new car on the fly would've almost been cheaper.

And this morning, when Taylor had announced she was taking the day off work—which he suspected was a monumental occurrence itself—he'd apparently caught the temporary insanity bug.

They'd stayed in her bed for most of the day, emerging from her room exactly twice, both incidents food-related. Taylor had put her robe on once to bring the mail in—and systematically sorted and either stacked or thrown away each piece, opening herself up to an OCD joke or two. They'd slept a lot, and interrupted their sleep with sex.

All in all, every man's idea of the perfect day.

What was the saying? Something about good things coming to an end?

The clock was ticking. Alex was having a harder time ignoring reality, the world outside their lust cave. He knew the longer he stayed, the more likely Taylor—okay, both of them—would get too used to being together. Though the past day and night had rocked his world, he was beginning to get antsy.

AN HOUR LATER, TAYLOR climbed out of the shower while Alex stayed in to rinse the last of the soap off. It turned out two could indeed fit into both the new shower and the one in the master bath. A little crowded but that'd just made things more interesting. Forced them to get more creative.

As she dried herself, she knew their mind-blowing love retreat had to end soon, even though neither of them had mentioned the subject. Once Alex walked out of here, there was no telling when she'd see him next. Before he left, there was something she needed to address, and she tried to figure out the best way of handling it.

Naked was not it, she decided with a flushed smile.

She peeked behind the shower curtain to feast her eyes on his beautiful body—scars and all—

one last time and hurried out of the bathroom before she lost her resolve to get dressed. She'd never had so much sex in her life and yet...she wanted more? With Alex, it would never get old. As inexperienced as she'd been before him, she instinctively knew this.

Taylor threw on jeans and a plain coral V-neck T-shirt before heading through the house. She went down the stairs to the basement and opened the now neatly organized closet in the family room. Quinn's duffel bag hung from a hook and she grabbed it. Went into the other room to the gun cabinet. Her hand shook as she unlocked the door.

The cabinet was half empty, as she'd expected. Alex had managed to sell five or six of Quinn's guns to people he knew. The one she sought was on the far right side by itself. She had no idea what exactly it was other than scary and ugly, but she knew it had been Quinn's favorite—the one Alex had pointed out the day they took inventory.

Alex had hesitated to take it then but he was the only one who should inherit it. It'd been one of Quinn's most treasured possessions, and while Taylor could appreciate the sentimentality of it, she had no desire to own it, look at it. Touch it.

She noticed the gloves on the shelf and put them on. She wasn't altogether sure why it was necessary but she'd never seen Quinn—or Alex, for that matter—skip using them.

Reminding herself the gun was unloaded, she picked it up, awed and more than a little freaked out by the thought of what this hunk of metal and plastic was capable of.

She carefully placed the gun in the bag, zipped it and hurried upstairs, eager to get rid of the goods. Yes, it was irrational to be scared to touch an unloaded gun, but the same could be said for touching garter snakes. Neither was her thing.

When Alex came out of her bedroom, dressed in the clothes he'd worn on the marathon house tour yesterday, she was sitting in the living room on the couch, the bag at her feet.

"What's going on?" he asked, walking down the hall toward her.

"I've been meaning to do this for a while." Taylor leaned over and widened the opening of the bag as he lowered himself to the couch next to her. She forced herself to pick up the piece of killing steel instead of making him grab it himself. She held out the gun to him, careful to point it away from both of them just in case.

Alex stared at it then looked away.

"Take it, Alex. It's yours. He'd want you to have it."

"Why today?"

She couldn't face, even privately, the nagging fear that he might treat her differently after today. Might distance himself from her. With the house projects finished, it could be weeks before she saw him again. She blinked and swallowed against that possibility.

"I'll be moving soon if the offer on my house comes through. Time to take care of things like this." Just business. *Sure.*

She half expected him to argue, but he nodded. Took the gun from her. Nodded again.

"Thank you." He raised it and looked through the scope. "It's a hell of a rifle."

"If you say so."

He lowered it, held it in both hands above his lap, examined it more closely. She saw him swallow hard and understood a little of what he was going through. Holding something that had been so much a part of her brother made it seem as if Quinn himself should come strutting through the door with a smart-aleck remark.

Wishing she could spare him the pain, she put her hand on his thigh.

Alex pointed the gun down, pulled the back part of it and looked into the chamber on the side. She assumed he was double-checking for ammunition. Apparently satisfied with what he saw, he set the gun on the floor by the bag.

He sat back and drew Taylor toward him, so she crawled on his lap. Arms around each other, they quietly grieved, and for the first time, Taylor felt that maybe the pain wouldn't suffocate her if she let herself think about her brother. She felt as if, together, she and Alex could get through the darkest times. Closing her eyes, she clung to the connection that hummed between them. Minutes passed without them moving or speaking.

Then Alex went from still and comforting to fidgety. Taylor reluctantly untangled herself from him, moved to the side. Best to get the rest over with.

"I know you're probably ready to get home..." she began. She cleared her throat. "But would you go somewhere with me first?"

"Where?" Alex's eyes were damp.

Seeing him like that twisted her up inside.

If she answered his question, he might refuse to go. "You'll see when we get there. It's not far."

He shrugged. "I've got nothing planned."

She'd take that as a yes, lack of enthusiasm or not. It wasn't a happy errand anyway. But something had changed in the air between them in the past five minutes. Something that she couldn't name, but it scared her. The closeness of the past day had vanished.

Her hair was only half-dry, but she merely ran

a comb through it. They put their shoes on and Taylor grabbed her keys and purse, all without a word between them.

Fifteen minutes later, when she turned her car into the boat-storage lot located near the lakeshore, Alex's eyes bored into the side of her head. She refused to meet his gaze. He undoubtedly remembered this was where Quinn stored his fishing boat. Still, he didn't say anything.

Taylor hadn't been here before and had no idea where to find Quinn's shed. She took a right at the first row and drove slowly so she could see the numbers.

"It's the other way," Alex said. "Row closest to the shore."

She turned the car around and followed his directions to find number seventy-three. Pulled up right outside of it and turned off the engine. It wasn't until she was out the door and about to try the key in the garage lock that she noticed Alex hadn't moved. He sat with his head back against the headrest, eyes closed.

Taylor trudged to the passenger side and opened the door. "Are you coming?" she asked gently.

Alex sat there for several more seconds without moving, without opening his eyes. Taylor leaned on the frame of the door, waiting. Finally he nodded, met her gaze. She wanted to hold out her hand for him but didn't want to be rejected. Instead, she stood back while he pulled his long body out of the compact front seat.

She bent down to the lock, stuck the key in and turned it. Together they raised the mini-garage door to reveal the fishing craft sitting on a trailer. The sight of it didn't hit her the way so many other of Quinn's possessions had. She'd seen the boat when it was new, years ago, but had never been out on the water with him. Quinn and Alex had always been fishing enthusiasts but she'd had no interest.

But Alex...she watched him as he walked alongside it, running his hand over the top and just staring. She knew he was being barraged by a thousand memories. She wasn't sure he even noticed when she sidled up next to him, wishing this wasn't hurting him. That wasn't the reason she'd brought him out here.

She waited until he shifted, became aware she was there, and then she held out the keys to the storage unit and the boat. "It's yours. I'm paying the storage for another year, but if you want to sell the boat, I understand."

"Not sure I can sell it." His voice was heavy with sadness. "Not sure I can use it."

"That's your decision. I'd forgotten all about it until I got the storage renewal bill in the mail today. I keep wondering what other reminders will show up out of nowhere."

He shoved the key ring in his pocket and strode out of the garage as if she'd said the wrong thing. As he hung a left and disappeared instead of climbing into the car, Taylor wilted against the inside wall.

Emerging from the garage two minutes later, she searched for Alex but didn't see him. She followed the line of garages, all of them connected so there was nowhere to go but the end of the row. Once she cleared the long structure, she spotted him twenty yards away on top of an old wooden picnic table close to the water. He stared toward the middle of the lake, at nothing if she had to guess. She headed toward him, refusing to pay heed to a heavy sense of foreboding.

The table wobbled when she stepped up on the bench seat to join him.

"Maybe it's time for a diet," she said, trying to lighten the mood a little.

He didn't reply.

They sat side by side watching the boats in the distance. A determined bird hidden in the trees to their left serenaded them, the song mixing with the periodic slosh of water on the rocks. The sun had started its final descent for the evening and the air had cooled a few degrees. The evening would be perfect—if there wasn't so much hanging unspoken between them. It went beyond grief, at least in Taylor's mind.

A ski boat with a group of noisy teens and an older man sped by then turned, cut its speed and made its way to the boat ramp farther down, just on the other side of the storage compound. Taylor and Alex both watched as the group efficiently loaded the boat on a waiting trailer and left. The absence of raucous, happy sounds from the waterskiers emphasized the quiet between them.

"Thank you for giving me his boat," Alex said several minutes later, still staring out at the water. "And the rifle."

"I didn't do it to upset you."

"I'm not upset." He wove his fingers together and corrected himself. "No more upset now than usual."

"I know."

He'd weathered his personal storm of self-blame and sadness for months by himself. Taylor believed with every fiber of her being that she could help him work through things if only he'd let her. But she didn't know how to start.

"Alex."

Her heart beat several times as she waited for him to acknowledge that she'd spoken. Finally, he shot a fleeting glance her way, not even meeting her eyes.

"If you don't mind, I need a few minutes alone." His voice was a monotone. Detached.

"If you'd talk about it, maybe it would help—"

"Nothing will help, Taylor," he snapped. He bowed his head. "Please."

She clamped her jaw shut against the sting of his words. Staring at him, she gave him ample time, endless chances to soften what he'd said. He didn't speak another word.

Really? After their closeness of the past day and a half? The months leading up to it? He could shut her down so coldly? Not being ready to talk was one thing, but shutting her out like that…

Taylor climbed down from the table without a word and made her way to the car. She surprised herself with the force she used to slam the door shut, then hit the inside for good measure.

Slumping in her semireclined seat, she closed her eyes against the tears that were gathering. It didn't help. They spilled out from the corners and ran down the sides of her face into her hair.

It had been risky to spend more time with him, especially after admitting her feelings to herself, but she'd thought she could handle it. Had thought that the realization that they wouldn't end up with a happily-ever-after would leave her prepared.

Able to stave off the hurt when he went on his way, whether to the army or another woman.

Taylor allowed herself three minutes to purge the tears that had built up. She refused to let Alex find her wailing and licking her wounds when he finally returned to the car.

When her three minutes were up, she raised the seat and caught a glimpse of herself in the rearview mirror. Her hair was tangled from driving with the car windows down. Her green eyes stood out, partly because they were damp and partly because she no longer wore her glasses. There was a hint of color in her cheeks and it wasn't from an embarrassed flush for once but just from living.

She barely recognized the woman who stared back at her for a moment, but then she tucked her hair behind her ear and looked more closely. *This* was who she'd become in the past few weeks.

Without really noticing it, she'd changed inside to match the external metamorphosis. She'd worked her way out of her shell, pushed herself, with Vienna's help, to try new situations. Forced herself repeatedly outside of her comfort zone. She'd met people, gotten to know a few. Dated. Survived being treated like dirt by a man and not blamed herself as she once would have. She'd turned into a more confident person who wasted less time fretting over what others thought.

She'd become someone she liked. Only now did it hit her that maybe in the past she hadn't been able to love herself. Now she could. And she believed others could love her, as well.

Like Alex.

You didn't spend thirty-some hours straight with a woman unless you had feelings for her. Sure, sex skewed things a bit, but it hadn't been just sex for either of them.

There were the things he'd said to her in a low voice, in the early-morning hours, when she'd joked about her campaign to meet the perfect man. There was the way he'd insisted on getting up and making breakfast for them, refusing her help. She knew he hated to cook, but he'd come back to the bedroom with a bowl full of scrambled eggs and a stack of whole-wheat toast. Tea for her, with the right amount of lemon.

She'd never told him how much lemon she liked in her tea.

He'd let her choose the movie they'd watched in bed, on her laptop. Hadn't grumbled when she'd opted for a romantic comedy.

He'd watched out for her all these weeks. Been protective of her, bordering on overprotective, and while he maintained it was all because of Quinn, she no longer believed that.

What she believed was that he cared more about

her than he'd let on. More than he'd admitted to her…and maybe to himself.

She was no longer the girl who was afraid to love him. There was something pretty amazing between them, and it was time for him to face up to it, as well.

For the first time, she allowed herself to believe they could have a future together. Just as soon as she told him what she thought of his own cowardice.

Taylor got out and slammed the door, a new determination—and an underlying hope—propelling her back to the shore.

CHAPTER TWENTY-SEVEN

ALEX HAD SPENT the twenty-five minutes since Taylor had stormed off debating with himself. Get the hell out of here on foot, without telling her? Or stay and face the inevitable confrontation? He'd been seconds away from walking several times, but the thought of her face when she realized he was gone had rooted him to his spot on the table.

Now he'd apparently waited too long.

He didn't turn around when he heard her approaching behind him, though his leg was starting to stiffen up. Guess that was the price you paid for a night of mattress aerobics. A sore leg and a woman with a bone to pick, if her quick, deliberate steps through the sandy grass were any indication.

"We need to talk."

The four most dreaded words in the English language. He supposed he deserved them several times over.

"Here?" He'd prefer anywhere else. Tahoe. Brazil. Anything to put off talking about Quinn again. Or last night. Or whatever the hell it was she was so intent on discussing. All the talk in the world wasn't going to change how badly he'd screwed up.

She stepped directly in front of him, nearly at eye level with him because of the way he was hunched over. When he met her gaze, there was fire in those green eyes of hers and he knew he was in trouble.

He should've taken off when he'd had the chance.

"I swore to myself a hundred times over I would never tell you this, Alex," she said, touching his knee lightly. "But it occurred to me that that was letting you off easy." She looked to the side, her chest rising as she inhaled. Then she pegged him with a direct stare again. "I guess I'm not a fan of easy anymore. I'm in love with you."

He closed his eyes. No. That wasn't supposed to happen. He'd been foolish to stay over last night, dumber still to hang around all day, but he hadn't expected Taylor to throw this at him.

Before he could come up with an acceptable response, she carried on.

"That's exactly what I expected you to say."

He furrowed his forehead in confusion. "I didn't say anything."

"Exactly. But that's okay because I have a lot

of things to get out so you can just sit there and listen till your ears bleed."

Any other time he'd notice how cute she was when she was mad, but now he was too overwhelmed with hating himself to think anything positive.

"I have a theory," she continued. "I suspect you actually love me, too. But you're too stubborn to see it or admit it. Big burly army guy who's afraid of so little and yet won't face up to his feelings. Ironic, isn't it? I'm the one who's supposed to be afraid of so much...."

She crossed her arms over her chest, and stared him down expectantly.

"Taylor..."

She nodded once, as if he'd proved her point. "That's what I thought."

"Stop..."

"Maybe it would be smart for me to stop, but this time I'm not going to play it smart. You're so worried about what Quinn would think, but you have it all wrong. All Quinn would ever want is for me to be happy."

"I'm not that guy, Taylor."

"If I'm wrong and you really don't love me, okay. I'll eventually accept that. I'll be able to live with myself knowing I leveled with you."

"I can't love you," he said quietly when she paused to take a breath. "I can't love anyone. I'm trying to figure out how to live with myself. I'd do nothing but hurt you. Hurt you more."

Narrowing her eyes, she studied him, defiant at first, then less confident. She bit the corner of her bottom lip and he had to look away before her expression turned to hurt. This was exactly what he'd hoped to avoid.

The old Taylor would've backed down, but this new, determined one surprised him.

"You know what I think, Alex? I think you're stuck." She uncrossed her arms emphatically. Clenched her jaw momentarily. "Yes, something horrible happened to you and Quinn and everyone on that helicopter. We lost a really good guy that day." Her voice cracked, but she pushed on. "It wasn't your fault and I suspect deep down you know that. But it's time—*past* time—to embrace that. You need to stop using the accident as an excuse not to live."

Taylor stared at him a moment longer, shook her head and walked away.

"Don't bother waiting," he called after her. "I'll find my own ride home."

"Works for me." She didn't even look back when she answered.

TAYLOR DIDN'T SHED A TEAR on the drive home. Nor did she feel in the least bit guilty about leaving Alex by the lake.

She pulled her car into the garage dry-eyed. Walked, unseeing, across the driveway and the deck. Let herself in the house and blew out a long, shaky breath. Congratulated herself for handling that confrontation and the aftermath so well.

The kitchen was a mess from their slumber party so she set her purse down and immediately started tidying, rinsing dishes, stacking them in the dishwasher. Busy work. Blessed busy work.

As she moved one of the dirty plates Alex had used to serve their breakfast, she discovered the egg carton sitting on the counter beneath it. She flipped the top open. Three eggs remained. They'd sat out on the counter all day, at room temperature.

That was all it took.

Sobs burst from her with the power of Niagara Falls. She shoved the remaining dishes—and the eggs—out of her way and leaned over the counter, blinded by tears.

The back door opened and Taylor froze, automatically thinking it was Alex. She wiped her hands over her face and turned around before she could reason with herself that there was no way he could get here that fast.

"Taylor, honey, what's wrong?" Vienna rushed toward her, eyes wide with alarm.

At the sight of her friend's face, Taylor let go

of the ounce of control she'd mustered, unable to hold it together for another second.

Vienna pulled her into a hug and let her cry. "What happened, Tay?"

Taylor tried to get a full breath, tried to slow down so she wouldn't hyperventilate. "He... he...left the e-eggs out. I have to th-throw them awa-a-ay."

"Who left the eggs out?"

She couldn't bring herself to say his name. She felt Vienna nod after a few seconds.

"Alex? Did he do it?"

Taylor cried harder, if that was possible.

"Was Alex here all day? That's why I came over. He won't answer his cell."

Taylor tried to convey an affirmative answer, pulling away and covering her face with both hands.

"Come here," Vienna said, guiding her to the living room. She eased Taylor onto the couch and sat next to her, hugged her and let Taylor get it all out.

Minutes later—Ten? Thirty?—Taylor's embarrassing outpouring had slowed to a periodic hiccup.

"I'm sorry," Taylor said, wiping her eyes on her shirt.

"I'm guessing this isn't about the eggs."

Taylor tried to laugh but it sounded like a dying animal. "Not about the eggs."

Several seconds passed and Taylor closed her eyes, breathed as deeply as she could. Then she explained about the past two days, starting with the graduation party and ending with her declaration of love out at the lake.

"You said that to him?" Vienna asked when she was done. "About using the accident as an excuse?"

Taylor nodded, a rock settling in her gut. "I left him there. Maybe you should go see if he's still stranded."

Vienna waved off the idea. "He's a big boy. He can call a taxi for all I care. I'm proud of you for saying all that. It needed to be said."

"I'm not sure. I knew the rules going into this. Love wasn't ever supposed to be part of the deal."

"Seems like that's when it usually happens."

"How stupid am I to try to tell him *he* loves *me?*" She squeezed her eyes shut, all the conviction she'd felt earlier having seeped out of her, leaving her mired in doubt.

"Honestly, Tay? He's the stupid one." Vienna pulled her legs up under her. "He cares about you big-time. I'd have to be an idiot not to see that from where I stand. He's letting the best thing that could ever happen to him slip away because he's too scared to move on with his life. It makes me sad."

"Maybe he doesn't really care that much. It's not like I have all this experience with men to be a good judge of it. Maybe it was just a physical thing for him."

Vienna shook her head adamantly. "If he'd just wanted sex, he'd pick up some chick he'd never see again. My brother is stupid on many levels, but I refuse to believe he's dumb enough to go there with you."

"Well...I guess it doesn't matter in the end. He made his decision and it wasn't me."

"I'm sorry, Taylor. I never would have encouraged you if I'd known this would happen."

"I had to try," Taylor said quietly.

"At the risk of sounding condescending, I'm proud of you, girlfriend. Three months ago, you never would have had the nerve for any of this. Now you're telling army guys what's what and who's who."

Taylor forced a half smile. "Yay me." She didn't even try to sound convincing.

Vienna hopped up off the couch. "Come on," she said. "You need to cut loose for a little while."

"Oh, no. I have to work in the morning. No hangovers for me."

"Not alcohol. Just a drive with the windows

down, the music up, and chocolate to get you through."

The last thing Taylor wanted to do was go anywhere. But the thought of how quiet this house would be the second Vienna left propelled her off the couch. "I look like hell."

"Where we're going, that doesn't matter." She linked her arm with Taylor's. "Hair doesn't matter, calories don't count, and you might as well prepare to lose a little piece of your hearing, too. Time for a dose of break-up therapy, Vienna-style."

Taylor had no hope it would help, but it sure beat lying in her lonely bed and listening to the silent house.

CHAPTER TWENTY-EIGHT

ALEX WALKED OUT OF his doctor's office on the east side of Madison wondering what the hell was wrong with him. Dr. Hennings had finally, after all these months of hellacious therapy and rehab, given him the all clear on his leg. He'd managed as close to a full recovery as he was going to get and, more important, was given the okay to fly. All that remained was getting the army's flight surgeons to agree.

The joy Alex had expected to feel was seriously MIA.

As he headed down the wide main walkway from the clinic, he glanced around for Vienna's car. His appointment had taken longer than he'd expected so she should be waiting to give him a ride home.

"You requested a driver?" Marshall shot the smart-aleck remark from the bench along the sidewalk.

Hell. Last person he was in the mood for.

"I can call a cab." Alex walked a few steps farther then pulled out his phone.

Marshall fell in beside him. "Vienna was delayed at the mall so she asked me to cover for her. I'm here. Happy to give you a lift."

The attitude was gone and Alex was low on cash so he looked for the Acura. "You been drinking?"

"I'm sober. I'd breathe on you to prove it but I don't care to have you kick my ass again."

Alex studied him. Marshall's eyes were clear and focused, albeit rimmed by faint yellow bruising, courtesy of Alex's fist, and his stance was steady. Alex shrugged and headed for the car.

Once they were both in the front seat, they sat there in silence. The keys were in the ignition, but Marshall didn't start the engine.

"Well?" Alex said.

"I gave up drinking. Cleaned out the house. Haven't had a drop for almost two weeks."

"What happened to make you stop?"

Marshall scoffed. "Asshole brother of mine broke my nose, for one thing. Hurt like hell. I spent the next three days medicating with Jack. Woke up the fourth day and it hit me."

"What did?"

"Everything. Things you said, Mom pleading with me. After seventy-two hours of nothing but drunk, I still ached from fighting you. The liquor hadn't done a thing."

"It's unreliable that way." Alex watched a

woman and three little kids walk down the sidewalk. "So you just decided? Just like that?"

"Went cold turkey. I've been looking for a job."

That made Alex turn his head. "Yeah?"

"Got a couple of good leads. We'll see what happens."

Alex noticed his brother had gotten a haircut. Shaved. Maybe he was serious about straightening up.

"Anyway," Marshall said, "Just wanted to say thanks."

"Thanks for breaking your nose?"

"No, I'm still pissed about that." Marshall fiddled with the keys dangling from the ignition. "For having your act together, I guess."

Alex laughed. "Dude, I'm not the Worth sibling with anything resembling an act together."

"That's bull."

He scowled. "What house have you lived in for the past thirty-whatever years?"

"I'll give you, you were a screwup in school. When you went into the military, though, you figured it out. Made up for lost time."

Alex reclined his seat enough so he could put a foot up on the dash, earning a frown of disapproval from his brother. "Not so sure about that. I was given a purpose. I learned to fly helicopters. That's different from you and Vee."

Marshall's stare burned into the side of his face but he refused to make eye contact. The whole subject made him uncomfortable as hell. What man liked to talk about his weaknesses?

"You really still think like that, don't you?" Marshall asked.

"Like what?"

"Like you're not good enough. You've always compared yourself to us. So we knew what we wanted to do before we finished high school. So we went to college. So what?"

Alex shook his head.

"For what it's worth, I respect the hell out of what you do." Marshall's voice was quiet. Sincere.

It surprised Alex into looking at him.

"What?" Marshall said.

Again, Alex shook his head.

"You want to compare? Okay, we'll compare, and then I'm shutting the hell up because I don't want your head getting any bigger. I write magazine articles about lakes and bird species. You?" He chuckled. "You shoot down bad guys."

"Until a bad guy shoots me down." He forced his mind not to go there. Not right now.

"You're a damn hero. With medals."

Some hero. What kind of a "hero" treated his best friend's sister the way he'd treated Taylor? He wasn't any damn hero.

"Look at you," Marshall continued, and Alex began to think maybe it was better when they weren't on speaking terms. The guy didn't shut up when he got a dumb idea. "Look what you've been through. I lost a stinking job. A company. And I nearly let it do me in. You lost a best friend. Maybe a career. And you've been fighting your way back the whole time."

"My therapist discharged me yesterday. Doctor just agreed with her. All that's left is convincing the army docs."

"What's that mean exactly?"

"Means I'm recovered. As good as I'm going to get. They both think I won't have any trouble flying."

"And you're just now mentioning this?"

"You started in with all this sappy rah-rah shit," Alex said. "Couldn't get a word in edgewise." He looked at his watch, an idea taking shape. "Do me a favor. Drive me over to the airport instead of home."

"What for?"

"Because I can fly. I've got a connection there, retired army officer who gives flying lessons. Long time ago he told me anytime I wanted to take one of his birds out, to let him know."

"You ready for that?"

The first buzz of excitement zipped through

Alex and his palms started sweating at the thought of being in a cockpit again. Like the rotors of a Blackhawk when they first started up, his heart gradually accelerated till it was racing in anticipation. "Ready like you wouldn't believe. You ever been in a bird?"

"No."

"Want to go up on your first helicopter ride?"

Marshall stared out the windshield, considering it. "I'm more of a desk-job kind of guy but... maybe I could write an article about the experience or something. Let's go. I'll give it a try."

An article. Alex grinned and shook his head. He and his brother were back to being different as day and night. But for the first time, he realized maybe that was all right.

OUT WITH THE OLD, TAYLOR thought as she surveyed the endless boxes in the living room of the bungalow. The proverb had reverberated through her mind all day.

This move was probably long overdue and it really had come to symbolize breaking ties to her past. Quinn. Her mom. Even her dad to an extent, though her memories of him in that house were limited.

Alex.

His name echoed in her head without her permission, but he was part of the past, as well. A fleeting part.

The old house held ghosts and she'd clung to them for long enough. The sight of Quinn's empty bedroom every day did nothing to lessen the loneliness that had become even worse these past three weeks since she'd blurted her feelings to Alex and scared him away. It had taken her a while to realize that selling it wouldn't make the good memories disappear. She could take those with her wherever she went.

Someone knocked on the front door behind her and she wondered if the moving crew had forgotten something. They had her money—and their help had been worth every penny. All she'd done was watch and direct.

Before she could get to the door she'd just shut, Vienna opened it and poked her head in.

"Is it safe to enter?" Vienna wore a black business suit, conservative heels and more makeup than usual. She carried a bag on her shoulder, likely some comfortable clothes to change into.

"It's as safe as it's going to get," Taylor said. "The big burly moving men just left."

"Pity. Any list guys?"

"The list is dead. You know that. Though the lead mover was kind of cute. Nice guy."

"Oh? And?" Vienna kicked off her heels and pushed them to the wall.

"And nothing. I've been rejected enough for the next decade. Instead of a husband I have the cutest house on the block."

"And boxes." Vienna made a face as she looked around. "I can't wait to get out of these clothes. Is the bathroom accessible?"

"It's the one box-free room in the house." Only because the front bathroom was too small to hold any. "How was the interview?"

Vienna left the door to the bathroom open as she changed clothes and hollered her reply. "It was fine, I guess. But I don't have great feelings about it."

Taylor spotted a box in the living room marked *Office* so she picked it up and carried it to the front bedroom. "Why not?" she asked as she passed the doorway to the bathroom.

Vienna joined her in the office-to-be, still tying the drawstring on her shorts. She wrinkled her nose and shook her head. "Just...felt like the whole thing was canned. If I had to guess, they have the person they want and they're just going through interviews to fill a quota."

"I hate it when they do that. It's unfair and misleading." Taylor sat on her desk chair and swiveled to look at all the boxes in this room. She'd be unpacking for a week just to get her office in order. Already she was feeling twitchy without her trusty computer hooked up, but first she'd have to locate it.

"I wasn't in love with that job anyway," Vienna said. "Though I am starting to stress out just a bit. It's September, Taylor. School has started up again. I'm not there and…I'm not working. I don't know what I'm going to do."

"It's early yet. We could start up our rounds of the professional groups again, only this time forget the checklist part of it."

"Maybe." Vienna wandered around, reading the labels of the boxes. "Have you talked to Alex at all?"

Just hearing his name out loud shot a searing pain through Taylor. She was tired, so very tired of hurting. "What do you think?"

Vienna faced her. Took a deep breath. "He's flying out Monday to see if the medical board will approve him to go back to active duty."

Taylor propelled herself off the chair and over to the top box on the closest stack. She worked her fingernail under the tape until she could rip it open, unaware and uncaring which box she'd chosen.

So many different emotions reeled through her and held on to the entire stack of boxes and closed her eyes for a moment, her back to Vienna. The news meant he'd gotten through his therapy as he'd hoped. She knew how important that was to him, and she was both proud of him and happy for him. But twisted up with those positive emotions were dark ones.

"I didn't think you knew," her friend said. "Thought I'd tell you in case..."

The box was open now and Taylor pulled out items that belonged on the top of her desk. Pencil holder. Mouse pad. Pop-up sticky-note holder. None of which she saw as she set them on the desk. "In case what?"

"I don't know. Maybe you want to see him one more time before he goes?"

The thought of facing him made her stomach knot up.

"Vienna." She continued to set items on the desk without bothering to consider where they belonged. "I did everything I can. I told him everything. I made a fool of myself insisting that he felt the same way." She couldn't handle it. "I don't want to see him again."

Vienna came over and started to help her. "I'm sorry, Taylor. I understand completely. I just thought you should know."

"What if he gets killed over there?" The fear popped out before Taylor could stop it.

Vienna let out a long, noisy breath and sat on the top of the desk. "I know. I hate it. But Alex is good at what he does. He has to be or *everyone* on that helicopter would have been dead."

Taylor nodded, trying to take solace in what she knew was the truth. Alex would be okay.

The bigger question was…would she?

"It's going to get easier."

"When?" Taylor asked.

"Umm, not today, I guess." Vienna hugged her. "You're moving forward, though. New house. New life. You're going to be okay."

"I'm holding you to that," Taylor mumbled.

As soon as she got her computer connected, she was going online to find a plaque for her wall.

Out with the old, in with the new.

She just hoped the new was better than the old.

CHAPTER TWENTY-NINE

USING THE ACCIDENT as an excuse not to live.

Like hell.

Alex stalked off the wide dock where he'd tied the boat, the late-afternoon sun casting a long shadow on the pavement in front of him.

He was doing everything he could to get *back* to his life. Tomorrow, he flew out to be evaluated by the army's medical board, and if they approved him, things would move fast. He felt good about his chances. His doctor here had been amazed at his progress, said he never would have guessed Alex could get so much muscle control back.

So the future was looking promising, like he'd soon be exactly where he'd wanted to be—flying overseas in the middle of the action again.

He told himself his lack of enthusiasm was just nerves. Completely normal after what had happened the last time he'd been in a Blackhawk. All the counseling in the world wouldn't be able to prevent a few jitters.

Still, Taylor's accusations continued to bother him, no matter how much he attempted to block them out and just go on with his life the way he'd planned.

After parking the boat trailer and the pickup truck he'd borrowed from Mr. Mooney, their neighbor, Alex jogged back down to the dock and hopped into Quinn's boat. *His* boat. He ignored any trepidation about taking out Quinn's boat without him. He could face up to this just fine.

He'd brought his tackle box along with a rod and reel, just in case he felt inclined to put a line in, but mostly this was about proving he could go out in the boat. Marshall, who liked fishing about as much as he liked getting a root canal, had offered to come along. Alex had refused. This was something he had to do alone.

He started the motor, steered away from the dock and stopped thinking. The worries, the memories, the uneasiness, they all fell away as he slipped into auto-pilot mode. He allowed the peace of being on the water after all this time to envelop him. Lost himself in it. Didn't make a single conscious decision. Within minutes, he realized he'd taken the boat to one of the secluded, brush-covered coves that he and Quinn had favored for bass fishing.

Alex let the boat drift in the calm water. Leaning back as far as the seat would let him, he stretched his legs out, relaxed. Soaked up the sunshine and the familiar chirps and buzzes of birds and insects, the periodic splash or ripple in the water. He absently removed the cover from the storage compartment next to him and glanced down.

I'll be damned.

Quinn's high-dollar aviator sunglasses, the ones he'd thought he'd lost in an airport when he was on leave last year. Ugliest glasses Alex had ever seen, and he'd told his friend that frequently. Pointed out he was better off without them.

And here they were.

Alex chuckled aloud as he stared at them. He took off his own shades and put them on. Looked at himself in the reflection of the glasses he'd taken off. Nope. They were still ugly. Quinn had always maintained they were ugly on everyone but him and maybe he'd had a point.

Alex switched glasses again and tried to ignore that his eyes had gone damp. He took a deep breath and looked up at the bright-blue, cloudless sky.

"Shitty day for fishing," Quinn would have said. Alex could hear his voice, clear as day, as if he was there in the boat beside him. They'd always preferred cool, cloudy weather.

Alex shook his head and leaned forward, perching his forearms on his knees. A lump the size of a hand grenade filled his throat. He squeezed his eyes shut, knowing suddenly what it must feel like to have a nearby explosion knock you back a hundred feet and onto your ass.

Sucking in air and trying to ignore the physical pain, he stood up in the boat and grabbed his pole. He hadn't planned to actually drop a line, so he didn't have any live bait, but he had a lure or two that would work here. He prepped his line, then cast it close to a branch that protruded from the water.

He was going to catch enough damn fish for two.

He spent a good ten minutes slowly reeling in the line and casting it back out before he gave up. Propped the pole up with the line still in the water, not caring if it tangled in the branches beneath the water's surface. He doubted he'd catch a thing that way, but when you got down to it, that didn't really matter, did it? There *weren't* two men here. Just him and a ghost.

He swallowed several times. Cleared his throat. "I'm so damn sorry, man."

Quinn was buried here in Madison, Alex knew, but he'd never been to visit his grave. This was why.

Maybe Taylor had been right, after all.

He *was* stuck. Not moving on. Because he

was too much of a coward to face the memory of Quinn. Scratch that, to face his own jumble of guilt and regret.

Well, to hell with that.

He picked up Quinn's sunglasses again and cracked another sad grin just looking at them.

"You should still be here," he said to no one. "God willing, I'm heading back to fight the fight soon, just like you would've done." His voice sounded strange, loud in the peaceful setting.

"I'll never in a thousand years be as noble about the whole thing as you were. You know I've always been more interested in playing with the big toys than fighting for freedom." He paused, needing to get control of himself even though there was no one around but a few birds to see his breakdown. "You were one hell of a soldier. The best..."

And he'd died for the cause. Died doing what he was made to do, fighting for what he'd believed in more than just about anything. Taylor's insistence on that point came back to him now like a flaming boomerang. No way he could miss it this time.

Being KIA was what it was all about for Quinn. Not that he'd have chosen to die—he'd never been one of those crazy SOBs who had a death wish and always pushed the limits, took unnecessary risks. Quinn had wanted to fight for his country till the fight was over. And he'd died doing what he, more than just about any guy Alex knew, had lived for.

Quinn would have sat back and gotten that satisfied grin on his face, nodded emphatically at the way things had ended.

And he'd kick Alex's ass for taking this long to understand that.

"It's a war," Quinn had said one early morning in this very boat. "People can die. You and I could die." He'd stared off at the trees on the shore, lost in thought. "Hell of a lot better than getting hit by a truck crossing the street on the way to the convenience store if you ask me."

Alex remembered the conversation like it was last week, not nine or ten years ago. Even then, *especially* then, Quinn had been all about the cause. Nine-eleven had spurred him on, made his patriotism burn. He'd campaigned to get Alex to join with him and Alex had finally decided to give it a try. That discussion had been Quinn's way of making sure Alex was cool with what they were getting into. He'd wanted his buddy to experience it with him, but only if Alex really wanted to.

At that point, Alex had. He'd drifted around after high school, knowing college wasn't for him but not knowing what was, and when Quinn announced his plans, Alex had been ready for a change. He'd known there had to be more out there, something that clicked for him, and he hadn't been able to find it here in Madison, Wisconsin.

He'd never thought about flying anything until he'd come across the possibility in basic training. The idea had sparked something in him, an interest he hadn't felt for much of anything besides high-school sports and girls.

For him, from then on, it was all about being several thousand feet off the ground, the controls in his hands and under his feet. When you got down to it, he didn't need a Blackhawk. He just loved to fly. Army or not.

Suddenly he could hear Quinn's voice in his head again, pointing out that he could fly anywhere, just as Marshall had insisted. Without sleeping on a rock-hard bunk or checking his boots for cobras or scorpions. Without much chance of getting shot out of the sky.

And even more, he could hear Quinn telling him he was a damn idiot for doing what Quinn would want to do instead of what *he* wanted.

Alex stood and realized there was nowhere to pace.

He sat back down and reeled in his line until it got tangled. Instead of fighting with it, he cut it. There were more important things to worry about.

CHAPTER THIRTY

TAYLOR WAS KNOWLEDGEABLE about a lot of different subjects, but flower bulbs was decidedly not one of them. Lucky for her, some glorious person had had the foresight to write a book on how to plant them.

Like the old house, the landscaping at the new one was minimal. Cared-for but uninspired. It had never bothered her before, but now that she owned her very own adorable bungalow, she was determined to make it a real home.

She was turning her sights forward, making a satisfying future for herself. Letting go of past misconceptions, from the fear of not being good enough to the belief she needed a man to be happy. The past few months had changed her, and though the summer hadn't exactly been a breeze, she was more comfortable with herself. Despite the dating disasters, she had plenty of positive experiences, as well.

She belonged to a new math club that she anticipated going to every month. She'd gained a new confidence for handling dates—not that she'd had any lately. But she wouldn't get so scared she'd want to hurl the next time she did. New house, new friend, new attitude, new decorating challenge, new landscaping objectives.

By spring, if the how-to book could be believed, she'd have a host of tulips, irises and daffodils, not necessarily in that order. To her, the bloom-filled spring symbolized hope. The new, improved, independent Taylor, who did more than work twelve-hour days and hide in her office. The one who was fine without a man.

She could do this.

"That has to be the biggest mess you've ever made in your life."

The familiar male voice froze her heart for a moment, then released it like a racehorse out of the blocks.

Alex.

He'd come to tell her goodbye.

The strong, independent rah-rah talk she'd been giving herself thirty seconds ago went out the window, so to speak. Squeezing her eyes tightly shut before facing him, she coached herself to breathe. Not to let this break her down. She'd exposed herself in front of him already—he didn't need to see her cry again.

Taylor glanced around her, avoiding him, and realized he was right. Various gardening tools,

he gloves she'd shed in frustration, the prescrip-
on sunglasses that were overkill now that she
ore contacts, and a sports bottle half-full of iced
ea were scattered all over the flower bed and the
alkway in front of it. She'd managed to track,
pread and splatter loose dirt everywhere.

"They say messiness is a sign of genius." She
icked some dirt back into the bed. "I've always
anted to use that line. Never had the chance be-
ore."

Everything they'd been through and here she
as, babbling like a fool.

Alex reached her walkway then and she finally
aced him.

Drat. He still knocked her off her proverbial
eet. Three weeks hadn't done a thing to dull that
esponse.

He wore cargos again, but for the first time, they
ere shorts. An old T-shirt showed he hadn't put
lot of thought into looking good for her, even
hough he looked so good in her opinion she
anted to cry. He held a small unmarked paper
ack in one hand.

His hair looked windblown, his unshaven face
anned. His eyes were just as penetrating as al-
ays, though they no longer made her feel dis-
oncerted. Much. His dark eyebrows arched as if
e were asking if it was okay for them to talk.

"I owe you an apology, or twelve," he said in a low voice as he approached her. He thought to glance around and ensure their privacy.

She silently willed him to talk fast, unsure how long her composure would hold out. She had half a mind to tell him he didn't owe her anything, but this could be the last time she saw him. It was best to get everything out in the open—she knew that from experience.

"I'm sorry about the day at the lake," he said, moving closer still until she could smell him, outdoorsy, virile.

She must smell like soil and earthworms. The least he could have done was warned her he was coming over. Of course, then she would have been hard-pressed to stick around long enough to see him.

"There's nothing to—"

"Yes. There is. I didn't handle that well at all. I could make a dozen excuses, but what it comes down to is that I hurt you. I regret that."

His voice lulled her. It lured her into remembering the sound of it in the early-morning hours, the feel of his breath on her ear as they'd talked for hours after...

Yeah. She was not going there.

"I'm also sorry for using your brother as an excuse for not letting myself really be with you."

Oh, lord, she didn't want to go through this right now. Right here. The last thing she needed was for her neighbors to see the new girl losing it in front of her house.

"It's okay, Alex," she said hoarsely. "I'm not mad at you. You don't have to say all this."

"And I'm sorry for sneaking away from you that first night before the sun came up—"

"Stop. Please."

"I'm messing this up, aren't I?"

"Messing what up?"

He looked at the dirty ground, a half grin on his face. "You used to be the one who was tongue-tied. You're not that girl anymore, are you?"

She tilted her head, wondering if he'd been sniffing household chemicals. "No? I mean kind of." She smiled in spite of herself at the way she was tangling her words now. "That same girl is still in here. Obviously."

He nodded, studying her closely. "I like her. Both hers. The tongue-tied Taylor and the upgraded model."

"Alex, what…"

"I love you, Taylor."

Her mouth closed and her eyes widened. She had the sensation of falling backward and having the breath knocked out of her.

"You…what?"

He took her hand in his empty one, ran his thumb gently, lovingly over her fingers. "I'm an idiot."

"That's not what you said."

"Both are true. I love you. And I'm an idiot for not letting myself love you sooner."

All the blood in her body rushed into her chest. Chills shot through her. Maybe this was how it felt to inhale too much helium, she thought. Then she laughed.

"Ouch," he said, lacing their fingers together. "And women wonder why guys don't talk about their feelings."

"One more time," she said. "Tell me."

First, he told her without words. He leaned down and closed the few inches between them as he pressed his lips to hers. It was somehow the most tender, emotional touch they'd shared yet, even though it lasted mere seconds and was chaste enough the neighbors wouldn't get the wrong idea.

"I love you, Taylor McCabe. Scarlet, too." He breathed the words over her temple, into her ear, and she let them sink in.

"Umm…" She feasted her eyes on his face, his straight nose, square chin, angled cheeks. Giddiness was threatening to incapacitate her but she needed to understand before she gave in. "You said you…couldn't."

"I couldn't let myself. Or that's what I thought. urns out you were right."

"I was right," she repeated, trying to slow the ope that was blossoming inside of her.

"I was stuck."

A slow smile tugged at her lips. "Did I say at?"

"I was using the accident as an excuse not to ve."

The smile disappeared. "And now? What's anged?"

"I found Quinn's sunglasses," he said, taking em from his belt loop or his back pocket where e'd apparently hooked them.

"The ones he lost. He must have emailed me n times asking if I'd found them."

"They were in the boat. In the side storage com- artment."

"Okay. And…they held the secret to the uni- erse?"

"Something like that. Did anyone ever tell you ou've got a little of your brother's smart-aleck- ess in you?"

"Never. Alex?"

"I'm getting to it." He took her by the hand and d her to the wide steps of the front porch. He sat n the top one and pulled her down next to him. et's just say I faced up to some ghosts I'd been

avoiding. Figured out some things. The abridge
version is that I was going back to the army fo
the wrong reasons."

Her hope dipped. "And now you're going fo
the right reasons?"

"I'm not going. I'm resigning my commission.

She waited for him to explain, on the verge o
jumping out of her skin.

"Flying is what I love, Taylor. A distant secon
after you," he added quickly with a sheepish grin
"I'm not like Quinn. I don't love the military. I'v
got a couple of leads on opportunities here flyin;
helicopters. I want to be with you."

"You're over the Quinn thing? Thinking h
wouldn't approve?"

"It's like he was on that boat with me and h
knocked me over the head. I understand now tha
there's a difference between messing around wit
your best friend's little sister and falling in lov
with her. He would have called me on it long ago
He would've been the first in line to see us to
gether…as long as I make you happy. As I sai
before, I was an idiot."

"You were, kind of," Taylor agreed.

"I deserved that."

"But I've always admired a man who can lear
from his mistakes. Usually in my experience it'

been in a lab or on a computer, but boats work, too."

He angled toward her and kissed her, deeply, thoroughly this time. She pulled him close and they fell backward, laughing, onto the porch floor, Alex partly on top of her. To heck with what the neighbors thought.

The sack he'd been holding clunked to the step in front of him and they ignored it, their lips seeking each other hungrily, playfully. As seconds, maybe minutes, passed, and the urgency between them grew, Taylor became aware that she did in fact have limits as to what she wanted the neighbors to witness. She broke the kiss and propped herself up on her elbow.

"What's in the sack?" she asked, attempting to breathe evenly.

Alex looked momentarily embarrassed, something she'd never seen before. He sat up and retrieved the sack but didn't open it. "Well, it's Sunday night," he said unnecessarily. "I was planning on leaving town tomorrow until about two hours ago, so I had to think fast to do something that might...mean something to you."

"Okaaay." She narrowed her eyes at him, curious.

"I haven't picked out a ring yet..." He set the

bag on the step next to him and took her hands in his.

Her eyes popped wider and she might have made an embarrassing squealing noise.

"Will you marry me, Taylor?"

She definitely squealed and crawled up on his lap, throwing her arms around him. "Yes. Unequivocally yes, I will marry you, Alex Worth." Kissing him, she settled into his body, his arms around her, enveloping her in safety and, at long last, love.

"We'll pick out a ring as beautiful as you tomorrow," he said, brushing her hair off her cheek. "But I do have something for you now. Something practical."

He picked up the bag and took out a book.

"Wedding Planning Basics," she read. "The bride-to-be's guide."

Tears fell from Taylor's eyes before she could stop them. She buried her face in Alex's shirt. "You know me so well," she said into his chest. "But…"

"What's wrong?"

"Nothing," she said quickly. "Not a thing. But a book on weddings? It's kind of making it black and white. And I've been trying something new. Less planning. More gray area. Someone once told me that love isn't black and white."

Alex laughed and kissed her temple so tenderly she almost expired right there on the porch steps.

"Someone, huh?"

Taylor nodded, unable to stop the gargantuan grin on her face.

"Sounds like a really smart someone."

She stared into his eyes. "Absolutely. He's brilliant. So what do you say? Would it be okay if we put the book on the shelf and tried going on instinct?"

He trailed his finger over her lower lip before pressing another kiss there. "Whatever it takes to make my brainy beauty happy."

"I'd give serious thought to composing a list for you about that, but actually, you've got it covered. Perfectly."

* * * * *